THE
UNPLEASANTNESS
AT
BASKERVILLE
HALL

CHRIS DOLLEY

Book View Café

THE UNPLEASANTNESS AT BASKERVILLE HALL

Published by Book View Café

Book View Café Publishing Cooperative
P.O. Box 1624
Cedar Crest, NM 87008-1624

www.bookviewcafe.com

ISBN 13: 978-1-61138-553-3

Cover art by Mark Hammermeister
Cover design by Chris Dolley

First printing, February, 2016

THE
UNPLEASANTNESS
AT
BASKERVILLE HALL

Books by Chris Dolley

Reeves & Worcester Steampunk Mysteries

What Ho, Automata

The Unpleasantness at Baskerville Hall

Other Books

Resonance

Shift

French Fried

An Unsafe Pair Of Hands

Medium Dead

Magical Crimes

International Kittens of Mystery

How Possession Can Help You Lose Weight

ONE

"Do you believe in star cross'd lovers, Reeves?"

"Sir?"

"Romeo and Juliet, Reeves. I fear that's what's happening to me and Emmeline. Minus the asp."

"The asp was Cleopatra, sir."

"Really? I didn't know the asp had a name. Family pet, was it?"

The things one learns when one's valet has a giant steam-powered brain. I puffed on a contemplative cheroot while Reeves mixed my mid-morning cocktail.

"Am I to understand that your aunt Bertha remains opposed to the match, sir?"

"If anything her opinion has hardened, Reeves. I have spent the last hour being lectured as to what is, and what is not, acceptable behaviour for prospective Mrs Reginald Worcesters. Chaining oneself to railings – even in the better neighbourhoods – features strongly in the unacceptable pile. Top billing, though, is reserved for having one's photograph appear in the *Tatler*."

"Your aunt is opposed to that illustrated magazine, sir?"

"Far from it, Reeves. Aunt Bertha is much taken with the *Tatler*. As are her circle. I should have said it's not so much having one's picture published as to the content of said picture. Being dragged off the Home Secretary by a burly policeman whilst attempting to give the former a ripe one across the mazard with a furled parasol is apparently the height of bad form."

"Miss Emmeline *is* a very spirited young lady, sir."

"That's what *I* said. Give her the vote and all would be

1

sweetness and light. Home Secretaries would be safe to walk the streets once more and the only casualties would be the purveyors of fine gauge chains for the progressive woman."

"Indeed, sir. Have you heard from Miss Emmeline since her departure?"

"I have not, Reeves. Which worries me greatly."

It wasn't only Aunt Bertha who'd taken against the match. The Dreadnought clan and, in particular, Emmeline's mother, had decided that her daughter could do better. Two days ago they'd packed her off to Baskerville Hall for a fortnight in the country with the hope she'd bag the heir to the Baskerville-Smythe title.

Not that she had gone willingly. Words had been exchanged. Food had been refused, and a small barricade – which she'd manned for a full twenty-four hours! – had been constructed around her bedroom door.

It took Reeves – perched on a ladder propped up outside her bedroom window – to persuade the young firebrand that feigned acquiescence was the best way to thwart her family's designs.

Reeves has always been big on feigned acquiescence.

But I had my doubts. Reeves may have thought the family would soon tire of trying to marry her off to every Lord Tom, Dick and Algernon, but what if they didn't? And what if she fell for one of these suitors? Emmeline had promised to write to me every day, but it was two days now and I hadn't received a single letter!

"I am a worried man, Reeves. What if this Baskerville-Smythe chap has turned her head? It's always happening in books. Modern girls rarely marry the chap they're engaged to on page seven."

"Miss Emmeline is a stalwart and strong-minded young lady, sir."

"So was Lady Sybil in *The Ravishing Sporran.* But one sight of a man in a kilt and she was undone, Reeves. Putty in his roving Highland hands. Do they wear kilts in Devonshire?"

"Not that I have heard, sir."

"Well that's *one* stroke of luck."

I took a long sip of fortifying cocktail before rising from my armchair. This Baskerville-Smythe chap would probably rate an entry in *Milady's Form Guide to Young Gentlemen*. What better way to discover what I was up against?

I found the guide in the bookcase and leafed through it until I found the entry for Henry Baskerville-Smythe. It read:

Dashing and well turned out colt. Excellent pedigree, good conformation. Unraced for two years as has been out of the country. Not expected to be riderless for long! Very fast on the gallops.

"I don't like the sound of this, Reeves. Have you seen it?"

I handed him the form guide.

"H'm," said Reeves.

"What do you mean 'h'm,' Reeves? Is that a good 'h'm' or a bad 'h'm'?"

"I think this is a positive development, sir."

"You do? How do you work that out?"

"An entry such as this, sir, is likely to attract a large number of young ladies and their families. Miss Emmeline will have stiff competition."

"She will?"

"I would expect there to be *several* young ladies staying at Baskerville Hall this very fortnight, sir, each with instructions to monopolise Mr Baskerville-Smythe's attention."

"I don't know, Reeves. I can't bear another twelve days like this, imagining the worst. We Worcesters are men of action. Pack my bags, Reeves. We leave for Baskerville Hall within the hour."

Reeves gave me his disapproving face. "I would strongly counsel against such a move, sir. Miss Emmeline *did* say that the Baskerville-Smythes had been given firm instructions to turn you away should you happen to call."

I waved a dismissive hand at Reeves' objections. "A mere formality, Reeves. We shall go in disguise."

Reeves coughed.

"It's all right, Reeves. I'm not contemplating a long beard and a parrot. A false name should suffice. None of the Baskerville-Smythes have ever met me. I shall once more become Nebuchadnezzar Blenkinsop. And you can be my valet Montmorency."

Reeves' left eyebrow rose like a restrained, but clearly startled, salmon.

"I think not, sir. It has been my observation that families are loathe to extend hospitality to strangers who arrive unannounced."

"Then I'll introduce myself as a distant relative – one cannot turn away family. I should know."

Reeves was still unconvinced, but at least he'd wrestled back control of his eyebrows.

"It would have to be a *very* distant relative, sir. Questions will be asked, and suspicions aroused should your knowledge of family matters fall short of expectations."

A good point. I took a long sip of my mid-morning bracer and waited for the restorative nectar to pep up the little grey cells.

"How about an imaginary scion, Reeves? Most families have a third or fourth son sent out to the colonies to find their fortune. I'll be the product of a secret marriage conducted in the Australian outback."

~

A quick perusal of *Who's Who* uncovered a wealth of Baskerville-Smythes, but few of them were extant. Henry was an only son, and his father, Sir Robert – a widower for nigh on ten years – had outlived both his wife and three brothers. The only relative above ground at Baskerville Hall was a Lady Julia Noseley, Sir Robert's sister-in-law.

"It says here that Henry's in South Africa serving with his regiment," I said.

"That *is* last year's edition, sir. *Milady's Form Guide to Young Gentlemen* did mention that mister Henry had recently returned from abroad."

"I don't like this, Reeves. He'll have a uniform. They're worse than kilts!"

I read further, desperate to find a suitable distant relative of the right age. One of Sir Robert's brothers, Cuthbert, had moved to South America. That was certainly distant enough. He'd married a local girl and had a son, Roderick. Cuthbert had then died of yellow fever and his wife had died of scarlet fever. Roderick had managed to survive both his parents – presumably because the local fevers had run out of colours – but was believed to have died a few years later when he was struck by the Buenos Aires to Mar del Plata express.

"These Baskerville-Smythes are a very unlucky bunch, Reeves. It's a wonder there are any of them left."

I was then struck with a notion. Roderick Baskerville-Smythe was only *presumed* dead. And he was born within a year or two of me. And he'd stayed in Argentina – no doubt with his mother's family – after he'd been orphaned. It was unlikely he'd ever met anyone from his father's side of the family.

"I have it, Reeves! Send a telegram to Baskerville Hall at once. Roderick Baskerville-Smythe has returned from South America!"

Reeves appeared not to share the young master's enthusiasm.

"I would not recommend such an action, sir. The appearance – as if from nowhere – of a long lost and, hitherto, believed deceased, relative, would, in my opinion, be viewed with great suspicion."

"Nonsense, Reeves. It would be an occasion of great joy. Fatted calves would be called for. There's even a passage in the Bible. Joseph, wasn't it? The one with the oofy coat? Returning home after seven years of high living abroad and being treated by his father to a fatted calf supper? And Joseph hadn't even had a close shave with the Cairo to Antioch express!"

"In the parable of the Prodigal Son, sir, to which I believe you allude, the young gentleman was only received favourably by his father. His brother, Esau, was somewhat vexed. You would be returning to an uncle, an aunt and a cousin. I fear they would side with Esau upon this matter, and speculate upon the motive behind your reappearance."

"They might think I was there to touch 'em for a few quid?"

"Indeed, sir."

"Well, that's easily solved. I'll introduce myself as a man of means from the start. Diamonds, I think. No one frowns upon a rich relative turning up on the doorstep."

TWO

A reluctant Reeves sent off the telegram announcing my imminent return to the family bosom, and off we set on the long train journey from London to deepest, darkest Devonshire. The journey was made even longer by Reeves's disposition, which was as gloomy as the weather outside.

That's the problem with having a giant brain – it's never satisfied. When it's not picking holes in perfectly good plans, it's wasting time searching for something better. I've always been a strong believer in the old proverb – too many thoughts spoil the child. Far better to come up with something that'll get one's foot over the threshold and then extemporise. After all, no plan survives first contact with a family member.

We arrived in the late afternoon at a place called Grimdark – which Reeves assured me was the closest station to Baskerville Hall. All I can say is that if the Eskimos have forty words for snow, the denizens of Grimdark must have at least fifty for grim. I'd never seen such a place. Everything was damp, grey and dripping. The grey granite walls, the grey slate roofs, the leaden sky. My face and clothes were coated in a fine mist the moment I stepped off the train.

I asked the porter if there was such a thing as a cab we could hire.

"A cab you say? B'ain't be no cabs round 'ere. Where you be 'eading?" said the porter in an accent that could only be described as below-decks pirate.

"Baskerville Hall," I said.

The porter took his cap off to scratch his head. "Ain't

seen Tom all day. They always send Tom to pick up visitors. They know you're comin'?"

"I sent a telegram. Did you mention what time we'd be arriving, Reeves?"

"I did, sir. Perhaps I should send another telegram to say that we have arrived?"

The porter shook his head, sending a light spray of moisture flying in all directions. "There be no telegraph at the 'all, sirs. Line stops 'ere. We 'as a boy who takes the messages back 'an forth on 'is 'orse, but by the time 'e got a message to Tom, be close on dark. An' Tom won't cross the moor in the dark. No one round 'ere would. I'll 'ave a word with me brother. 'E 'as a cart, an' if you don't mind a bit o' dirt, e'll get you, and your bags, to the 'all next to no time."

The porter's brother, swaddled in a voluminous felt cape and perched upon an ancient cart drawn by an equally ancient horse, arrived five minutes later. We stowed our bags in the back and climbed aboard.

"How far is it to the Hall?" I asked.

"Five mile."

It was a long and uncomfortable five miles. The road turned into a rutted track as soon as it left the village. From there it descended down a steep valley to a rickety bridge over a small but boisterous river. Then it climbed up onto what our driver told us was the beginning of the high moor. Not that we could see much of it. There was a persistent mist and the occasional patch of low cloud.

"That's the 'all, up ahead on the 'igh ground to the left." said our driver. "An' that – on the right – is Great Grimdark Mire. Whatever you do, gents, stay well clear. Bottomless 'tis. Swallow an 'orse an' cart like this in seconds. An' the more you struggle, the faster t'will eat you up."

I half-expected the driver to cross himself.

I couldn't see where the mire began and the moor ended. They both looked the same to me. Everything to the right of the track was bleak and flat, barely a tree to be seen anywhere. An expanse of brown grasses, mosses and heather that stretched as far as the mist allowed the eye to see.

"Is this all Grimdark Mire?" I asked.

The driver shook his head. "Grimdark grows and shrinks with the rain. 'Tis three square mile in the winter. A path that's safe in July will kill you in January."

"Lucky it's nearly May, then," I said, deciding it was time to lighten the mood.

"Been a wet spring," said the driver. "Followin' an awful wet winter."

"Ah, well. Soon be summer," I said.

"Then there's the piskies," said the driver.

"Piskies?"

"Little folk. They live on the moor. Mischievous creatures, they be. Nothin' they like better than to trick some poor unfortunate soul into strayin' into the mire. You take heed, gents. If you see a light dancin' on Grimdark, or hear distant singin' on the wind ... you stay where you be. Don't go off investigatin'. It'll be the last thing you do."

Baskerville Hall was marginally less gloomy than our driver. It was one of those grey gothic piles with mock battlements and stone mullioned windows. The kind of place Edgar Allen Poe would have liked. But at least the grounds had trees and lawns – a little oasis of cultivation sitting on a raised plateau above a sea of wild and dismal browns – though it looked like someone had gone overboard on the topiary. One of the lawns was surrounded by a wild menagerie sculpted in yew.

~

I trotted up the stone steps and pulled the doorbell. An age passed. I pulled at my cuffs, craned my neck mire-wards in search of piskies, and blew on my hands for warmth. Then the door opened to reveal one of the tallest and thinnest butlers I'd ever seen. Whether his hair was white or had attracted a fine dusting of snow from the altitude, one couldn't tell. He looked down at me from a great height and spoke.

"Yes?"

"Roderick Baskerville-Smythe, estranged scion of this parish," I replied. "I believe I'm expected."

"Oh," said the venerable b. "You've come, have you?"

I thought his tone a bit familiar for a butler, but then I'd never been to Devonshire before. Maybe this was the local custom.

"It's not *him*, is it, Berrymore?" said a female voice from the depths of the Hall.

"I fear so, milady," said the butler.

"Well bring him in, and let's have a look at him." said the woman, who I deduced – there being no other candidates – was Lady Julia.

The butler opened the door wider and stood aside. I removed my hat and strode into the hallway. Lady Julia and a chap of the same vintage, who had to be Sir Robert, were peering down at me from a first floor landing.

"What ho, what ho, what ho," I said. "I'm Roderick, your long lost relation – risen from the sidings, so to speak. Reports of my flattening greatly exaggerated, what? Takes more than the 4:10 from Buenos Aires to keep a good Baskerville-Smythe down."

Silence. I was reminded of the stunned reception I received two Christmases ago when I was given the wrong cue at the Gussage St. Crispin village show. Mrs Enderby-Slapp was on stage handwringing her way through Lady Macbeth's soliloquy when on bounced R Worcester, clutching his racquet, and uttering a cheery 'anyone for tennis?'

"You don't look like Cuthbert," said Sir Robert, breaking the silence.

"No, I'm *Roderick*, sir, not Cuthbert. Cuthbert was my father."

"Is he an idiot?" Lady Julia asked her brother-in-law. "Of course we know you're not Cuthbert. Sir Robert was pointing out that you don't look like him."

This was not going as well as I'd hoped. Lady Julia had a way of looking at a chap that made one feel like the lowest form of pond life.

"That's because I'm younger, Lady Julia. More hair, don't you know..." I gripped the rim of my hat harder, and tried to stop babbling. "And ... and, besides, I take after my mother."

"She was an idiot too, was she?" asked Lady Julia.

I could tell that Lady Julia was going to be somewhat of a

problem. A winning smile and a breezy turn of phrase was not going to cut it.

"Don't be so hard on the boy, Julia," said Sir Robert. "He *is* an orphan."

"And I was hit by a train," I added, deciding to play the sympathy card. "A big one."

"You don't look like you've been hit by a train," said Lady Julia. "You don't even have a limp. And why were we told you were dead?"

All good questions. I was sure I'd rehearsed an answer, but there was something of the Medusa in Lady Julia that turned all my little grey cells to stone.

"If I may be of assistance, your lord and ladyship," said Reeves, stepping forward.

"Who's that with you?" Lady Julia asked me. "The train driver?"

Reeves coughed. "I'm Mr Baskerville-Smythe's personal gentleman, milady. My master has little recollection of the train crash, or the events that followed, as he was unconscious for more than a week. One of his fellow passengers was misidentified as Mister Roderick by the investigating authorities, and it was *his* demise that was reported. *Our* Mister Roderick was thrown clear when the train hit the stagecoach and, fortuitously, landed on his head – thus escaping further physical damage."

"H'm," said Lady Julia. She didn't look entirely convinced, but she looked mildly swayed.

"It's true," I said. "It took me months to remember who I was."

"So why didn't you write when you *did* remember?"

"Mister Roderick was destitute after the crash, milady. He had no identity, no home, and no resources. So he travelled inland to seek his fortune. By the time he regained his memory, he was hundreds of miles from the nearest telegraphic station."

"Did you find your fortune?" asked Sir Robert.

"Rather! I have five diamond mines. I'm pretty big in amethysts too. So, don't worry, I'm not here to touch you for a few quid."

"Why *are* you here?" asked Lady Julia.

"To see the family seat. Do a spot of sightseeing before I toddle off back to South America. Not knowing about one's roots can cause a big hole in a chap's life."

"H'm," said Lady Julia. I'm not an expert on hums, but I felt this to be a warmer hum than the previous one.

"I think he may be Roderick, Julia," said Sir Robert. "Cuthbert was always a bit odd. And you can't turn the boy away on a night like this. Welcome to Baskerville Hall, my boy. Berrymore will show you to your room. We dine at eight."

~

"Is Miss Dreadnought on the premises, Berrymore?" I asked casually when we reached the door to my room.

"I believe she's in the library, sir."

"With my cousin?"

"Mister Henry is at the studio, sir."

My heart soared. Emmeline was not with Henry! And here was my chance to see her before dinner and explain my unexpected arrival ... and change of name.

I left Reeves unpacking and oiled down the stairs in search of the library. It took me three doors to find it. But where was Emmeline? There was a girl reading in a high-backed chair by the window, but it wasn't her.

"Oh," I said. "Sorry to disturb and all that, but I was told Miss Dreadnought was in here. Have you seen her?"

"I am Miss Dreadnought."

"Really?" I thought I'd met all the Dreadnoughts, but I'd never clapped eyes on this one. "Roderick Baskerville-Smythe," I said, adding a deferential bow. "Is your sister about? Emmeline, that is."

"I *am* Emmeline, Mr Baskerville-Smythe."

If she'd produced a wet halibut and slapped me across the face with it, I couldn't have been more shocked. If you recall it was only last month that I'd seen H. G. Wells turn into his sister before my very eyes! Was it happening again? That 'changing the timeline' thingy. Reeves said the time machine was safely back in the future, but what if someone had brought it back and rewritten history again?

"Are you feeling unwell, Mr Baskerville-Smythe?" this new Emmeline asked.

"What? No, I've just had a long day. I've only just arrived from South America. Um ... do you know H. G. Wells?" It was worth a shot. The last time the time machine had gone missing, it had been his aunt who'd stolen it.

"I've heard of him. I prefer Jules Verne though. That's who I'm reading now." She showed me her book, *Twenty Thousand Leagues Under the Sea*.

"Does Jules Verne have a time machine?" I asked.

"Not that I've read."

"You haven't seen a strange automobile with a giant parasol on the back around here, have you?"

"No. Though there might be one at the studio. There's all sorts of unusual props there."

"Ah. And the studio would be ... where?"

"It's at the old quarry. I'm sure Henry or Sir Robert will take you there tomorrow. They're besotted with the place."

"Right ho," I said. "I'll be beetling off then. Enjoy your book."

I positively *flew* out of the room, swooshed up the stairs two at a time, and burst through the door to my room. If anyone could put the timeline back together, Reeves was the man. His steam-powered brain was one of the wonders of the modern world.

"Reeves!" I cried, in between ragged breaths. "It's happening again. The timeline. Emmie's not Emmie any more. She's changed."

"Most distressing, sir," said that calm rock of logic as he folded the Worcester socks. "In what way has Miss Emmeline changed?"

"In every way! She says she's Emmie, but she doesn't look anything like her. She's blonde. And shorter. And fuller in the face."

"Did she recognise you, sir?"

"No! She didn't know me from Adam. Have you noticed anything strange, Reeves? Conflicting memories of historical events? An extra wife for Henry VIII perhaps?"

"I have not, sir. Is it possible that the young lady is engaging in a practical joke and is pretending to be Miss Emmeline?"

"Why ever would she do that?"

"Unfathomable is the way of young ladies, sir. Perchance Miss Emmeline observed your arrival and persuaded an acquaintance to play a prank upon you."

"Emmie wouldn't do that."

"Given the choice between a young lady engaging in a merry jape and the timeline being changed, I think that I, like William of Ockham, would err on the side of the simple explanation, sir."

"I'm not sure where William of Ockham fits into all this, Reeves, but if he'd read as much detective fiction as I have, he'd know the simplest solution is invariably wrong. It's always the most complex solution that turns out to be the true one."

"Works of *fiction*, sir, are works of entertainment, ergo the popularity of the more complex solution. Real life favours the mundane."

I felt like that chap in the book. I forget its name, but no one believed him. He spent two hundred pages trying to convince everyone that someone was trying to murder him. All his friends and family thought he was touched. Until they found him nailed to the gazebo. I can tell you they all felt pretty silly then.

"You'll not find me nailed to a gazebo, Reeves."

"Sir?"

"Put down that sock, Reeves, and follow me. I'll show you I'm right."

I returned to the library a little more sedately than I'd left. Reeves has his standards, and 'running whilst indoors' was one of his particular dislikes.

"Prepare yourself for a shock, Reeves," I said as I grasped the library door handle.

It would have taken a shoal of wet halibut across the mazard to come close to the shock I experienced when opening that door.

It wasn't Emmeline sitting in the chair by the window. Or her blonde replacement.

It was ... an orang-utan!

THREE

"Emmie!" I cried, rushing over. "What's happened? It's me – Reggie. Can you speak?"

I stared into the orang-utan's eyes trying to find some glimpse of Emmeline. Surely she had to be in there somewhere!

The ape drew back a little and gave me a look that showed neither love nor recognition. If anything it verged on the supercilious.

Ever since reading *The Murders in the Rue Morgue* I'd had a fascination with orang-utans. But never had I expected my fiancée to turn into one!

"This is worse than I thought, Reeves. She's regressed. Someone must have taken the time machine back thousands of years!"

"William of Ockham, sir–"

"Reeves!" I interrupted. "Please stop this obsession with William of Ockham. The man wouldn't last five minutes at Scotland Yard. And having one's fiancé turned into an ape is as far removed from mundane as it is possible to achieve!"

It is a characteristic of the Worcester family to find silver linings in the direst of situations. So it was on this occasion. Given Emmeline's new station, her family might decide that R Worcester esq. was not such a bad match after all.

But could I bring myself to marry an orang-utan?

And if I didn't, would I be sued for breach of promise!

It was at that moment that Emmeline – or Cheetah or whatever name she was going under at that instance – reached out and grabbed my hand.

"She remembers me, Reeves!"

And she had such a firm grip. And such leathery hands.

"I very much doubt, sir, that–"

"It's no good, Reeves. I can't back out now. A promise is a promise. In sickness and in ... change of species, but ... I don't want to live in an apiary!"

"That's bees, sir."

"What's bees?"

"That live in apiaries, sir."

"Do they? Where do apes live?"

"I believe Africa is very popular, sir."

"I can't live in Africa," I wailed.

"I very much doubt that you will have to, sir. I believe this orang-utan goes by the name of Lupin."

"Lupin?"

"Yes, sir. Mr Berrymore told me that Mister Henry had formed an attachment to this animal whilst serving in South Africa. He purchased him from a fellow officer and brought him back to England where he now has the run of the house. Mr Berrymore is of the opinion that Lupin is somewhat cunning and unpredictable, and should be avoided if at all possible."

"Ah," I said, snatching my hand away and stepping back. "Not Emmeline then?"

"No, sir."

I waited for William of Ockham to make an entrance, but Reeves – wisely, I thought – chose restraint.

~

We backed out of the room, keeping a steady eye on Lupin, who was keeping an even steadier eye upon us. The more I looked upon his face, the more convinced I became that Berrymore had it right. There *was* a devious intelligence behind Lupin's eyes. He looked like the kind of orang-utan who'd always have an alibi – having been playing cards at the time in a tree of ill-repute.

My knees trembled all the way to the hallway and didn't stop until we'd closed the library door.

"Eep!" A strange squeak sounded out of nowhere.

I swivelled round – looked hither, then thither – but saw

nothing.

"What on earth was that, Reeves?"

"I believe it originated from the landing, sir."

I couldn't see anyone on the landing.

"Psst!"

"Are you sure it's not you, Reeves? Is your pressure in need of regulation?"

"I believe the hiss to have also originated from the landing, sir."

"You don't think it's a snake, do you? Henry didn't bring a menagerie back from South Africa, did he?"

"One hopes not, sir."

"Maybe a Boer Constrictor, what?"

I waited for an appreciative comment – a quarter inch upward curl to the Reeves' lips, perhaps – but was rewarded with nothing.

"That was a joke, Reeves."

"So I feared, sir."

"Psst!"

There it was again, louder this time.

"I believe someone on the landing is attempting to attract your attention, sir."

I ankled up the stairs and onto the landing, keeping a wary eye out for snakes.

"What ho?" I said. "Anyone there?"

Emmeline – the *real* Emmeline – darted out from around a corner. My heart swelled, but ... she looked worried.

"Ssh!" she hissed. "Quick, follow me. Lady Julia will call the police if she sees you!"

I bounced after Emmie, following her into a corridor off the main landing.

"It's all right," I said. "Lady Julia's already given me the third degree."

"And you're still alive?"

"Veritably resurrected. Oh, and I'm not Reggie. I'm Roderick Baskerville-Smythe, Sir Robert's nephew from South America. Long story. Lots of trains."

"And I'm not Emmeline. I'm Lily Fossett. No trains though. But what *are* you doing here? You're not on a case are you?"

"No, I'm here because you said you'd write every day, and I haven't received a single letter. I thought you'd been eaten by bears!"

"But I *have* written every day!" She paused. I could see her perfectly formed little grey cells positively whirring. "Lady Julia!" she exclaimed. "She must have told the servants to look out for any letter addressed to you, and hand them over to her. I bet she burned them. They'll be ashes in her grate."

"Wait, so who's the blonde girl who calls herself Emmeline?"

"That's the real Lily. We swapped places. You've met her?"

"Ten minutes ago. Why have you swapped places?"

"So I can avoid Henry without having it reported back to mother. I thought Lady Julia might send her daily reports."

"And Lily doesn't mind all this subterfuge?"

"Not at all. She's an old friend and ... did you know that Henry's father is a moving picture producer?"

"No."

"Well that was the clincher. Lily's always wanted to be an actress, but her family won't allow her on the stage. So when I told her we'd be staying at Baskerville Hall she jumped at the chance to swap places. Apparently this is the home of Quarrywood – the biggest moving picture studio in England."

"Is it?" I'd seen the odd moving picture show at the theatre, but never thought to enquire where they were made.

"So I told mother that I simply *had* to have a companion if I were to spend two weeks at Baskerville Hall or I'd raise the barricades in my bedroom again."

"So your mother swung the invite for Lily?"

"Exactly. Lily's been having a great time. Henry's given her a part in his new film. He's in moving pictures now too. Sir Robert's made him a director. And prepare yourself for dinner tonight because moving pictures is *all* anyone ever talks about. One of the other house guests is a producer from America, and wait 'til you see Dr Morrow – he's a mad scientist creating all kinds of prometheans for Quarrywood."

I made a mental note to order a new edition of *Who's Who*. None of this moving picture business had got a mention in my old edition.

"Isn't there a slight flaw in your cunning plan?" I asked.

"What?" said Emmeline looking concerned.

"I'm thinking about what happens in two weeks time when you and Lily swap back. Won't Henry be somewhat peeved to find his leading lady and love interest is someone else. Not to mention your mother walking past a theatre and seeing the name Emmeline Dreadnought written in lights above the door."

Emmeline smiled. "That will *not* be a problem. No one in moving pictures uses their real name. And as for Henry's love interest, no one stands a chance with Ida Spurgeon around."

I wondered if Henry had brought a pet fish back with him from South Africa.

"Ida Spurgeon?"

"She's the daughter of T. Everett Spurgeon, the American moving picture producer I told you about. She doesn't let anyone else get a look in with Henry. Lily says Ida deliberately tripped her during one of her scenes this morning, and then complained to Henry how clumsy Lily was!"

"What's Henry like?" I asked nonchalantly.

"He's quite sweet really ... but he'd never solve a murder."

I positively glowed. Say what one will about the modern woman, one can't fault their priorities.

A cough came from the landing.

"Hello, Reeves," said Emmeline.

"Good evening, miss," said Reeves, appearing from around the corner. "I think it may be judicious to select an alternative venue for this conversation as people will be dressing for dinner soon."

"There's bags of time yet, Reeves," said Emmeline. "And most of the rooms in this wing are empty. I think that's why they put me here – to keep me out of the way. Are you pretending to be South American too, Reeves?"

"No, miss."

"I think you should. Don't you, Reggie?"

I kept quiet. 'Never antagonise the man who is about to

lay out one's clothes for dinner' is a family motto.

"And we'll have to give you an interesting past," said Emmeline. "I know! You're an Argentinean tango instructor fallen upon hard times."

"I think not, miss."

Emmeline did not appear to be listening. "We can't call you Reeves either. How about Reevero? Reevero Gaucho – that's a better name."

I decided to intervene before Reeves popped a rivet.

"You'll never guess who I met in the library just now," I said. "An orang-utan!"

As I had hoped, an orang-utan in a library trumped a cornered valet every time.

"Lupin!" said Emmeline. "What do you think of him? Did he look at you as though he was working out the best way to stuff your body up a chimney?"

"I'd say he'd already worked that out and was perfecting his alibi. Is it true he has the run of the house?"

"Completely. Some evenings he even dines with us! Henry dotes upon him."

The thought of dining with Lady Julia *and* Lupin brought a momentary tremble to the Worcester knees.

"The thing is," said Emmeline, suddenly looking a little serious "It's not just Lupin. There's something ... *off* about this place. I can't put my finger on what. I just ... can't shake this feeling that something bad is about to happen. You do know the family's cursed?"

"Is it?"

"Henry told Lily all about it. It dates back to 1782 when Theodosia Baskerville-Smythe saw something unpleasant in the woodshed."

"Did she say what?"

"Not a word. Though it must have been something to do with her nephew, because she cursed him and all his heirs. And she never ate a parsnip again for the rest of her life."

The mind boggled.

"Ever since then she's walked the Hall the night before the head of the family dies. And dragged him off to Hell on the very next day."

FOUR

Back in my room, I stretched out in a chair and settled back for a bit of pre-prandial contemplation. I prefer to contemplate with a glass in my hand, but – the room being dry – the little grey cells had to rough it.

All in all, I thought things had progressed well. A bit of a mid-season wobble with the orang-utan, and I could have done without the ghostly Theodosia, but otherwise all was tickety-boo. I had gained entry to the Hall. The mystery of the missing letters had been explained. And Emmeline and I, although as star cross'd as ever, were still united in our desire to tie the matrimonial clove hitch.

"Would you prefer to return to London by tomorrow's morning or afternoon train, sir," said Reeves.

"What?" I said. "Steady on, Reeves. We've only just arrived."

"My apologies, sir. I was under the impression that our mission here was complete. Miss Emmeline's affections remain steadfast, and Mister Henry's attentions are engaged elsewhere. I assumed our plan would be to withdraw at the first opportunity before our subterfuge was discovered."

"You presume to assume, Reeves. This is the gift horse that doesn't like its mouth prodded. Emmeline and I have the chance of spending a whole one and a half weeks together without anyone raising an objection or throwing a kilted gigolo in our path."

Reeves may not have coughed, but one of his eyebrows quivered censoriously.

"A risky stratagem, sir. It is my belief that Lady Julia will be observing you extremely closely."

"Then Emmeline and I shall go for long, brisk walks. Lady Julia can't be everywhere, Reeves. She has to keep an eye on the other Emmeline, remember."

~

I toddled downstairs a good twenty minutes before dinner. Everyone was gathered in the drawing room and all conversation stopped the moment I appeared.

"What ho," I said, a little nervously as eighteen eyeballs swivelled my way.

"This is Robert's nephew, Roderick," said Lady Julia. "You'll have to excuse him. He was hit on the head by a train."

"Really?" said Henry.

"A glancing blow," I said. "A little concussion. A sore ear. Right as rain now though."

Sir Robert made the introductions. I recognised Henry from his entry in *Milady's Form Guide to Young Gentlemen.* He was indeed dashing and well-turned out. He shook my hand enthusiastically.

"Welcome to England, coz," he said. "Do you tread the boards? I've got just the part for you in my moving picture."

T. Everett Spurgeon had a part for me in his moving picture too – if I was ever in New York. His fleshy hand enveloped mine and pumped it with almost as much enthusiasm as Henry had.

"Have you ever thought of investing in moving pictures, Roderick?" asked T. Everett. "Sir Robert says you're big in diamonds."

"Pretty big," I said.

"You must be awfully clever to find all those diamonds," said Ida Spurgeon, appearing alongside and sliding her arm through mine.

"One would think so," I said, trying unsuccessfully to uncouple my arm from hers. "But, no, I'm not brainy at all. Instinct is what one needs for prospecting, not brains. Did Isaac Newton ever find any diamonds? I think not. Pretty hot with apples, not so good with gems."

Emmeline annexed my other arm.

"I bet you still have funny turns, don't you?" she asked, giving me a meaningful look. "Being hit on the head with a train must take its toll. Do you froth at the mouth every full moon?"

"Only those months with an 'r' in them," I said, playing along.

Ida grasped my arm tighter and pulled me closer. The adjective 'frothing' was obviously a silent one when interposed between the words 'rich' and 'husband.'

"I think you're very brave," she said. "Do you own a yacht?"

"No," I said. "No yachts."

"I expect you get terribly sea sick," said Emmeline, "...in between the frothing."

I had the feeling I was seconds away from having my continence called into question. My embarrassment was saved by the intervention of John Stapleford, one of Sir Robert's neighbours.

"How *do* you find diamonds though," asked Stapleford. "Do you have to dig them out of the ground with a pick?"

The salvation of my embarrassment was brief. How *did* you find diamonds? And where was Reeves in my hour of need? He'd know everything you wanted to know about diamonds, and quite a bit about what you'd rather not.

"I ... pan for them," I said, looking longingly for the nearest decanter. Some chaps may swear by *in vino veritas,* but I found a stiff one worked even better when one was lying.

"Pan, you say?" said Stapleford. "How does that work? Are diamonds denser than the native rock?"

I shrugged – as much as a person with both arms securely pinned could. "Don't ask me. All I know is that it works. Others may disagree, but I swear by it. One can't make one's fortune without getting one's feet wet. Many a month I've spent knee deep in the Orinoco."

"I thought you found your fortune in Argentina," said Stapleford, looking more and more like Weaselly Beasley, the class swot from my old prep school. "Isn't the Orinoco in Venezuela?"

"It's a long river," I said. The room was far from warm, but I could feel the first bead of perspiration forming on the Worcester brow.

"I expect Roderick gets very confused with names," said Emmeline. "I know if I were hit by a train I wouldn't know the Thames from the Severn."

"I'm sure Roderick wouldn't get confused about the name of his intended though," said Ida. "You *do* have a fiancée back in Argentina, don't you?"

I had a strong urge to feign a heart attack. This was the horniest dilemma I'd ever been impaled upon. If I invented an Argentinean fiancée, I wouldn't be able to monopolise Emmeline without being labelled a bounder by the Baskerville-Smythes. And If I denied any betrothal, I'd spend the next ten days fending off the formidable Ida!

And I had a strong feeling that even a feigned heart attack would not dislodge Ida from my arm. She'd probably volunteer to nurse me back to health!

I opened my mouth in the vain hope that something clever might make an appearance.

It rarely does.

"Perhaps she was hit by a train too?" suggested Lady Julia.

"Or," said Emmeline. "Perhaps she broke off the engagement because she didn't like living in a shack over your diamond mine in the middle of nowhere."

"Yes!" I said. I could have hugged Emmie. If I'd had a spare arm.

"You're a veritable mind reader, Miss Fossett," I continued. "Conchita – that was my fiancée – wanted me to buy an estate in Buenos Aires, but I'm too fond of my old home. We fell out over it, and parted brass rags. It was a painful episode. But I'm sure *you'd* appreciate my humble home, Miss Spurgeon. The way the corrugated iron catches the sun at dawn... And we rarely have yellow fever in the camp now."

Ida's grip slackened.

"I doubt you have that many head hunters these days either," said Emmeline.

"Not since the crocodiles ate them all."

~

I was free of Ida, and no longer the centre of attention. The Stapleford cove gave me the odd look or two, and Lady Julia unleashed a couple of withering looks that would have cowed a lesser man. But I was a chap whose skin had been thickened by repeated exposure to disapproving aunts.

And I had Emmeline on my arm.

Ten minutes later though something odd happened. Henry was talking about his new moving picture when he suddenly stopped.

"Do you hear that?" he said, looking towards the windows.

Everyone stopped and inclined an ear. There was a faint wailing noise. Henry ran to the nearest window and opened it. The wailing noise grew. I'd never heard anything like it.

"It's the siren," said Henry. "Someone's escaped."

"Escaped from where?" asked T. Everett.

"Dartmoor prison," said Henry. "It's six miles away across the moor."

"Don't worry, they won't come here," said Sir Robert. "Grimdark Mire stands between us and the prison. Anyone heading this way will be swallowed whole and never seen again."

"Aye," said Stapleford. "Grimdark never gives up its dead."

"I wouldn't like to be out on a night like this," said Henry, peering into the dark. "Berrymore says there's a storm coming, and the wind certainly looks to be picking up."

"Do close the window, Henry," said Lady Julia. "Before we all perish from the cold."

No sooner had Henry closed the window when the dinner gong sounded.

"Is that the dinner gong?" I asked. "Or has one of the maids escaped?"

Everyone laughed, except Lady Julia, who I suspected had taken an oath at an early age not to smile in public.

Presently, the door to the dining room opened and

everyone began to file through. Except Lady Julia, who lurked in the doorway.

"A word, Roderick," she said as I approached. "You too, Lily."

I swallowed hard. Lady Julia waited until everyone else was out of earshot.

"I do not know what you are up to, young man," said Lady Julia. "But I am *watching* you. *Both* of you. Come, Lily, dear. You will sit next to me at dinner. I feel as if I have been neglecting you of late."

~

I had hoped to sit next to Emmeline during dinner but, with everyone already seated, I found myself down the other end of the table, wedged between T. Everett Spurgeon and Henry. Emmeline would have to face her inquisition alone.

"You look like a man who knows a good investment when he sees one, Roderick," said T. Everett.

"I should say so," I said. "I might take a spin around the moors tomorrow. See if the old nose can sniff out a gem or two. I thought I caught a slight whiff of emerald on the ride over."

"Really? Well, I know of something even better," said T. "A sure-fire winner just crying out for a little extra seed money. Ain't I right, Henry?"

"I've been trying to get the governor to invest," said Henry.

"In what?" I asked.

"Ride-in movies," said T. Everett, writing the words in the air with a stubby finger. "They're really taking off back home. You ever heard of Thomas Edison?"

"No, I can't say that I have."

"He is the devil, Roderick. A greedier or more ruthless man has never lived. He's sewn up the movie industry in New York. He wants to control everything – from the cameras you use to shoot the movies to the theatres where you show them. Anyone stands in his way, they get sued or bought out. That's why people like me are looking to move out of New York."

T. Everett paused while a footman placed a bowl of soup in front of him.

"Edison may have the East Coast sewn up, but he's nobody out west. Or over here. And when you think about it, why do you need a theatre to put on a picture show? All you need is a screen and a projector.

"That's the beauty of the ride-in," continued T. "It's like a travelling show. All you need is a projector and a roll of white canvas. You travel the country, set up your equipment on the edge of town, tell all the folks to come on by and charge them a nickel a time. You don't even have to provide any seats because they bring their own."

"They bring their own seats?" I said.

"Their horses," said T. "That's why it's called a ride-in. And the best bit is you make more on the concessions than you do from admission."

"What's a concession?"

"Food and drink. And, boy, do those horses eat. We make as much money on the rolled oats as we do on the popcorn!"

"It seems a corker to me," said Henry. "No draughty theatres to buy or maintain."

"What about the weather?" I asked. "I can see these ride-ins being very popular in the sunnier climes, but what about when it's raining?"

T. Everett positively beamed. "That's the really exciting bit. And why England is just perfect for this new development. The fly-in."

"With zeppelins," added Henry.

"That's right," said T. "It may be raining on the ground, but it's sunny above the clouds. Can't you just see the possibilities, Roderick? All those zeppelins parked high above the clouds, enjoying the sun and Quarrywood's next hit movie."

"What about the screen?" I asked.

"We use the side of a zeppelin!" said T.

"Or a cloud," said Henry. "If it's one of those white, fluffy ones."

"The possibilities are endless," said T. "England's the richest country in the world. And the cloudiest. Think of all those private zeppelin owners just crying out for somewhere new to go. We'll make the fly-in *the* most fashionable place to be seen. All we need are investors."

I slurped a contemplative spoonful of mulligatawny. I may not have had five diamond mines, but neither was I short of a few bob. As oofiness went, I was high to middling. Should I invest a few thou? I could see my fellow sloths being first in the queue for a fly-in over Piccadilly.

"And that's not the best bit," said T. "The beauty of the fly-in is that we can hold them anywhere. And if we hold them outside the three-mile limit, it's all tax free! No tax. No duty. Everything we make is pure profit!"

I'm sure there was a downside, but dashed if I could see it. I'd have a word with Reeves at the first opportunity.

T. Everett was a veritable fountain of ideas. Over the next two courses he regaled me with all manner of money-making schemes.

"It's all in the concessions," he said. "And the better-heeled the customer, the bigger the profit. Have you ever been to the opera, Roderick?"

"Does Gilbert and Sullivan count?"

"If they have opera glasses they do. How can you see how fat the fat lady really is if you don't have opera glasses? It'll be the same at a fly-in, except ... how can you fly a zeppelin without flying goggles?"

All good questions.

"So we combine the two," said T. Everett. "And sell everyone our very own fly-in movie goggles. No one'll dare miss out."

"Tell him about the cloud ice cube dispenser," said Henry.

"Think of all those clouds up there, Roderick," said T. "Full of the purest water imaginable. And all those thirsty patrons just crying out for ice in their drinks. I know a guy in New Jersey who has a patent for seeding clouds to make it rain. If he can make rain, he sure as shootin' oughta be able to make ice too, don't you think?"

Once again his logic was faultless.

"We'll call it Cloud Ice," continued T. "And we'll add some kinda scoop to our concessions zeppelin to collect it all. It'll be swell."

"Of course," said Henry, "None of this can get off the ground without a steady stream of hit movies to show. Which is where Quarrywood comes in. Have you seen any of our movies, Roderick? *The Quarry That Time Forgot*, *The Quarry of the Apes*. We're shooting *The Creature from 20,000 Leagues Under the Quarry* at the moment."

I sensed a theme.

"Isn't it *20,000 Leagues Under the Sea*?" I said.

"That's the book," said Henry. "But the sea's twenty miles away and the quarry's right here."

"The movie is a very different creature to a book, Roderick," said T. "It takes days to read a book. A movie's over in twenty minutes."

"Exactly," said Henry. "One can't afford to dawdle. Being a moving picture director is a bit like producing a village show when one only has the hall booked for twenty minutes, and the audience is packed with the local toughs, each one armed to the gills with rotten tomatoes. One can't send out old Mr Trumpington to stutter and repeat himself through all thirty-seven verses of *Observations of Flowers in the Vicinity of Matterstock Parva*. They'd kill him."

I may never have met old Mr Trumpington, but I'd sat through many a recitation by a close relative.

"No," said Henry. "One simply has to cut out all the Trumpingtons, and floral observations, when adapting a book for a one-reeler. People want action these days – lots of chases, monsters and murders. And if the book doesn't have enough monsters then I say 'add them.' Don't you think *The Importance of Being Earnest* would be improved by having a few more murders?"

"I didn't know there were *any* murders in *The Importance of Being Earnest*."

"I think you'll find there's *one*. Doesn't Lady Bracknell brain someone with a handbag?"

"Not in the productions I've seen."

Though I had to admit a certain desire to see one.

~

I caught a glimpse of Emmeline as Lady Julia led her and the other ladies into the drawing room after dinner. She smiled wanly in my direction before a tug from Lady Julia dragged her away.

Stapleford left soon afterwards too, citing the imminent storm and a prisoner on the loose as good reasons to head home. Apparently he lived a mile away at High Dudgeon Farm and the track home skirted the dreaded Grimdark Mire.

The remainder of the party gathered around our end of the dining table. Sir Robert bringing a rather fine decanter of port with him and Dr Morrow breaking out the cigars.

"How long are you planning to stay in England, Roderick?" asked Dr Morrow.

"Not long at all," I said. "Two weeks and I'll be pining for the Pampas."

"You're not intending to buy a house here then?"

"No, this is but a fleeting visit."

"Seems an awfully long way to come for a fleeting visit," said the doctor. "Why not stay for the summer?"

"Capital idea!" said Henry. "You could star in your own movie. *Journey to The Centre of The Diamond Quarry*. I'm sure the station master at Grimdark would let us borrow a train for the concussion scene."

I didn't like the sound of 'concussion scene.'

"You'd be in no danger," said Dr Morrow. "We'd use a double for the actual impact."

"You haven't seen the good doctor's doubles, have you?" said Henry. "They are *remarkably* realistic."

"It's what makes Quarrywood movies stand out from the rest," said Sir Robert. "Other moving pictures look contrived and pedestrian compared to ours."

"It's true," said T. Everett. "The first time I saw a Quarrywood movie – *The Quarry of the Apes*, I think it was – I couldn't believe my eyes. Apes were having sword fights – on horseback! – and guys were having their arms lopped off! I've never seen a theatre audience so enthralled. We sold more vials of smelling salts that evening than we did orange juice."

"Of course they weren't real apes," said Dr Morrow. "Or real people having their arms lopped off. They were automata and prometheans. Have you heard of prometheans, Roderick? Corpses sewn back together and reanimated?"

"I'm on first name terms with several," I said. "I've even exchanged words with Guy Fawkes."

"Wasn't he reanimated in London?" said Dr Morrow. "And then incarcerated by the police. I thought this was your first visit to England, Roderick?"

There was slight rise in the Worcester heart-rate, but a fleeting one. My little grey cells were fully lubricated by this time of the evening, steeped in fine Burgundy and the first flush of the Old Ruby.

"Ah, you're thinking of the gunpowder plot Guy Fawkes," I said. "I'm talking about the Argentinean one. He has two Fs in his name. Two Gs as well, I think. Rum fellow. He was a pirate, you know? Grief-stricken when they couldn't reanimate his parrot."

I think I got away with it. Dr Morrow gave me a strange look but, as a person who'd been collecting strange looks for most of his life, I found it little stranger than most.

"They're a lot cheaper than actors," said Sir Robert, returning the conversation back to his beloved Quarrywood. "Prometheans. And less trouble. Tell an actor his part calls for an arm lopping and he'll hand in his notice. Not so with these *réanimé* chappies."

"Of course, I *do* sew their arms back on," said Dr Morrow. "After all, they've all been sewn together so many times, what's one more?"

"Quite," I said. "I don't suppose you *need* any real actors in your moving pictures, do you? You could use prometheans for every role."

"Not really," said Henry. "They do have their limitations. If one wants someone to be stabbed, or have a tree fall on them, they have no equal. But they can't act. One needs an expressive face for close-ups. Prometheans don't have the range."

"Or the intellect," said Dr Morrow, looking at me a little more closely than I was comfortable with. "I can't see any scarring on your head, Roderick, from when that train struck you."

"It *was* a glancing blow," I said. "The train hit the stagecoach I was travelling in, and I was thrown out. It was more a case of a dull thump as my head hit the ground than a whack from a charging train."

"I think we'll lose the stagecoach for the movie," said Henry. "It'll look better if the train gives you a good whack and sends you flying high through the air. And we'll have to give you a good reason for being on the tracks in the first place."

"He could be tied to the tracks," said T. Everett.

"Capital!" said Henry. "The Lizard Man ties Roderick to the railway tracks then, just as Roderick frees himself – whack! – along comes the train."

I had to ask. "Did you say Lizard Man?"

"Quarrywood is famous for its Lizard Men," said T.

"We try to use them in all our films," said Henry. "They make excellent villains. They look like men, but they have these big dinosaur heads and tails."

"People don't realise how hard it is to portray villainy," said Sir Robert. "Or how long it takes. When one only has twenty minutes, one can't afford to keep pausing the action for a close up of the actor so he can twirl his moustaches in a menacing fashion."

"In the States we use the hat," said T. Everett. "If an actor's wearing a white hat, he's a good guy. If he's wearing a black hat, he's bad."

"What about tan hats?" I asked.

"They're for bystanders," said T. Everett. "They're only there to make up the numbers."

"We tried hats in *The Quarry of the Apes*," said Sir Robert. "Didn't look right."

"Especially on the Lizard Men," said Henry. "Dashed difficult to feel threatened by a Lizard Man wearing a sombrero."

"Even a black one," said Sir Robert. "We had to re-shoot every scene."

"But now we have the balance right," said Henry. "One

only needs a glimpse of a Lizard Man to know he's up to no good. No need for hats or close-ups of twirling moustaches. It lets the action run much smoother."

~

The ladies returned just before midnight. I didn't see Emmeline at first. Naturally my first thought was that she'd tied herself to a stout table – probably using a curtain she'd pulled from its rings – but, no, she was merely hanging back to increase the space between her and Lady Julia.

Fortunately, Lady Julia favoured early nights, and only stayed long enough to glare at me twice before exiting stage left.

I counted to five before ambling over to Emmeline, adding a nonchalant whistle to convey an aura of detached innocence in case anyone was watching.

"She's like a terrier," said Emmeline, keeping her voice low. "She didn't stop all evening. Questioning me about my family, friends, you."

"Me?"

"She's not sure if I'm an impressionable, silly girl or your partner in crime! And I can't be beastly back to her because everyone thinks I'm Lily. I can't get Lily into trouble, so I have to sit back and take it."

"She'll relent," I said, trying to sound a good deal more confident than I felt.

"I hope so. I can't sit through another evening like tonight. I'll explode!"

"I'll have a word with Reeves. He'll come up with a plan, I'm sure."

We couldn't talk privately after that. Henry came over, swiftly followed by Ida, and from then on the conversation switched to all things Quarrywood.

Until a woman's scream stopped all conversation dead.

FIVE

We all ran to the source of the scream, and found Lily standing in the hallway, staring up at the landing, one hand clasped to her mouth.

I followed her gaze and started. Was it a ghost? It looked like a ghost. Its face was a glowing skull – a ghostly, shimmering, greenish glow – shining out from beneath a hood. She, or it, wore a long black dress and was oiling along the ill-lit landing.

"It's Theodosia!" said Henry. "She's the image of her portrait."

Henry looked at his father, whose face had turned ashen. "It can't be," said Sir Robert.

Henry set off up the stairs at a fair lick. I followed. The ghost had turned into the very corridor that Emmeline and I had had our earlier conversation.

But when Henry and I reached the corridor, it was empty. Every door in the corridor was closed, save one: the nearest on the right, which was wide open.

The Worcester heart was beating at a considerable rate. The room in front of us was dark, the only light coming from a single gas lamp on the landing behind us. If the ghost was inside the room, it was hiding its glowing face.

A footman arrived with a lamp. Henry took it and slowly entered the room, holding the lamp high in front of him. We all shuffled after him.

Then there was a collective gasp. There was a message on the mirror over the chimney breast.

Written in rouge, it said in large letters, 'He dies tomorrow!'

~

We searched the entire bedroom. There was no sign of the ghost, and nowhere anyone pretending to be a ghost could have gone. Both windows were locked, and Sir Robert was adamant there were no secret passages.

"Our family have lived here for generations. If there was a secret passage, I'd know about it."

"I searched high and low for secret passages when I was a boy," said Henry. "I measured the house inside and out. There are no spaces unaccounted for."

"You're not saying it's a real ghost?" asked Emmeline.

"Of course not," said Henry. "But... I can't see how anyone could have run in here, written that message, then disappeared. There wasn't time."

Reeves, for who else could it have been, coughed from the corridor.

"This is my man Reeves," I said. "Do you have an observation?"

"I do, sir. Mister Henry is correct in his assertion that there was insufficient time to write that message and effect an escape, ergo the message was written earlier."

Words are insufficient to encapsulate the enormity of Reeves' brain. Perhaps a hieroglyph could do it justice – an extra large one with an all-seeing eye and a couple of fish.

"Go on, Reeves," I said. "What else do you deduce?"

"I suspect, sir, that the open door to this room, and the message inside, were what is commonly called a red herring, designed to detain his or her pursuers while the perpetrator made good their escape elsewhere."

"Then they're still in this wing," said Henry. "No one could have doubled back down this corridor. We'd have seen them. Come on. We'll search every room."

Every room off the corridor was searched. Nothing was found. No ghost, no abandoned black dress, and no further missives written on mirrors.

"Could the ghost have been a projection?" asked Sir Robert.

"I don't think so, Sir Robert," said T. Everett. "There

would have been a cone of light from the projector to the image. There wasn't one. I looked."

"So how did they escape?" said Henry. "Every window is locked."

Cometh the locked room mystery, cometh the cough.

"Not *every* window, sir," said Reeves as a roomful of eyes swivelled his way. "I did notice that one, although closed, was unlatched."

"Which one?"

"The one in the room opposite to the one with the message, sir."

I'm not sure how many there were of us, but by this time we were a sizeable party of guests and servants, and all of us followed Henry into the room with the unlatched window.

Henry hoisted up the lower pane of the sash window and let in half a gale that lifted both curtains towards the ceiling.

"I can't see anything," said Henry, leaning out into the night. "There's no ladder or anything to climb down on."

"May I borrow your lamp?" I asked Henry. "I have some experience in this line of work."

I took the lamp, and leaned out of the window. Henry was right about the lack of anything nearby to climb down on. No drainpipe, no handy tree or climbing shrub. If someone had left by this window they'd have needed a ladder. And if our driver had been right about it having been a wet spring and winter, then a ladder would have left two distinctive marks in the lawn below.

I led the house party outside and around the Hall to the East Wing. The weather was wild but, thankfully, the rain was holding off.

"That's the window," said Henry. "The second one along from where the wing meets the old house."

I advanced cautiously towards the spot where any ladder would have been placed, checking the ground for those telltale signs much beloved by us consulting detectives – the imprint of an unusual boot, the hole left by a wooden leg – but found nothing.

Neither did I find any marks left by the feet of a ladder. And yet, the ground was decidedly soft.

"I can't see any signs of a ladder," said Henry. "Can you?"

I extended the search area. What if the ladder had been exceedingly long and placed further away from the wall? I scrutinised the entire area, stooping low with the lamp to examine the minutest blade of grass.

Nothing.

"Would a woman's weight on the ladder be sufficient to make a mark?" asked Sir Robert.

"It would," said Emmeline. "Look, my heels are sinking into the lawn."

"Mine aren't," said Ida. "But then ... I'm not as heavy as you."

"Yes, you are!" said Emmeline.

"No, I'm not! Am I, Henry? Only yesterday you remarked how dainty I was."

For a good second or two Henry looked like a chap about to feign a heart attack. But he recovered. "Both of you are, of course, exceedingly dainty, but our ladders are not. And this ground is as soft as I've ever seen it. I can't see even a cat being able to climb a ladder here without leaving a mark."

Ida wasn't finished.

"What about a ghost?" she said haughtily. "They don't weigh anything at all. Couldn't a ghost climb down the ladder without making a mark?"

"A ghost wouldn't *need* a ladder!" said Emmeline, a little more pointedly than is usual in polite society.

"A ghost wouldn't leave footprints in the lawn either!" said Ida. "Because *they* don't plod like a carthorse."

"I don't *plod –*"

In the interest of preserving decorum – and the crime scene – I thought it wise to intervene.

"Wait!" I said "There's another place the ladder could have been erected."

Emmeline and Ida drew back from each other and turned my way.

"Where?" said Henry.

"If the ladder was long enough, it could have been propped up against the main house and angled such that it passed by the window in the East Wing."

"Running parallel to the wing, you mean?" said Henry.

"Yes."

We searched along the base of the East Wing, but again found nothing. And then it began to pour down – a veritable cloud burst with accompanying thunder and lightning.

"We'll continue this investigation in the morning," said Henry. "There's nothing more we can do tonight."

Once inside the Hall, I drew Emmeline and Reeves aside.

"I didn't say anything earlier," I said, keeping my voice low. "But have either of you seen Lupin this evening?"

"I knew it!" whispered Emmeline. "The moment Henry said there was no ladder or anything to climb down, I knew you'd suspect Lupin. I haven't seen him at all this evening."

"The figure purporting to be a ghost did not ambulate like Lupin, sir. It was also taller."

"I think you underestimate Lupin, Reeves. I expect he can walk like a deb if the mood takes him. And that glowing head was obviously false. Lupin was probably wearing it like a hat."

"If you say so, sir."

SIX

I had somewhat of a disturbed night what with the continual lightning flashes, thunder claps, and rain lashing against the windows. It was more like one of those wild storms one experiences in the south of France than the more genteel English variant. I half-expected Reeves to waken me for breakfast wearing a sou'wester.

"Has it stopped raining, Reeves?" I asked as he drew back the curtains.

"The weather appears most clement, sir. Mr Berrymore is of the opinion that the day will be a sunny one."

"Something of an expert is he, Reeves? The owner of one of those meteorological bunions, perhaps?"

"I really couldn't say, sir."

"Any sightings of Lupin this morning?"

"He is taking breakfast with the family, sir."

"Really? What about spectral sightings? Have there been any more overnight?"

"None, sir, though opinion in the servants' hall is that last night's visitation was not a dissimulation. There is considerable concern for Sir Robert. Mr Berrymore remembers the last time the ghost appeared, and that was on the eve of Sir Robert's father's death."

"We don't believe in ghosts though, do we, Reeves?"

"No, sir."

That was a relief.

A little later I toddled down to breakfast. If the day were to be a sunny one, Emmeline and I could go for a walk. We'd have to set off at different times to avoid the gimlet-eye of Lady Julia, but we could soon meet up at some pre-arranged local landmark. And there was always the chance that, after last night's ghostly manifestation, Lady Julia's attention might be directed elsewhere.

I breezed into the dining room.

"What ho, what ho, what ho," I said, waggling four welcoming fingers and a companionable thumb.

"Are *you* responsible for that abomination last night?" snapped Lady Julia.

"I told you, Aunt Julia," said Henry. "Roderick never left my side all evening. It can't have been him."

Lady Julia appeared unswayed.

"Doesn't anyone else find it strange that it happened within hours of his arrival?" she said.

"Henry's right, Julia," said Sir Robert. "We were all there. We all saw Roderick follow Henry up the stairs in pursuit of the apparition. It wasn't him."

"What about Lily?" said Lady Julia. "Where was she?"

"Lily and I were talking in the dining room when the ghost appeared," said Henry. "It wasn't her either."

Every head at the table nodded in agreement with the exception of Lupin and Lady Julia. Emmeline gave me a reassuring smile. Lupin smirked.

I noticed the line of serving domes on the breakfast sideboard and ankled over. I hoped there'd be a kipper or two left. I had the feeling that my little grey cells were going to need every assistance if I were to survive the day unscathed.

I found the kippers and pondered over whether to take two or three. Three would give my brain a good fillip, but it would probably elicit a biting comment from Lady Julia concerning gluttony.

I piled two on my plate and headed for the dining table. As one of the available seats was next to Lupin, I chose the one on the far side of the table, next to Ida.

"Do you think it was a real ghost last night, Roderick?" asked Ida.

"I do not," I said, giving Lupin – who was sitting opposite – the kind of challenging look that Sherlock Holmes would have given Professor Moriarty had they met over a kipper. "I think the 'ghost' is very much alive ... and under this very roof as we speak."

Lupin narrowed his eyes, put down his banana, and slowly slid off his chair.

"Who do you think it is?" asked Ida.

I was too distracted with Lupin's disappearance to reply immediately. Where had he gone? What was he doing under the table? I feared for my legs, and all stations south.

I was not alone in my apprehension. Several heads darted this way and that, trying to discern where Lupin might surface.

"He likes playing under the table," said Henry. "He can stay there for hours. Do you have a suspect, Roderick?"

A large unseen hand grasped my knee. "No," I said, nudging the upper tenor register. "It could be anyone."

A second large unseen hand grasped my other knee, then a third hand curled around my foot. How many orang-utans were down there?

The next second I had the answer – none – for Lupin burst out from beneath the table, leaped onto my lap and sent both me and the chair flying backwards. The chair and I soon parted company, but not Lupin and I. We remained entangled, rolling across the floor.

"Don't worry," said Henry. "He's only playing. The two of us wrestle a lot."

I hadn't wrestled since I was a child. And I'd never wrestled anyone with four hands! Lupin was also deceptively strong. He may have been half my size, but he was the stronger.

"He must really like you," said Henry. "I've never seen him wrestle anyone else."

"I expect he's excited at finally meeting his intellectual equal," said Lady Julia.

I'm sure Lady Julia meant it as an insult, but as I lay pinned to the floor, staring up into Lupin's eyes, I could see the fearsome intellect of a simian Moriarty perched upon my chest.

Lily screamed. "He's ripped Roderick's hand off!"

Ida echoed Lily's scream. "She's right. Look!"

If I'd had any air left in my lungs, I'd have screamed too. I swivelled my head instead, following the track of Ida's finger. There, a foot away from my nose, lay a severed hand!

I screamed airlessly. How? When? I had no pain from either hand – both as far as I could tell were pinned to the floor by Lupin – but ... the evidence of my mutilation was before my very eyes!

Lupin observed the severed hand too. He jumped off me, snatched the hand and bounded towards the window. I took the opportunity to raise both wrists from the floor...

Both my hands were where they should be. I was whole.

Emmeline was the first to reach me. I suspected she might have cantered over the top of the dining table, as one of her heels had spiked a kipper.

She knelt by my side, ashen-faced, staring at my hands. "You're not hurt!" she said. "I thought..."

She stifled a sob, turning it into a relieved laugh.

"If it's not *your* hand, whose is it?" said Henry. "Lupin! Come down from there!"

Lupin had taken refuge on the pelmet above the window. He sniffed the severed hand and didn't seem to find the experience pleasant.

Henry and Sir Robert stood under the window remonstrating with Lupin. Lady Julia was the only one of our party to remain seated. She shook her head in a despairing fashion and pronged a kipper.

"There's another one!" said Emmeline pointing under the dining table.

"Another what?" I asked, scooting backwards on hands and heels. Not another orang-utan, I hoped.

"Another hand," she said.

"Berrymore," said Lady Julia. "Would you kindly ascertain if there are any more body parts beneath the table."

Berrymore delegated the bending and crawling to a footman, who reported no further sightings. The footman retrieved the hand that Emmeline had spotted and, somewhat gingerly, presented it to Henry.

"It's an automaton's hand," said Henry, giving the hand the old once over.

I was just dusting myself off when Lupin threw the other hand at me. It missed, but it too showed the metallic innards protruding from the wrist.

"Where's the rest of him?" asked Emmeline.

A good question.

"Are any of the servants automata?" I asked.

"We don't allow them in the house," said Lady Julia.

"Two of the gardeners are automata," said Henry. "And several of our actors, but they're stored at the studio."

My thoughts took a dark turn. There was one automaton who *was* in the house – Reeves! I'd never thought to introduce him as one. He was a superior model – indistinguishable from the real thing. Had someone lopped off his hands?

"Could someone send for my man Reeves?" I asked. "He's an expert on all things automata."

A footman was despatched. Emmeline and I exchanged concerned looks. Reeves could not abide untidiness. He'd be mortified to appear in public without hands.

But what if it he'd lost more than his hands?

I began to feel a little faint. I couldn't lose Reeves!

"Bit of a brainbox, is he?" asked Henry. "He certainly seemed to know his stuff last night."

"Yes," I said, looking wanly towards the door. "He's the brainiest chap I know."

It felt like the footman had been gone for hours. Lupin was coaxed down from the pelmet. Another footman was sent to ask Trelawny the gardener to count the hands of his under gardeners. Emmeline removed the kipper from her heel.

And I stared at the two severed hands, unable to deduce a thing. I expect Sherlock Holmes would have been similarly unmanned at the sight of a severed piece of Watson.

And then the door opened.

SEVEN

It was Reeves – alive! – and sporting the requisite number of hands.

"Reeves!" I exclaimed, a little effusively perhaps, but, I think, understandable given the circs.

"We have a mystery, Reeves," I continued.

"Indeed, sir?"

"Namely these." I raised the two severed hands. "They were found under the dining table."

"Most unfortunate, sir," said Reeves shimmering over for a better view.

He scrutinised the hands from every angle. He peered. He prodded. He took them to the window for a better look. He even held them to his ear.

"They have been removed with an axe," he pronounced.

"Aha," I said. "Do the gardeners have an axe?"

"They do," said Sir Robert. "Trelawny keeps two axes in the woodshed."

The second footman returned at that very moment with news from this Trelawny.

"Mr Trelawny says Pasco's missing, sir," said the breathless footman.

"Pasco?" I enquired.

"One of the under gardeners," said Sir Robert.

"An *automaton* under gardener," said Henry.

~

Off we went – all of us except Lady Julia, that is, who considered it unseemly to search for an under gardener.

"That is what servants are for," she pronounced and, with

head held high, sailed into the drawing room.

"I think we need to visit the woodshed first," I said. "To count those axes. One of them may have evidence on the blade. Do automata bleed oil, Reeves?"

"I believe this model does have a small reservoir of oil in the hand and wrist to facilitate smooth articulation, sir. But, in this case, both amputations were slightly higher on the wrist and missed the reservoir."

"That's as maybe, Reeves, but who knows what else has been lopped off?"

We picked our way across the damp, yielding lawn. The going had turned decidedly heavy overnight after all that rain, and not all our party were dressed for the conditions. Ida and Lily had to hitch up their dresses and Emmeline threw a shoe.

We couldn't all fit into the woodshed either. Half the party had to remain outside, crowded around the door and single window.

"Both axes are here," said Sir Robert.

Henry picked up the first axe and ran a finger along the cutting edge.

"I can't feel any oil," he said.

"Let Reeves have a look," I said. "His powers of observation are legendary."

"I don't think that will be necessary, sir."

I was amazed. With all the people crowded around the door and window, there was barely enough light to see by.

"You can see all from over there?" I asked.

"No, sir. I don't believe an examination of these axes will yield anything germane to the investigation. The boot however–"

"What boot?"

"I cannot help but notice a boot protruding from the pile of logs in the corner, sir."

We all shuffled position for a better look. Reeves was right! There was a definite boot sticking out from beneath the log pile.

"What's happening?" said Ida from outside.

"They've found a boot," said Lily.

"Is it Pasco's?"

"I can't see."

We began to dismantle the log pile, forming two chains to carefully move the logs from one part of the small shed to another.

Gradually, the body was uncovered. It *was* Pasco, minus his hands ... and head.

And he was only wearing boots.

I'd never seen a trouserless automaton before. I don't know what Theodosia Baskerville-Smythe's 'something unpleasant in the woodshed' had been, but this one rattled me.

"You've had your turn at the window, Emmeline," said Ida. "Let me look."

"No! Don't look, Ida," said her father. "Cover your eyes."

"Why?"

"Just cover your eyes."

A pensive, and decidedly uneasy, silence descended upon those of us within the shed.

"Well..." said Henry, and I think he spoke for all of us.

"Indeed," I said deciding it best to move swiftly on. "At least there's no question about cause of death. Beheading tends to get the job done every time."

"Decapitation was not the cause of his demise, sir," said Reeves. "The head in this model stores the memory, but the motor functions are controlled from the torso."

"So what was the cause of death?" I asked.

"If you observe, sir, he has been stabbed in the turbines."

"Pardon?"

"You can see the large stake protruding from the lower torso, sir."

"Oh, that's what that is!"

Thank God for that.

"Who could have done this?" asked Sir Robert. "And why? Pasco's a machine. He has no enemies."

"It has to be that escaped convict," said Henry. "Berry-more, take the women back to the house. We have to search the grounds."

~

A search of the grounds yielded nothing. Tom, the coach-man, was despatched to Grimdark to fetch the police while Sir Robert, Henry, Dr Morrow, T. Everett and a couple of stout footmen ventured out to check the Quarrywood studio.

"Are you coming, Roderick?" asked Henry.

I declined. I wanted to search the house. Both hands had been found in the dining room; was the head nearby too?

"How's your pressure, Reeves?" I asked as we crossed the lawn on the way to the dining room. "I gather from Lady Julia they don't allow automata in the house."

"That is true, sir. I anticipated the contingency and have endeavoured to keep my situation secret from the servants."

"What about the steam though? You're not likely to keel over in the next five minutes, are you?"

"No, sir. I elicited the information from Berrymore that there was a steam outlet in the old stable block. I availed myself of the facilities prior to waking you this morning."

"The old stable block is close to the woodshed, isn't it?" I asked.

"Yes, sir. I had not realised the significance of the wood-shed during my earlier visit, but I can attest that I witnessed nothing of note. There was no evidence of anyone else being abroad between the hours of four and five."

Emmeline came rushing over as soon as we left the east lawn.

"Have you found anything?" she asked.

"Not yet. We're about to search the dining room."

She slipped her arm in mine. "That's just in case you have any misplaced notion to tell Berrymore to escort me to a place of safety."

"I wouldn't dream of it," I said.

The three of us paused outside the dining room door before opening it. I braced myself for a flying Lupin to hit me amidships, then opened the door.

The room looked empty.

"Is Lupin still here?" I asked, having a cautious look hither and thither.

We looked under every table, checked the curtains and even opened one or two drawers. No Lupin.

"Do you really suspect Lupin?" asked Emmeline.

I did. And yet ... wasn't he the obvious suspect? Butlers and orang-utans – it was usually one or the other that did it.

"I think he knows more than he's letting on," I said. "He found the hands. But where did he find them? Under the table, or out in the woodshed? He's strong enough to wield an axe, and dextrous enough I'd imagine."

But how does one question an orang-utan? He can't speak English, and if one gave him a pencil, God knows what he'd do with it.

"Is this even a murder?" I asked. "Can a machine be murdered?"

"If that was Reeves under the log pile, you'd call it murder," said Emmeline.

"That goes without saying," I said. "No log would go un-turned. But, philosophically, would it be murder? Automata can be repaired."

Reeves coughed. It wasn't a philosophical cough.

"If I may contribute to your musings, sir, I would point out that humans can be reanimated."

"I don't think that's quite the same, Reeves," I said.

Reeves expression turned distinctly sniffy. I wouldn't have liked to have met either of his eyebrows in a dark alleyway.

"Would that be because automata are not regarded as having souls, sir?"

"Reggie knows *you* have a soul, Reeves," said Emmeline. "I expect yours is one of the largest on record, don't you agree, Reggie?"

"Of course."

"I think all creatures have souls," continued Emmeline. "Except wasps."

I decided to guide the conversation back towards the investigation.

"Could Pasco be repaired and asked who killed him?" I said.

"If we find the head undamaged, sir, there would be a high probability that the memory of his demise could indeed be recovered."

I was struck by an idea.

"I wonder if that's why the head was removed – so no one could find out who killed him?"

"A simpler solution, sir, would have been to crush the head *in situ* with the blunt end of the axe."

"And why cut off the hands?" asked Emmeline.

"Do automata have fingerprints, Reeves?"

"No, sir. Ordinarily the removal of the head and hands would indicate a desire to hide the victim's identity, but I fail to see the necessity in this case."

"That's because you're looking at this from the perspective of a giant brain, Reeves. Murders are rarely logical. I can see two perfectly good reasons that explain all."

"What are they?" asked Emmeline.

"One, the murderer – and I'm thinking Lupin here – wanted something to play with. A memento, perhaps? He *is* an orang-utan, Emmie. Who knows what devilish thoughts his little furry grey cells can come up with."

"What's the other?" she asked.

"That the body is not Pasco."

~

We searched for the missing head in the dining room, the library, the hallway, and the parlour. Then Reeves and I searched below stairs whilst Emmeline braved Lady Julia to conduct a refined search of the drawing room.

We didn't even find an ear.

"Was Lady Julia very scathing?" I asked when we all met up by the foot of the stairs.

"She would have been if I'd said I was looking for a servant's head," said Emmeline. "I told her I was searching for some embroidery I'd mislaid yesterday."

Our conversation was interrupted by the return of Sir Robert and his party.

"No sign of anything untoward at the studio," said Sir Robert, taking off his overcoat and giving it a good shake. "Everything was locked up and in its place. The police should be here momentarily. We saw Tom's cart coming down the track."

Ida and Lily must have been listening out for Sir Robert's return for they positively flew out of the drawing room. "What's happened?" asked Ida. "Where's Henry?"

"He's outside," said Sir Robert. "Waiting for Tom and the police."

But Tom hadn't brought the police. Last night's rains had caused the River Angst to burst its banks and wash away the bridge. He'd had to turn back.

"It could be days before the river's safe to cross," Henry told us.

"What are we going to do?" asked Ida. "Have you got a gun, Henry?"

"I don't think it's going to come to that, Ida," said Henry. "I can't see this convict hanging around. He'll want to be as far away from the prison as he can. He may have sought shelter here last night in an outbuilding – that's undoubtedly where he ran across poor Pasco – but he'll be long gone by now. After the incident with Pasco, he'd have even more reason to clear off sharpish."

"What do you think, Roderick?" asked Sir Robert.

"I think there may be more to this than meets the eyeball," I said. "The escaped convict is the obvious suspect, but has anyone actually seen him?"

"Pasco must have," said Henry. "That's why he was killed."

"But why lop off his head and hands?" I said. "Seems rummy to me. Why would a convict try to hide Pasco's identity?"

"Dartmoor's a notorious prison, Roderick," said Sir Robert. "All the worst kinds of murderers are sent there. Chopping heads and hands off his victims is probably second nature to this villain."

Sir Robert had a point.

"That's true," I said. "Consulting detectives call it *modus operandi*. Every murderer has one, don't they Reeves."

"So it is widely held, sir. Murderers are creatures of habit. Once they find a method that suits, they are loathe to try another."

"There you are then," said Henry. "This convict is an assassin used to tidying up after himself. All the more reason for him to be long gone from here."

"Do you think the ghost was prophesying Pasco's death?" asked Lily.

"I don't think there *was* a ghost, Emmeline," said Sir Robert. "I've talked with Henry about this, and we're certain it was a servant's prank. One of the younger ones. I imagine they are feeling much chastened by subsequent events, and I'm sure we will not see a reoccurrence. Best to put the matter behind us."

"Well," said Henry, rubbing his hands. "Tempus fugit. Let's get changed and meet back here in ... thirty minutes? It's a sunny day, and we have an important scene to shoot. Don't want to waste the light."

"Are you sure we'll be safe?" asked Lily.

"Positive," he said. "But I'll take a shotgun along with us just in case."

~

Sir Robert and all the houseguests, with the exception of Emmeline and myself, left for the quarry.

"Are you sure you won't join us, Roderick? Lily? I can find parts for both of you," said Henry before leaving.

"Maybe later," I said. "I'd like to do a little sleuthing first. See if I can find Pasco's head."

"And I'm going to do a little sketching," lied Emmeline extremely convincingly. "The Hall looks quite magnificent with the early morning sun upon it."

Now all we had to do was steer clear of Lady Julia and we'd have the entire crime scene to ourselves!

"Time, I think, to learn more about this Pasco," I said. "Where was he last night, and who saw him last?"

EIGHT

We set off across the lawn in search of Trelawny, the gardener. Emmeline and I were better attired this time – in tweeds and walking shoes. I'd favoured a bold red tartan sock myself, but Reeves was adamant that an understated pastel was more suitable sleuthing attire.

We found Trelawny in the walled garden. He was a short, wiry individual with a weather-beaten face and a worrying shortage of teeth. I rather thought he had the look of a man who'd been aged for twelve years in an oak cask. He told us he was in the middle of forcing rhubarb. To do what, he didn't say, and I thought it best not to enquire.

"Did you see or hear anything unusual last night?" I asked, getting right down to it.

"Only the storm, Master Roderick. 'Twas a howlin' an' a thunderin' all night."

On to the next question. "What about Pasco? When was the last time you saw him?"

"That'd be sunset. We always stop work at sunset. I goes to me cottage, and Pasco 'e goes to the ol' stable block for 'is steam. 'E's a machine, you know? Sir Robert put a boiler in the ol' stable block last year when 'e bought Pasco 'an Silas."

"Silas?" I asked.

"'E's another one of they machines. A right fancy one 'an all. 'E's over the back now, mowing the lawn ... with his feet."

Trelawny laughed to himself, a cackling wheezy kind of laugh.

"He's one of the newer gardening models," said Emmeline. "I thought I was seeing things when I first saw him. I asked Henry about him. He has all these attachments. Silas, that is, not Henry. He has these pronged cutters on his feet for mowing the lawn, and the same on his hands for trimming hedges."

"Oo arr," said Trelawny. "'E's got boots for ploughin' too, an' for sowin', an' 'ands that can saw logs. Got 'tachments for everythin'."

"So," I said. "Where would Pasco have gone after he'd brought himself back up to pressure?"

"Nowhere," said Trelawny. "That's where 'e spends the night. 'Im an' Silas together."

I looked at Reeves. Had Pasco been in the old stable block when Reeves had been there this morning? Reeves raised an eyebrow. Whether one eyebrow signified 'yes' or a surge of activity in his steam-powered grey cells, I had no idea.

"Does anyone else sleep in the old stable block?" I asked Trelawny.

"No. Tom an' Jethro sleep over the new stables. Dan an' Jimmy sleep up at the quarry these days."

"Right ho," I said. "Thank you for your time, Trelawny. We'll beetle off and have a word with Silas."

"You can try, Master Roderick, but you won't get no sense out of 'im. You can tell 'im what to do, but that's it. 'E's not one of they clever machines like Pasco. 'E just does what 'e's told."

"I believe I am familiar with the model, sir," said Reeves. "It's more of an intelligent tool than an automaton."

"Not much of a conversationalist then?" I said.

"No, sir."

~

"Well, Reeves?" I asked as soon as we'd moved out of earshot. "Were Pasco and Silas in the old stable block when you were there this morning?"

"Silas was, sir, but Pasco was not."

"So, Pasco was probably killed sometime between sunset and four."

"That would be my assumption, sir."

"What about this Silas, Reeves? Did he look worried? Wave a saw at you and point tremulously at the woodshed?"

"No, sir. The model in question does not communicate. It does not even have a head. It is designed to work, not to resemble a human."

"What about its attachments?" asked Emmeline. "Did it have any unusual ones? Like revolving axes? I've heard Henry and Sir Robert say that Stapleford's a marvel with machines. He's always coming up with new ways to modify automata for their moving pictures."

"I did not notice anything unusual, miss."

I wanted to have a look at this Silas myself. We followed the rattling sound to the back lawn where we found him mowing. It was fascinating, and not a little disturbing, to see him shuffling across the sward sending a shower of cut grass streaming in his wake. I'd never seen such sharp toenails.

"How does he do it, Reeves? Surely no blade could be that sharp."

"I believe it is what is called a finger bar mower, sir. A steam-powered sickle bar is driven back and forth across a stationary finger bar, and the grass is cut between the blades."

I watched mesmerised. Silas was the size of a child – a rather squat, headless child with large feet and hands. And a large single eye on a flexible stalk.

"Could he wield an axe, do you think?" I asked.

"Not with sufficient force to sever Pasco's head, sir. This model is essentially a slow one, built for strength and dexterity. With a grasping mechanism attached it can lift heavy weights and open gates, but the arm lacks the speed to swing an axe with deadly force. Besides, the hedge-trimming attachment is more than capable of amputating a head. The wound on Pasco, however, would have been very different."

I decided to visit the old stable block next. Had the killer stumbled into the old stable block looking for shelter, found Pasco and killed him? Or had Pasco heard a noise and ventured out? If there'd been a struggle on the soft ground there could be traces.

We quartered the area between the old stable block and the woodshed. There was plenty of evidence of the two dozen feet that had visited the woodshed after breakfast, but no obvious signs of a struggle. And there was a flagstone path between the stables and the shed.

The old stable block didn't provide any clues either. There were no signs of a struggle inside. I checked the hayloft and every stall, looking for the unexpected – a crumpled note, a discarded banana, mysterious carved runes, a convict's striped clothes...

Nothing.

"If the killer was this convict," I said. "It might explain why Pasco was debagged. A man in a striped uniform is going to attract attention. He'd get a lot farther with new clothes."

"So there should be a pile of prison clothes somewhere," said Emmeline.

"Exactly," I said. "I haven't seen any. Have you?"

"No," said Emmeline. "He couldn't have burnt them – not with the rain last night. He might have buried them though."

Reeves coughed. "There is a furnace that heats the copper boiler, miss."

I looked at Reeves in awe. I may have the occasional issue with his eyebrows, but the man's brain was immense.

We returned at speed to the old stable block and stood back while Reeves opened the furnace door.

"Any sign of a stripe?" I asked.

Reeves raked the embers with a rather lethal looking poker.

"No, sir. It *is* possible that the cloth has been completely incinerated. If Pasco was killed in the early hours of the night, there may have been time."

Such is the detective's lot. There are highs. There are lows. There are even times when one finds oneself wrestling orang-utans on dining room carpets. All one can do is dust off one's brogues and press on.

I decided another look at the woodshed was called for.

"Do you know if they've moved the body?" I asked

Reeves.

"I overheard Berrymore say that Sir Robert had not given him any instructions on the matter, sir. And that Pasco was to remain where he was until Sir Robert returned."

"Ah, well, brace yourselves then. You don't have to come in, Emmie."

"Nonsense," she said. "I saw it all earlier."

Well, I certainly braced myself. A naked under gardener was disconcerting at the best of times, and this would be my second viewing on an empty stomach.

I opened the door, and peered in.

Pasco had gone.

NINE

I looked at the log pile we'd moved earlier.

"He's not been buried again, has he?" I said.

The three of us began moving the log pile, one log at a time, back to its original position. As soon as we reached the bottom layer we knew the answer. Pasco was not there.

"He *was* dead, wasn't he?" I asked.

"He was certainly not operational, sir, neither could he have been repaired this quickly. He'd require new turbines, or a new torso. He'd also require his head reattached, and at least thirty minutes on the steam outlet."

"Why would someone move him?" asked Emmeline. "We've already seen him."

I may not have had my kipper breakfast, but my little grey cells were in mid-season form. "I see all," I said.

"You do?" said Emmeline.

"Indubitably. That is the right word, isn't it, Reeves?"

"I suspect so, sir."

"Good. The killer has taken some risk in moving the body in broad daylight, therefore one can deduce that it is of vital importance."

"Go on," said Emmeline. "I adore it when you deduce."

"So, although we *though*t we had seen all there was to see this morning, we were mistaken. There must be something about the body that we missed. And the killer has risked all to make sure that his, her – or, indeed, its – mistake was rectified."

~

We sleuthed for another hour, checking all the outbuildings for any sign of Pasco.

"He couldn't be in the Hall, could he?" I asked. "Is it possible to stroll through the servants' entrance carrying a naked under gardener without attracting comment?"

"I would very much doubt it, sir."

And I suspected it would be even harder to smuggle one through the main entrance. Claude 'Cicely' Sissinghurst had tried it once at the Sloths Club, and got nabbed in the back passage.

"Trelawny could have buried him in the garden," said Emmeline. "That's the only place I've seen where the soil looked disturbed."

"I don't think Trelawny's the kind of chap who'd appreciate us digging up his prize carrots. A man who takes a firm hand with rhubarb is likely to cut up rough."

"There is the mire, sir," said Reeves. "If one is looking for a place to dispose of a body, the mire would suit admirably.

"Reeves, you are beyond compare," I said.

"I think he gets brainier every day," said Emmeline.

"What was it Stapleford said last night?" I asked. "Grimdark never gives up its dead?"

"His very words," said Emmeline.

We all stood and looked toward the mire.

But, if Grimdark never gives up its dead, how were we going to find Pasco?

And then it came to me.

"There'll be footprints," I said. "If someone threw Pasco into the mire they'd have to walk through some pretty soft ground on the edge of the mire first. There'd be traces. We might even be able to get a grappling hook around the body and pull Pasco out."

We ankled down the gravel drive and onto the raised causeway that was the track to Grimdark village. The great mire stretched out before us. It looked far more colourful in the sun that it had done yesterday. There were tussocks of yellows and bright greens, and a myriad of small pools of water – some of them gleaming in the sun, some as black as pitch.

And far in the distance was another light.

"Is that a fire?" I asked, pointing just below the horizon.

"It must be a large fire," said Emmeline. "Is it in the mire or beyond?"

"It couldn't be piskies, could it?" I said. "Our driver told us to beware of lights in the mire."

"Piskies are a superstition, sir. *That* is a fire. A particularly *large* fire. Is the Quarrywood studio in that direction, miss?"

"No, the studio's in the opposite direction," said Emmeline. "That fire must be on the high moor. Henry says no one lives there. It's desolate."

For the next ten minutes we walked the mire's edge – or as close to the edge as we dared venture (which wasn't that close) – looking for footprints. Our attention wavered between the mire's edge and that distant fire. What was it? A warning beacon to attract our attention? Or the convict drying out his clothes and trying to get warm?

"Over here!" cried Emmeline. "Footprints!"

I rushed over.

"Look," she said. "There are lots of them, and they go right into the mire."

I had hoped to find a distinguishable boot print – something one could trace back to its owner. But the ground went from spongy tussock to soft mud. Most of the prints were deep and the mud had slopped in from the sides leaving a series of vaguely boot-shaped holes stretching ten, twenty yards into the mire.

"It looks like a path," said Emmeline. "Sir Robert said there were old paths across the mire, but none were safe as they shifted so."

"I would not advise any attempt to follow the footprints, sir."

"Don't worry, Reeves," I said. "Wild horses couldn't drag me into that mire. Well, of course, they could, but I wouldn't go willingly. And, thinking about it, if they were *dragging* me, wouldn't they get mired first? They'd really have to push me and I don't think wild horses are that good at pushing, do you, Reeves?"

"Quite, sir. I was wondering if you had noticed the gate on

the other side of the track."

I swung round. There was small wooden gate in the yew hedge opposite. It lined up perfectly with the path into the mire.

It was also, as we soon discovered, a well-used gate. The grass either side of the gate had been worn back to bare earth. There were dozens of imprints from all types and sizes of footwear.

We went through the gate into a partially wooded section of the grounds to the rear of the Hall. A path wound around a wooded slope and up towards the back lawn. The right hand edge of the path was bordered by a tall yew hedge. The left hand edge showed traces where a similar hedge had been, but there were only a handful of yew trees left and none of them had been trimmed for years.

I was baffled. Since the moment we'd arrived, everyone had told us how dangerous the mire was, and that no path was safe. And yet here was evidence of a well-trodden track between the Hall and the mire.

And at the other end of the track was a fire.

~

My stomach may have been rumbling but, for a consulting detective with the game afoot, that was a mere trifle.

"What's the quickest way to that fire?" I asked Emmeline. "To the left or right of the mire?"

"I don't know. I think this track bends round the north western edge of the mire, but I'm sure it stops at High Dudgeon Farm – that's where Stapleford lives. I don't know what the moor's like after that. Stapleford says there are lots of small bogs all over the high moor."

I preferred the idea of at least a part of our journey being along a navigable track.

"To the left it is then."

We followed the track as it began its long arc around the mire's edge. The moor on the left of the track rose and fell – rocky tors with the occasional stand of trees nestling in the valleys in between. On the right, the mire stretched out flat and treeless towards the higher moor on the horizon.

The fire still flickered and burned in the distance.

After half a mile, another path struck out from ours and headed towards a gap between two low hills on our left.

"That'll be the track to the studio," said Emmeline.

I half expected to see a zeppelin hovering over the distant horizon, but the sky was clear. There were no distant sounds either.

"How far is it to the studio?" I asked.

Emmeline shrugged. "I've never been there. I shouldn't think it's far."

We pressed on. Our track was now heading east, and every step was bringing us closer to the mysterious fire.

"I wonder if it's the killer burning evidence," said Emmeline.

"One would think, miss, that the mire would be a more convenient and less conspicuous location for the disposal of evidence."

"But what if the article in question wouldn't sink?" I said. "I know this may be a personal question, Reeves, but do automata weigh less than men?"

"No, sir. Pasco's body would indeed sink if placed in the mire."

I was still pondering the buoyancy of incriminating evidence when I caught sight of a figure hurrying towards us across the open moor to our left. Reeves' superior eyesight identified the individual as a policeman.

We stopped and waited for him to join us.

"Ho," he said, breathing a little hard. "Are you from the Hall?"

"We are," I said.

"I've been sent to warn you about the escaped convict," said the constable. "It's Harry Selden."

"Selden?" I said. "Not the psycho historian? The history prof who went berserk in the quad and took an axe to his students?"

"No, sir," said the constable. "It's the other one. The Clerkenwell Cat."

"Doesn't ring a bell. Have you heard of this Clerkenwell Cat, Reeves?"

"I believe so, sir. If I recall correctly he's a promethean – half human, half cat – he was notorious for leaving the body parts of his victims on his master's lawn."

"Really? Well, I'm sure the local gardeners will be relieved that Clerkenwell's one hundred miles to the east of here."

The constable shook his head. "But not his master, sir. He lives up at the Hall these days. A Dr Morrow. The chief constable reckons that's where Selden will make for."

Reeves raised a doubtful eyebrow.

"What is it, Reeves?"

"One hesitates to question the analysis of the Chief Constable, sir, but one would think that Mr Selden, having been incarcerated for several years, would be unaware as to the whereabouts of Dr Morrow."

"Oh, he knows very well where Dr Morrow is," said the constable. "That's what made him break out. One of the warders showed him a story about Quarrywood in the Daily Bugle and he went berserk. They hauled him off to the hospital wing, and thought they had him sedated, but next time the warders looked in on him, he'd gone. No Selden. No doctor. Just this large stomach and a pair of the doctor's shoes lying there in the middle of the floor."

TEN

Suddenly the fire on the moor seemed a good deal less important than it had a minute earlier.

"Dr Morrow's at the studio," said Emmeline. "If Selden's been watching the Hall, he'd know."

We had to warn everyone at the studio. And the Hall. The place was teeming with lawns.

The constable rushed off to take word to the Hall while we beetled off to the studio. The fire would have to wait.

The first indication that we were nearing the studio was a sign on the side of a rocky hill. QUARRYWOOD, it read in enormous capital letters – each letter having its own hoarding.

Our path widened and curled around said rocky hill, descending as it did so, the land on the left falling away into a valley covered in a yellow flowering shrub which Emmeline informed me was gorse.

We saw the quarry buildings first, a couple of two storey granite constructions built on a large levelled area ahead of us. One looked like a large house, the other a small warehouse or factory. Then, as the path completed its curve around the side of the hill, we saw the quarry face – a huge crescent-shaped cliff about two hundred feet high in the centre.

But our attention was swiftly drawn away from the cliff and towards what could only be ... a Lizard Man. It was barely fifty yards away and lumbering in a distinctly menacing fashion towards Lily, who was lying on the ground, shielding her face, and looking somewhat distrait.

At least *I* had an inkling of what I was looking at. Henry's description last night of a large man with a dinosaur head and tail was spot on. But what I hadn't realised was that Emmeline had never been party to any discussion viz Lizard Men.

Emmeline took off. Most young ladies of my acquaintance would have headed in the opposite direction to the Lizard Man. Emmeline is unlike most young ladies. Pausing only to pick up a good sized rock, she flew at the Lizard Man and caught him with a ripe one across the snout with her rock.

"Run for it, Lily," she cried. "I'll hold him off."

The Lizard Man turned a large, quizzical head towards Emmeline, who picked up another rock and let fly from close range. It was another ripe one on the snout. The Lizard Man uttered a kind of squawk, and waved his arms a bit. Emmeline reached for another rock. That was too much for the Lizard Man who turned and legged it. Emmeline gave chase.

"Cut!" shouted Sir Robert, who, up until that moment, I hadn't noticed. He was with a gaggle of others closeted around a camera off to our right.

"No! Keep cranking," said Henry. "This is much better."

The Lizard Man did not look like a sprinter. Or, by this time, particularly threatening. Whereas Emmeline...

She was a stone-throwing Amazon. And soon to be a club-wielding Amazon.

The Lizard Man darted towards the buildings, a path which took him past a pile of planks and assorted cut wood. Emmeline let fly with her last rock before availing herself of a stout length of timber.

"I think we should intervene, Reeves."

"I agree, sir. The Lizard Man has a height and weight advantage, but Miss Emmeline is fleeter and decidedly more determined."

"Not to say armed, Reeves. Do you think this Lizard Man is a promethean?"

"No, sir. Prometheans require viable bones and tissue. Dinosaurs have been extinct for sixty million years ergo the Lizard Man is an actor wearing a costume."

All the more reason for a swift intervention. "Emmie!" I

cried. "Stop!"

Reeves coughed. "Miss Emmeline is using the name Lily, sir."

"Lily!" I shouted, breaking into a run. "Stop! He's an actor, not a Lizard Man!"

The Lizard Man almost made it to the buildings, but I think he was having trouble maintaining his balance whilst running. The dinosaur head looked rather too large to me in proportion to the rest of his body. Over he toppled, rolling onto his back. Emmeline closed in and drew back her club.

"No!" I shouted. "Don't! He's an actor!"

"He can take it," shouted Henry. "Let him have it."

"No!" screamed the Lizard Man. "Don't hit me!"

Emmeline paused, club still raised, and looked over her shoulder. She must have seen the camera. And the assemblage of people clustered around said camera watching. Not to mention the two headless Lizard Men sitting on a pile of rocks smoking.

"Oh," she said. And then put one perfectly formed foot on the Lizard Man's chest and posed for the camera.

"Cut!" shouted Ida. "You ruined Emmeline's big scene, Lily!"

Ida was in a minority of one. Possibly two if you counted the Lizard Man.

I stopped running and joined in the applause that had broken out.

"She's a natural," said T. Everett, much to his daughter's displeasure.

~

I waited for the applause to die down before breaking the news about Selden.

"Sir Robert, Henry," I said, toddling over. "I'm afraid we have a problem."

"What kind of a problem?" asked Sir Robert.

I told him about the meeting with the constable.

"Morrow?" said Sir Robert, looking around for the doctor. "Is this true? Do you know this man Selden?"

Dr Morrow's face took on the hue of an ailing oyster. "I

do, Robert," he said, turning to me. "You're sure he said *Harry* Selden? Not some other Selden?"

"The constable called him the Clerkenwell Cat."

"That's him," said Morrow dejectedly.

"Will he really come looking for you, Morrow?" asked Henry.

"I fear he will. He has it in his head that I am his master – something which I assure you I never intended. It just ... happened."

"But how would he know you're here?" asked Stapleford. "You've only been here for six months."

I mentioned the Daily Bugle article, but kept quiet about the shoes and the stomach. The air was charged enough as it was, and we consulting detectives don't like to spread panic.

"Is he dangerous?" asked Ida.

Everyone looked at the unfortunate doctor. As did I. How does one say 'deranged homicidal cannibal' without causing panic?

The good doctor appeared lost for words, but, fortunately, I hit upon a few optimistic ones to fill the tense silence.

"The good news," I said. "Is that he *has* eaten."

"I don't understand," said Ida. "What's that got to do with anything?"

"Morrow?" said Sir Robert.

"Perhaps we should discuss this in private, Sir Robert," said Morrow. "There are ladies present."

Ida stamped her foot. "No! Lily already knows. If she can take it, so can I."

"Very well," said Morrow. "Selden is a troubled individual – delusional. He ... he thinks he's a cat."

"Did you say cat?" asked Sir Robert.

"I did. As I said, he's delusional and ... he kills people."

"Does he chop their heads off like he did to Pasco?" asked Ida.

I felt for Morrow. I've frequently been in a similar posish – wishing to put a gloss on a tricky sitch and finding no such *mot juste* exists.

"Not exactly," said Morrow.

"Out with it, man," said Henry. "We need to know what we're up against. Is he a strangler? A cut-throat? A brawler?"

"He ... kills like a cat," said Morrow.

There was a considerable intaking of breath from the gathering.

"But he *has* eaten," I said, deciding to move things along somewhat. "So no one's in immediate danger."

"When you say 'eaten' do you mean *eaten*?" said Stapleford.

"I think I do," I said.

"I don't understand," said Ida, looking puzzled. "Why's everyone talking about eating?"

"He kills like a cat, Ida," said Emmeline. "He leaves bodies on his master's lawn. Sometimes ... not all of the body."

"Oh," said Ida, looking not a little rattled. Indeed the entire company fell into a sombre, reflective mood.

I thought it timely to mention the good news again. "But he did have a good meal before he escaped. Pretty stuffed, I'd say, from what the constable said. I expect he'll be sleeping it off for hours yet. Probably curled up in a sunny spot miles from here."

"What does this Selden look like?" asked Henry. "Is he like one of your promethean creations?"

"He's not a true promethean," said Morrow. "He's never been dead. He's more of an augmented human. Most of the time he could pass for a man if he's wearing a hat and loose-fitting trousers."

"I don't understand," said Sir Robert. "How did you become involved with this individual in the first place?"

"It's a long story," said Morrow. "I read Vivisection at Oxford and was a member of the Young Alchemists Society. There I met Professor Jekyll and was much taken with the work he did with potions. I thought I could combine vivisection and potions to produce a human hybrid. A hybrid that would have all the best attributes of humans and animals. But I was young and foolish. I never once considered the ethics of what I was undertaking. I never considered the consequences, only the science."

"And Selden?" asked Sir Robert. "Was he one of these

Young Alchemists?"

"No. He was a patient at the Clerkenwell Asylum. Poor Selden. He had so many plans. He wanted to be a fashion designer, you know? Foundation garments. But his main obsession was with cats. He wanted to be one. When I met him he told me he felt like a cat trapped in a man's body. He was desperate, and I ... I thought I could help him. Though, looking back, I think perhaps I was fooling myself – whatever I told myself, it was the science I was more interested in, not the patient. I took risks that no man should ever have taken."

"Surely you blame yourself too much, Morrow?" said Sir Robert. "I have observed you these past six months and you have always taken the greatest care of our promethean actors. You treat them no different from the servants."

"I try to make amends for my youthful failings, Robert."

"What did you do to him?" asked Ida. "You didn't give him a cat's head, did you?"

"No, I gave him the ears of a lynx and the tail of a panther. He was very taken with them. As I said, most of the time he could pass for human as long as he covers them up."

"You say 'most of the time,'" said Stapleford. "What exactly does that mean?"

"Ah," said Morrow looking down at his feet – probably searching for another *mot juste*. "The potions I gave him affected his metabolism. It's mainly at night but, if he becomes distressed, it can happen at any time."

"What can happen at any time?" asked Henry.

"He changes into a beast – physically – half man, half giant tabby. He's not evil. You *must* understand that. He just ... thinks differently. Like a cat."

"We must return to the Hall," said Sir Robert. "We have enough guns to arm the footmen. We can mount a guard there until this Selden is apprehended."

"Let's not be hasty," said Henry. "It seems a shame to waste a sunny day like this. If Selden thinks he's a cat, he's going to wait until night to hunt. And Roderick says the man's already stuffed to the gills. You'll stay, won't you, Lily?

I have a corker of an idea for a new scene."

"I'll stay," said Ida. "I'm not frightened at all."

"Are you sure, Ida?" asked her father. "This Selden is a killer."

"I have every confidence in Henry, father. He'll protect me."

"What about you, Lily?" asked Henry.

Emmeline looked torn. She looked at me, and she looked at Lily before replying.

"No, Emmeline's the actress, not me," she said.

"Are you sure you won't reconsider?" said Henry.

"Let her go, Henry," said Ida. "Can't you see she's scared?"

I don't think Ida realised she was one rock away from being floored. Emmeline balled both fists and gave Ida a scathing look. "I am not scared, Ida, and I do *not* need Henry or *any* man to protect me!"

"Indeed not," I said. "After seeing you deal with that Lizard Man, I was rather hoping you'd come back to the Hall and protect us. Don't you agree, Sir Robert?"

"Indeed, so," chuckled Sir Robert.

Ida did not see anything to chuckle about. She returned Emmeline's scathing look with interest and I rather felt she'd have given a better account of herself than the Lizard Man had.

~

Most of the party opted to remain at the quarry. I had the feeling that Henry would have quite welcomed an appearance by Selden, regarding it as an opportunity to add an extra scene to his moving picture. He did post an armed guard though, handing a shotgun to one of the stouter Lizard Men and giving him strict instructions to keep his eyes peeled and his body out of the shot when they were filming.

The rest of us - Sir Robert, Morrow, Emmeline, Reeves and I - hastened up the track towards the Hall.

We were a silent bunch, deep in thought one would imagine, pondering giant tabbies whilst keeping a vigilant eye on the undergrowth.

After a minute or two, Morrow broke the silence with an unexpected, and troubling question.

"Why did you call Emmeline Lily," he asked Emmeline.

"Did I?" said Emmeline.

"You did," said Morrow. "When you saw her on the ground."

"Well, it *was* her nickname at school," said Emmeline. "I don't know why. One of the other girls started it and it stuck I suppose. I haven't called her Lily in ages though. Must have been the shock of seeing that monster about to attack her."

"And come to think of it," said Morrow. "Didn't you call Lily, Emmie, Roderick?"

"I don't think so," I said, not liking the direction this conversation was taking.

"I believe Mister Roderick did utter an invocation to the Argentinean saint, Madre Esmeralda, sir," said Reeves. "It is common in the mining camps to use the shortened form of her name utilising only the initial letters 'M' and 'E.'"

"That's right," I said, joining in the subterfuge. "She's our patron saint. I often feel called to invoke her name in times of stress, don't I, Reeves? Em Ee, I say."

"Indeed, sir."

"I've never heard of Saint Madre Esmeralda," said Morrow.

"Few people have," I said. "She didn't get out much. Bit of a hermit, I think. Lived in a cave."

"I can't see that fire any more," said Emmeline thankfully changing the subject.

"What fire?" said Sir Robert.

"There was a large fire on the high moor beyond the mire," said Emmeline. "We saw it on our walk earlier."

The fire had indeed gone out – or was burning lower. I scanned the far horizon and saw not even a wisp of smoke.

"I wouldn't pay any attention to any lights or fires you see on the mire or beyond," said Sir Robert. "We've all seen them. Stapleford says it's marsh gas. Berrymore says it's piskies. All I know is that it's best to stay well clear. The mire is no place for the curious."

ELEVEN

"Is the constable still here, Babbacombe?" Sir Robert asked the armed footman loitering by the main door to the Hall.

"What constable, sir?" said Babbacombe.

"The constable who brought the news about the escaped convict."

Babbacombe looked confused. "Ain't seen no constable, sir. Ain't seen nobody since Mister Roderick and Miss Lily left."

I had one of those forebodings that we consulting detectives get just before events turn rummy.

"He might have entered by the mire gate and knocked at the servants' door," said Morrow.

Sir Robert strode purposefully into the hall. "Berrymore!" he shouted.

The ancient b. appeared a few seconds later. I wasn't sure if it was his age or his extreme height, but Berrymore in motion always looked like a man walking into a strong headwind.

"Have *you* seen the constable, Berrymore?" asked Sir Robert.

"What constable, sir?" said Berrymore, tacking slightly to the left.

Sir Robert turned to me. "He *did* say he was coming straight here, didn't he?"

"He did. When we left him he was heading this way. He couldn't have been more than a half a mile from the Hall, wouldn't you say, Reeves?"

"Perhaps a thousand yards, sir, but no more than that."

"He wouldn't have strayed into the mire, would he?"

asked Emmeline.

"He'd have no reason to," said Morrow. "The track is straight and well marked. You can see the Hall tower from a mile away. He couldn't have got lost."

The drawing room door opened and out came Lady Julia. "What is the reason for this commotion?" she said. And then she noticed me and her eyes narrowed. "Oh, you're here, are you? I might have known. Who have you lost this time – the coachman?"

"No, a policeman," I said. "He was on his way here to warn everyone about the escaped convict."

Sir Robert brought his sister-in-law up to speed viz Selden and his unusual eating habits. She took the news considerably better than Berrymore, whose knees almost gave way the moment Selden's name was mentioned.

Sir Robert sent Berrymore off to question the servants about the missing policeman. Babbacombe was despatched to question the outdoor staff, and check the lawns for any signs of stomachs or regurgitated helmets.

"Did this policeman give his name?" asked Sir Robert.

"No," I said. "We didn't chat for long."

"I wonder if it was Hatherleigh," said Sir Robert. "Was he a large, square jawed chap with a ruddy complexion and a helmet.

"I wouldn't call him square jawed. Or of a ruddy complexion. But spot on about the helmet and being large."

"But where was he coming from?" asked Morrow. "You say he was coming across the moor from the north, but there's nothing to the north of here for fifteen miles."

"Perhaps, with the bridge down, that was the only way someone could get news to us," said Sir Robert. "Or he crossed the moor from the east – from the prison, perhaps – and took a circuitous route to avoid the mire."

"And perhaps Roderick made it all up," said Lady Julia. "Did anyone else see this policeman?"

"Reeves and I did," said Emmeline. "I expect there are footprints where we met to prove it."

"Size twelve footprints," I added.

"No one doubts Roderick's word, Julia," said Sir Robert.

"Morrow can vouch what he said about Selden is true. And we all heard the siren last night."

Reeves coughed.

"You have an observation, Reeves?" I asked.

"Indeed, sir. I was reflecting upon the constable's complexion."

I braced myself. It had been several hours since Reeves had last topped up his pressure, and this opening sentence didn't sound like Reeves in mid-season form. An automaton with low pressure was very much like Stiffy Trussington-Thripp after one too many bots of the good stuff – that is, prone to distraction and lengthy reminiscences of the inconsequential.

I feared William of Ockham might get an outing.

"Although one would not expect every constable to have a ruddy complexion," continued Reeves. "One would expect a modicum of facial colouring resultant from a life spent largely out of doors."

I considered intervening, but Lady Julia beat me to it.

"Why are we listening to a valet, Robert?" she said. "Has the world gone mad?"

"I apologise for my circumlocution, milady," said Reeves. "To get to the nub, is it possible that it was Selden, disguised as a constable, that we met upon the moor this morning? His prison pallor would explain his complexion's lack of ruddiness."

Well, just as I'd written him off, back came the old Reeves, firing on all cylinders.

"What *does* Selden look like?" Sir Robert asked Morrow. "We know about the ears, but is he a big chap?"

"Not large," said Morrow. "Five feet nine, I'd say, and lithe. Of course, I haven't seen him in ten years. He may have put on weight."

One would have thought, considering his ability to eat a fully grown doctor at a single sitting, that considerable weight may have been put on.

"The man I saw was closer to six feet," I said. "And far from lithe."

"What about his ears?" asked Sir Robert. "Did you get a

look at them?"

"I don't normally make a habit of observing policeman's ears," I said. "They don't like it. Besides he was wearing a helmet."

"What about his um ... trouser area?"

"They like that even less."

~

Berrymore returned to report that not a single policeman had been spotted by anyone below, above, or between stairs. And the laundry maid had been hanging out the washing during the critical period and hadn't seen a single helmet.

Babbacombe drew a similar blank. Neither Tom the coachman nor the gardeners had seen or heard anything. Every servant was accounted for, and the lawns were devoid of any unexpected additions.

I wanted to conduct my own search. Policemen do not disappear. Many a time I have wished otherwise, but it is one of those incontestable truths. Somewhere there would be a policeman or evidence as to where he'd beetled off to.

But it was time for luncheon and, as I'm sure you remember, the Worcester stomach had already been deprived of breakfast. To miss one meal may be regarded as a misfortune, to miss two is unconscionable.

Luncheon at the Baskerville-Smythe trough was somewhat of a subdued affair. Lady Julia made a point of seating herself between Emmeline and me, and conversation was far from sparkling. I did make one attempt to enliven the conversation, but was swatted down by my redoubtable neighbour with a comment I spent the rest of the meal trying to decipher. *Don't talk with your mouth open, dear.*

What did that mean? I wasn't sure if I'd been told to shut up or invited to amuse the gathering with a spot of ventriloquism!

Meanwhile at the other end of the table, Sir Robert and Morrow had convinced themselves Selden could not have been the constable.

"Where would he have obtained the uniform?" said Sir Robert. "They have warders at prisons, not policemen. Completely different uniform."

Morrow had an answer to the constable's failure to appear at the Hall too.

"The constable must have spotted Selden before reaching the Hall and given chase."

"Into the mire?" said Sir Robert.

"I doubt it. They'd both be dead if they did. I think it more likely they ran across the moor to the west."

I couldn't wait for the meal to end. I'd already formulated a plan for the afternoon. We'd return to the spot we'd last seen the constable and retrace his journey to the Hall from there. If he had hopped off the track in pursuit of anyone, there'd be a trail. The same went for if he'd been waylaid. One can't grapple with a custodian of the law without leaving a trace or two.

But Lady Julia had other ideas.

"You shall spend the afternoon in the drawing room with me," she announced as we arose from the table. "Both of you."

"But Lady Julia," I said. "There's important sleuthing to be done. The missing policeman. The escaped convict—"

"That is what servants are for," she said, interrupting. "I hear you like to sketch, Lily. I shall have a maid fetch a vase of flowers for you."

"Oh," said Emmeline. "How ... kind."

"And as for you, Roderick, you shall read an improving book. You can read, can't you?"

~

I don't recall if Sherlock Holmes had ever been locked in the drawing room by Mrs Hudson, but I doubted it. But then Holmes had never come up against anyone as formidable as Lady Julia. She had a way of narrowing her eyes that could freeze the corpuscles at thirty paces.

And as for her choice of improving literature, I'd never encountered such turgid rot. *Ethics*, it was called, by some chap named Spinoza. I read the entire book and still had no idea who the murderer was! I may have skipped the odd page, but still ... one expects classic literature to have a proper *dénouement*.

I don't think Emmeline fared any better. Staring at a vase of flowers for four hours is right up there with reading the Spinoza chap.

Our liberation came when the drawing room clock struck six.

"You may leave and dress for dinner now," said Lady Julia.

Out we went, closing the drawing room door firmly behind us. We didn't dare speak until we'd reached the landing in case Lady Julia's hearing was as formidable as her gaze.

"What are we going to do about her?" asked Emmeline, keeping her voice barely above a whisper. "She's going to stick to us like glue."

"Does she go out much? From what I've seen she seems to haunt the drawing room."

"I've seen her take a walk in the gardens, but I think she finds the weather too cold this time of year."

"Then we shall endeavour to spend more time out of doors."

"We could always volunteer our services to Henry," suggested Emmeline. "He *has* asked both of us to appear in his moving picture. And Henry's very amenable. We could always slip away whenever any sleuthing was required."

There are times when Emmeline can rival Reeves in the brains department.

"Emmie, you must have had kippers for breakfast."

"I had two."

~

Reeves was waiting for me in my room. The stout fellow had secured a generous quantity of the fortifying nectar and handed me a glass.

"You're a lifesaver, Reeves. I've just spent four hours reading Spinoza, and I can tell you that hard labour is a breeze compared to that. If judges had the option of sentencing criminals to four years of hard Spinozaring, there'd be far less crime in the world."

"If you say so, sir."

"Any news of the missing boy in blue?"

"No, sir. I did take the liberty of searching the grounds, but found no definitive trace. I did note additional footprints in the vicinity of the mire gate since our last observation of that area, but there was nothing to indicate their ownership."

"Not size twelve then?"

"No, sir, though I did not have occasion to gauge the size of the constable's boots. They may have been smaller than size twelve."

I shook the noggin.

"Unlikely, Reeves. I'm sure it's part of the entry requirement. Minimum height, minimum shoe size. The empire would collapse if they allowed small-footed men into the constabulary."

I made myself comfortable in the armchair by the window and took a contemplative sip of cocktail.

"Do you ever think there are more games afoot than one realises, Reeves?"

"Frequently, sir."

"I mean, here we are with a missing policeman, an escaped cannibal, a murdered under gardener – whose body is *also* now missing – and a missing ghost. Are these all the one game or many?"

"There is an insufficiency of evidence to say, sir."

I took a longer sip of the fortifier. Perhaps if I started at the beginning I could make better sense of the puzzle.

"What does below stairs think of Sir Robert's theory that last night's ghost was their handiwork?"

"The prevailing opinion is that Sir Robert is attempting to sweep the matter under the Axminster, sir. Most believe the ghost to be genuine, and Sir Robert's life to be in grave danger. Everyone, except the Berrymores, are convinced that the convict Selden is the murderer that the ghost foretold."

"Berrymores, Reeves? There are more than one?"

"Mr Berrymore's wife is the cook, sir."

"Oh, and these Berrymores, did they offer an alternative

candidate, or don't they think the ghost was genuine?"

"They both believe in the ghost, sir, but doubt Selden is its agent. Mrs Berrymore became rather distressed when she first heard of the identity of the escaped convict. Mr Berrymore says it was on account of her affection for cats."

"Well known for her affection for cats, is she?"

"Not that I had observed, sir, but I have only been here for the one day."

"The kitchen's not filled to the rafters with moggies then?"

"No, sir."

I finished my cocktail and waited while Reeves re-filled my glass from the jug.

"We still don't believe in ghosts, do we, Reeves?"

"No, sir."

"Which makes Lupin favourite for that role. No one else could have climbed out of that window."

Reeves gave one of his disapproving coughs, which I waved away.

"I know you're an orang-utan denier, Reeves, but once one has eliminated the impossible, whatever remains, however hairy, must be the truth."

"If you say so, sir."

"I jolly well do say so. Which brings us to Pasco. Why would anyone kill him, and then go to such great pains to hide his body – even after half the household had already seen it!"

"That *is* a puzzle, sir."

"Could Pasco be more important than people realise?"

I stared at the ceiling, sucked on an olive, and had a good ruminate.

And then, somewhere in between the cornice and the ceiling rose, it came to me.

"*The Mystery of the Twelve Carbuncles*, Reeves!"

"Sir?"

"The Sherlock Holmes adventure about the chap hiding stolen carbuncles inside Napoleon. What if someone had hidden stolen carbuncles inside Pasco?"

"To what end, sir?"

"What do you mean 'to what end?' To hide them of course. Imagine you're a jewel thief, Reeves. You've just grabbed a fistful of carbuncles, but the police have spotted you and are in hot pursuit. You run into the first building you see, and find yourself inside an automaton factory. They do have automaton factories, don't they, Reeves?"

"They do, sir."

"Good, that's sorted then. So, there you are – inside the automaton factory – apprehension imminent, and you spot a place you can hide your stash – inside Pasco, whose lying on the assembly line half assembled. You hide the carbuncles, leg it for the door, and get nabbed by the rozzers. Off you go to chokey, knowing that as soon as you get out, the carbuncles will be waiting for you safe inside this Pasco chap. What do you think, Reeves?"

"An imaginative theory, sir, but Selden was not a jewel thief."

"It doesn't have to be jewels, Reeves. It could be anything. You forget we're dealing with the mind of a cat. It might be a favourite toy, or a half-eaten mouse that he was particularly fond of."

"It is my recollection, sir, that Selden was apprehended in Clerkenwell, a district not well known for its automaton factories."

"It wouldn't have to be a factory. A repair shop would work just as well."

"But how would Selden, sir, having been incarcerated for ten years, be cognisant of Pasco's current whereabouts?"

"Mere details, Reeves. The theory is sound."

"If you say so, sir."

I put down my glass. I had to say something.

"Reeves, I have noticed you using that term a lot of late, and I don't think I like it."

"Sir?"

"This 'If you say so, sir' of yours. It smacks of condescension. I may not have a giant brain like yours, but it's surprisingly nimble. It flits, Reeves. It finds strange places to perch on. Places that few people even know exist. I may not always be right, but I'm not a chap with two left ears either."

"I apologise, sir. I will re-write that particular subroutine immediately."

"Thank you, Reeves. Now where were we?"

"You were theorising that Selden had left a dead mouse inside Pasco, sir."

I decided it time to move on.

"Next, we have the mystery of the *modus operandi*, Reeves."

"Sir?"

"Everything we've heard about Selden suggests a chap who thinks like a cat, but have you ever known a cat wield an axe?

"No, sir."

"Or stab a mouse in the turbines?"

"Indeed not, sir."

"Then why would Selden?"

"The evidence would suggest to me, sir, that Selden was not responsible for the attack on Pasco."

"You forget the dead mouse theory, Reeves."

"No, sir, I assure you that that particular theory is etched within memory."

I gave Reeves a hard stare. "I'm not saying it *has* to be a dead mouse, Reeves. It could be anything. But the only reason for Selden to change his modus operandi would be if he saw Pasco not as food to be played with, but as a container to be opened."

"That is one interpretation, sir, but it *is* predicated on the considerable coincidence of both Pasco and Dr Morrow residing in Clerkenwell and Baskerville Hall at the requisite times. And we have it from Trelawny, the gardener, that Pasco was purchased last year. I cannot envisage Sir Robert buying a second-hand under gardener, which would mean that Pasco would not have been built when Selden was last in Clerkenwell."

I couldn't imagine Sir Robert buying a second-hand under gardener either. Oh well, that's the nature of sleuthing – sometimes one's best theory crashes and burns. One draws a line through it and moves on.

"Something adventurous in the sock line tonight, I think,

Reeves. Have you laid out my evening dress?"

"No, sir. I will attend to it now."

Reeves shimmered off to the wardrobe while I drained my glass of the early evening fortifier.

"What is it, Reeves?" I asked. The chap appeared transfixed by something within the wardrobe. "You're not objecting to that red silk handkerchief again, are you? I have told you, even the Prince of Wales wears one in his waistcoat these days."

"No, sir. There appears to be a head in the wardrobe."

TWELVE

"A what in the wardrobe?"

"A head, sir. It appears to be glowing."

I don't know about you, but Reginald Worcester does not like the idea of glowing heads appearing in wardrobes. I hastened over at once.

"I suspect it may belong to Pasco, sir."

It was difficult to tell. The top of the head had received a considerable bash. And the face was covered in an odd greenish paint. But how many missing heads could there be?

"The rest of him's not in there, is it?" I asked.

We searched the wardrobe, then the rest of the room. I even looked under the bed and felt a little way up the chimney. We didn't find any more of Pasco, but we did find a tin of RadioGlo paint and a paint-stained brush concealed beneath my underlinen in a dressing table drawer.

"None of this was present this morning, sir."

I read the label on the RadioGlo tin.

"What's radioluminescent paint, Reeves? Is that another word for 'odd shade of green?'"

"It's a paint that glows in the dark, sir. I believe it to be a mixture of radium, copper and zinc sulphide. Pasco, or an accomplice, must have painted Pasco's face to give it a spectral glow."

One did not have to be a consulting detective to work out what for.

"So, Pasco was last night's ghost."

"So it would appear, sir."

"You don't sound convinced, Reeves."

"One doubts the reliability of any evidence that has been

planted, sir."

"Lock the door, Reeves," I said. "Whoever stowed this here is going to want this room searched pretty dashed soon. We need time to think."

And a generous refill of the thought restorative.

~

I had that warm feeling in the head that one gets when one's little grey cells are whizzing around with alcohol-fuelled vigour. And when Reginald Worcester's l g c's start whizzing there's nothing they can't accomplish.

"Might I suggest, sir, that we move the incriminating evidence to an alternative location? There are several empty rooms in this wing."

"Not yet, Reeves. That's exactly what they're hoping we'll do."

"Sir?"

"I see all, Reeves. We are, as I suspected earlier, dealing with a criminal mastermind."

"Oh," said one of Reeves' eyebrows. Not literally, of course, but figuratively. It rose a whole eighth of an inch.

"Indeed," I said. "It's a clever feint. They make us think that the plan is to have the incriminating evidence discovered in my possession. But it isn't."

"It isn't, sir?"

"No, Reeves. I could say 'I've never seen this severed head before in my life, officer.' People might not believe me – Lady Julia for one – but no one could prove otherwise. But if we move the evidence, especially if we do so in haste, fingerprints will be left, Reeves. And fingerprints *will* stand up in court these days."

"I shall wear gloves, sir."

"Of course it could be a double bluff. Or even a triple one. You can never tell with criminal masterminds. What if they were expecting us to relocate the evidence, and then panic when we realised about the fingerprints, and rush back and wipe the evidence clean?"

Reeves was unusually silent.

"You see what I'm getting at, Reeves."

"No, sir."

"Fiendishness, Reeves. Criminal masterminds like nothing better than to manipulate others into doing their dirty work for them. And they're risk takers. They may well have left their own fingerprints on the head knowing that we'd panic, and wipe the head clean for them. I expect they're sitting in their room now having a good chuckle at how close we were to determining their identity."

"I believe one can overthink a problem, sir. I hesitate to mention Ockham's razor, but feel it appropriate in this situation to-"

"Reeves," I held up my hand to stop him. "Does this razor to which you refer belong to William of Ockham perchance?"

"It's a metaphorical razor, sir, for shaving away unnecessary assumptions."

"Bearded chap, was he? This William of Ockham."

"I believe he is normally portrayed as clean-shaven, sir."

"Must have had two razors then. Or did the metaphorical one shave the other away?"

"I really cannot say, sir," said Reeves, airing his disapproving face.

I drew myself up to my full seated height.

"We shall examine the evidence for fingerprints, Reeves. Then we shall move said evidence to a place of safety."

Even a Reeves in the midst of low dudgeon could see the merit in that.

Reeves selected a white silk evening glove for the task ahead, and I inserted the Worcester digits therein. I then placed each of the three objects upon the corner of the dressing table where the light from the window was at its brightest.

I gave them all a good eyeball, from several angles, using my silver-mounted magnifying glass. Reeves then did the same.

"Can you see anything, Reeves? I can't."

"The tin and paintbrush handle are remarkably unblemished, sir. I would say that both have been deliberately wiped clean."

"And the head?"

"That is more difficult to say, sir. There is a smudge – which could be a fingerprint – in the large depression to the crown of the head. It is, regrettably, too faint to make an accurate sketch."

"Ha," I said. "Not too faint for Serge, *Le Patissier*."

"Sir?"

"You haven't read *The Poisoned Brioche*? *The Eccles Cake of Death*? *The Girl in The Baklava*?"

"No, sir. I have not had those pleasures."

"Amend that at your earliest convenience, Reeves. For, if you had, you'd know that there are ways to enhance fingerprints. Flour, for one. You dust it lightly over the print and – *voila* – things are brought up a treat. Serge always carries a bag of self-raising in his pocket just in case. He's a crime-fighting patisserie chef, you know?"

"I did not, sir."

"You would be staggered, Reeves, staggered at the number of people who have been murdered in his patisserie shop. A dozen at least. And that's just the novels I've read. But Serge solves every case, and every time it's the fingerprints that lead him to the guilty party."

"Most interesting, sir. I have read several learned treatises on the subject of fingerprints written by the world's foremost experts, but never encountered a mention of flour."

"I am not surprised, Reeves. Everyone knows that authors know far more about the latest crime-fighting techniques than any so-called expert."

I sent Reeves off to the kitchen for flour.

In the meantime – the little grey cells still warm and whizzing – I decided to engage in a little deduction. Clearly Pasco was the ghost, but could he have undertaken the task unaided? I very much doubted it. He wasn't one of those augmented automata – the ones with all manner of rummy attachments. He was an ordinary gardening model who'd need a ladder to climb down from that window like everyone else. And he'd leave a substantial imprint in the ground if he just jumped out the window.

Could Lupin have carried him down? Lupin was certainly strong, but was he strong enough to climb down *and* carry a fully grown under gardener?

And what was the significance of the large bash on the head? Pasco had already been decapitated and stabbed in the turbines, why another wound? Or was the bash the first injury?

I was still musing when Reeves returned with the flour. And a sieve.

"I thought it would improve the efficacy of the flour application, sir."

"Good thinking, Reeves."

I took the sieve, added a good quantity of flour, and gave it a gentle shaking over the head, concentrating on the depressed bit where Reeves had seen the smudge.

"Can you see anything yet, Reeves?"

Reeves leaned over the head and gave it a good scrutinise with the glass. "No, sir. The flour appears to have covered the smudge entirely."

I gave it the eyeball. Reeves was not wrong. I picked up the head and shook the flour back into the bag and tried again.

"Less flour this time, I think, Reeves."

That didn't work either. A light dusting revealed nothing. I couldn't understand it. This didn't happen in the books. One sift from Serge and every fingerprint revealed themselves instantly!

Maybe the smudge wasn't a fingerprint? I decided to dust the rest of the head. Serge often found fingerprints where the *Sûreté's* finest hadn't even spotted the merest smudge.

But the flour wouldn't stick. The more I sieved, the more slid off. I had a veritable flour mountain growing on the dressing table!

"I don't think this is working, sir."

A chap with whizzing l g c's does not give up lightly. Didn't something similar happen to Serge in an early book? *The Girl in The Baklava*, I think. The three-day-old poisoned macaroon that...

"An atomiser, Reeves!" I said. "We need to apply a fine spray of water to the surface prior to the flour."

"I would not recommend it, sir. One would suspect the

water would wash away any trace of fingerprint."

"Not if you use a fine spray, Reeves. Serge swears by it. It helps the flour bind to even the smoothest surface. Do you know where Emmeline's room is? She's bound to have an atomiser we could borrow."

Reeves returned in a matter of minutes, but not alone. Emmeline had insisted that if any game was afoot, her feet had to come along too.

"So that's Pasco's head," she said, hoving alongside me. "Why does it have that large dent?"

"I suspect that was the initial blow," I said. "It would have been dark, remember, and our murderer may not have known Pasco was an automaton. I think he whacked Pasco on the head thinking it would kill him, then, when Pasco kept on moving, he resorted to the stabbing and decapitating."

"A possible theory, sir, but the position of the wound suggests to me a deliberate action to destroy Pasco's memory."

"Does it?" I asked.

"It does, sir. A single blow to the top of the head is a most unusual one. Most blows to the head occur to the sides or the back. Pasco's memory boards, however, are located in the very spot that has been damaged."

"So the murderer must know a lot about automata," said Emmeline.

"Not necessarily, miss. They could have asked Pasco. This particular model is programmed to tell people the location of all their major parts, if asked, in order to facilitate repair. They are programmed to obey orders and be helpful. They have no thoughts of self-preservation."

"Is that *all* orders, Reeves?" I asked. "If some chap trotted up to Pasco with a dress and a pot of RadioGlo paint, and said, 'What ho, Pasco, would you mind awfully putting on this dress while I paint your face green?' that this Pasco would acquiesce?"

"Yes, sir. Pasco's model is a very basic one, designed for the garden where there will be minimum interaction with the general populace. Automata destined for work inside the house have more complex programming and, consequently, are more expensive to manufacture."

"So Pasco could be an unwitting accomplice," said Emmeline. "Someone could smuggle him into the house and order him to play the ghost?"

"Indeed, miss. And then, by destroying Pasco's memory, their secret would be safe."

"What about the shape of the dent, Reeves?" I said. "Any idea about the weapon?"

"I suspect the blunt end of the same axe that was used on his neck and hands, sir. One can discern a slight oval pattern in the dent which I am sure would match."

"Right ho," I said. "Have you got that atomiser, Emmie?"

"Yes, but it's half full."

Reeves unscrewed the top of the atomiser and drained the perfume into the only empty vessel he could find – my cocktail glass.

"I'll take the atomiser to the bathroom and fill it with water, sir. I suggest you lock the door while I'm gone."

I locked the door after Reeves' exit.

"You do realise," said Emmeline with a girlish smile, "that if anyone *does* choose to search the rooms now, it won't just be Pasco's head we'll be in trouble for."

"The paint tin, you mean?"

"No, silly. You've just locked me in your bedroom. Lady Julia will be scandalised."

I hadn't considered this. As scandalous behaviour went, locking an unmarried, and unchaperoned, young lady in one's bedroom outranked stowing an under gardener's head in the wardrobe any day.

"We could hide under the bed and pretend we're not here," I said.

"I think people searching rooms tend to look there first."

"Then I'd jump out the window and save your honour. You could say you heard a noise and thought it was Selden, so you ran into the nearest room and locked the door."

"How would you explain why you were lying on the lawn with a broken leg?"

"I'd say I'd never seen this broken leg before in my life. It was already there when I tripped over it. Probably Pasco's."

Emmeline laughed ... until there was a knock on the door.

We both jumped. Emmeline emitted a strangled 'eep' and I was ankling it at full speed towards the window, before the reassuring voice of Reeves stemmed the stampede.

"It is Reeves, sir," he said. "You may unlock the door now."

I let him in.

"We'll have to formulate some kind of door knocking code in future, Reeves. Two quick knocks followed by two slow ones means all's well."

"Very good, sir."

I took the atomiser and gave it a test puff or two. A pleasing cloud of fine vapour was produced both times.

"Perfect," I said. "Now watch this."

I sprayed Pasco's head in a fine mist, waited a second or two, then sieved on the flour. The flour stuck!

"Can you see anything, Reeves?"

"No, sir."

"Are you sure?"

"Positive, sir."

"I'll add some more flour."

"I would not advise it, sir."

"Nonsense, Reeves. If it works for Serge, it'll work for Reginald."

I added more flour, then more water, then more flour.

"Should it look like that?" asked Emmeline.

It looked a mess, which was not how it was described in the book. Pasco's head was covered in a sticky white goo.

"I think it might need time to settle," I said, hopefully.

"It looks more like pastry," said Emmeline.

We stood around the head waiting in a despondent silence. And then I sieved on some more flour. Then Reeves annoyed me with a lot of defeatist rot about giving up on the experiment, and I sieved on a lot more ... interspersed with generous sprays of water. We Worcesters do not yield in the face of adversity – even when that face is covered in pastry!

"Reggie," said Emmeline, placing her hand on my tiring sieving arm. "I think that's enough."

Sadly, I had to agree.

"I shall write a stiff letter to the publishers of *The Girl in The Baklava*, Emmie. Mark my words. *"*

Emmeline watched the corridor, while a gloved Reeves and I carried the incriminating pastry into an empty room at the far end of the corridor. I stashed the brush and paint tin in a dressing table drawer there. Reeves placed the pastry-covered head in the wardrobe. We then withdrew smartly.

"All clear," said Emmeline. "Sorry, but I must dash. The maid's running my bath. I'll see you at dinner, Reggie."

It was a dispirited Reginald Worcester that trudged back to his room. I'd even lost the will to get excited about socks, and, when I took a long and surprising sip of *Eau de Cologne*, it seemed to sum up my entire afternoon.

But we Worcesters can't stay down for long. We're rather like corks – always looking to spring back up the moment cruel fortune releases its grip. After an hour I could even see a silver lining to the *Eau de Cologne* incident – I'd have the sweetest smelling breath in the entire dining room!

~

It was ten to eight, by the time I trotted downstairs. Babbacombe was sitting in a hall chair by the door, cradling a shotgun, and looking pretty glum. I gave him an encouraging what ho, then proceeded to the drawing room.

"Good evening, Roderick," said T. Everett. "What's *your* take on this Selden crisis? Does he have a plan, do you think?"

"One would think he'd be looking for Dr Morrow," I said. I then noticed that the doctor wasn't present. "Where is the doctor?"

"He must still be in his room," said T. Everett. "Everyone's a little late tonight. Usually we're all here by half past."

"There are extenuating circumstances," said Lily.

"I think Selden's long gone," said Henry. "That business with Pasco will have shaken him."

Ida disagreed. "The maid told me that Pasco's body has gone missing," she said. "Berrymore sent the coachman to move the body this afternoon and he couldn't find it! The maid's sure Selden ate him."

"The maid doesn't know what she's talking about, Ida," said Henry. "There'll be a simple explanation. One of the servants must have moved the body without telling anyone."

"And there's a policeman gone missing too," said Ida. "The maid reckons he was dessert."

"Ida!" said her father. "Could we talk about something else?"

"I agree," said Lily. "I feel like we're all standing around waiting for Selden to make an appearance."

Emmeline floated into the room. It may be sappy, but I rather felt the room brightened. If there had been small birds present, they would have chirruped. Clouds – if one could fit a small brace of cumulus into a country house drawing room – would have parted.

"Just the person I wanted to see," said Henry. "Everett and I have come up with the perfect moving picture for you."

"You have?" said Emmeline.

"It's a corker," said Lily. "You've got to do it."

"We're going to call it the *The Perils of Poor Lily*," said Henry. "It'll be a quarry-based serial of cliff-hanging peril. Each weekly episode will end with you in the direst peril."

"Tied to a railway track with a train steaming towards you," said T. Everett.

"Or dangling from a cliff top," added Henry.

I had to say this didn't sound to me like a plum part.

"Goodness," said Emmeline.

"But every week you escape," said Henry. "Just when everyone in the audience is convinced you're a goner, in rides the hero to save the day."

"Can't I save myself?" asked Emmeline.

"That would never play in the Midwest, Lily," said T. Everett.

"So, I spend all my time getting into trouble, and then a man saves me?" asked Emmeline.

If I'd been Henry, I'd have stepped back a foot or two at this point.

"Audiences love a damsel in distress," said Henry. "But you wouldn't be an ordinary damsel in distress. You'd be as you were this morning – someone who'd see a Lizard Man and dive right in. The audience will love you. You'd be a free spirit, always getting into scrapes. But then, with five minutes to go, you get into a scrape that no one thinks even you can escape from."

"And then a man saves me," said Emmeline.

"Not just *any* man, Lily," said Henry. "He'll be a hero ... with a white hat. And there'll be plenty of male villains you can bash."

"You've been very quiet, Ida. What do you think of the idea?" asked her father.

"I think Miss Fossett was *born* to hang from a cliff. She has such stout arms."

"I do not!"

"You do!"

"Of course you don't," I said, strategically placing the Worcester body in between Emmeline and Ida. "Oh, look. Here's Morrow."

Heads turned, and the doctor, looking a little flushed and out of puff, hurried in.

"Sorry if I'm a little late," he said. "I lost track of time."

Which was understandable in the circs. If Reeves started eating postmen and leaving their internal organs on the doorstep, I'd be a little distracted too.

Morrow's arrival was swiftly followed by that of Lady Julia.

"Has anyone seen Robert?" she asked.

"I saw him half an hour ago," said Henry. "He and Berrymore were checking all the doors and windows were locked."

"But where is he now?" asked Lady Julia. "He should be here. He's not in his room or the library."

"It *is* an unusual day, Aunt Julia," said Henry. "I expect he's giving last-minute instructions to Berrymore."

The dinner gong sounded.

"Where *is* Robert?" said Lady Julia, sounding a tad more annoyed than concerned. "He's *never* late for dinner."

Berrymore emerged, pushing open the double doors through to the dining room.

"Have you seen my father, Berrymore?" asked Henry.

Berrymore looked surprised. "I saw Sir Robert ten minutes ago, sir. I was under the impression he was on his way here."

THIRTEEN

Dinner had to wait. According to Berrymore, Sir Robert had left the butler's pantry ten minutes ago en route for the drawing room. Babbacombe, on guard in the hallway – with a clear view of the door to the servants' quarters – had not seen Sir Robert emerge.

Even Lady Julia joined the party that followed Henry through the servants' door in search of Sir Robert.

An armed footman, who looked liked a younger version of Babbacombe, was sitting in a chair by the back door to the garden.

"Have you see my father, Witheridge?" asked Henry.

"I ... don't know, sir," said Witheridge, looking decidedly shifty.

"Either you have or you haven't, man. Which is it?" barked Henry.

"He told me not to tell anyone, sir."

"*Who* told you?"

"Sir Robert, sir. He said he was slipping out for five minutes and if anyone asked I was to say I'd never seen nothing."

Witheridge had a distinct 'rabbit in the lamp light' look.

"Are you saying he went *outside*?" said Henry.

"He took a gun with him," said Witheridge. "I offered to go with him, but he told me to stay at my post."

"This is ridiculous!" said Lady Julia. "Robert would never embark on some secret tryst minutes before dinner."

"Did he say *where* he was going? Or why?" Henry asked Witheridge.

"No, sir. He just told me to keep quiet about it."

A search party was swiftly organised. Two brace of shotguns were fetched from the gun room and passed around. I had one for about five seconds before Reeves appeared at my shoulder and insisted it was his job to carry it for me.

Witheridge and Babbacombe were ordered to stay behind and protect the ladies. This, not unexpectedly, raised the ire of Emmeline, who objected to being left behind, insisting the search party would need all the sharp eyes it could get.

"You're not dressed for it, girl," snapped Lady Julia.

Lady Julia did have a point. Billowy dresses and a couple of inches of heel were not ideal attire for scrabbling around in the dark.

"Besides," I said. "Someone has to stay behind and protect Witheridge and Babbacombe."

With lamps lit and passed around, the party left the back door and split up. It was twilight and rather misty. The mist was an odd species of mist, too – one could see patches of the denser stuff drifting over the lawns.

Henry and the others set off for the outbuildings, calling out for Sir Robert as they went. I decided to head across the back lawn toward the mire gate. If I were looking for a secret trysting place, that's the spot I'd have chosen.

The mist thickened and cleared around us. One second Reeves and I were in a pea souper, the next we could see almost one hundred yards. And as the lawns began to drop away, I saw the most unnerving sight. There, through a gap in the trees, I saw a hooded woman in a long black dress bent over a shape on the ground. She was eighty yards away at the bottom of the slope. And as I held up my lamp, she turned and looked my way. And then she was off, legging it at speed towards the mire gate.

We gave chase. I didn't trust the direct route. Another bank of fog was drifting in and the ground would be covered in scrub and spreading tree roots designed to up-end the over-hasty. And Reeves was carrying a loaded shotgun. So we ran the longer way via the Yew Walk. It wasn't until we were within ten yards that we recognised the shape on the ground that the woman had been bent over.

It was Sir Robert.

~

"Is he dead?" I asked, having a pretty good idea as to the answer. He was lying face down on the ground and hadn't moved an inch.

Reeves knelt beside him and felt for a pulse.

"Sir Robert is deceased, sir, but still warm. I would estimate his time of death as mere moments ago."

We both looked through the mist towards the mire gate. The woman had gone. All we could hear was the distant hoot of an owl and the calls of the searching parties.

"Should we give chase, sir?"

"Watch out for her footprints, Reeves. We don't want to destroy them. Keep to the side of the track."

We ran towards the gate. Ten yards short of our destination, I noticed a shotgun – presumably Sir Robert's – lying on the path. We ran past, not stopping until we reached the gate.

A thick fog hung over the mire. We looked up the track and down. No lights. No hurrying shapes. No sound of running feet. It was as though the woman had vanished into the mist itself.

"We still don't believe in ghosts, do we, Reeves?"

"No, sir."

"Good."

And then I shone the lamp over the ground by the gate, and had an even bigger shock. There were clear footprints in the soft earth superimposed upon the ones I'd seen earlier that day. They were not human.

"Is that a cloven hoof, Reeves?"

"It would appear so, sir. Most disturbing."

We followed their intermittent trail back to the body. One could see where the creature had stood over Sir Robert.

"Cats don't have cloven hooves, do they, Reeves?"

"No, sir."

I stood there, the Worcester mind boggling. What were we dealing with? Mrs Lucifer or a well-dressed goat?

"Have you ever seen anything like this?" I asked.

"No, sir. The imprint is far too large to be that of a deer.

The woman could be a promethean, but the choice of cloven feet is extremely odd."

"Could it be another of Morrow's experiments, do you think? Is there a Clerkenwell Goat?"

"Not that I have heard, sir."

I looked down at Sir Robert's body and took a deep breath. Time to stiffen the lip, and harden the gaze. We consulting detectives had to see the puzzle, not the man. It's one of the reasons we British make the best detectives – our innate detachment – that and being torn from the bosom of our families at a tender age and given seven years hard education at boarding school.

"What about this gun?" I said, retracing our steps back towards the gate. "Was it fired? I didn't hear any shots."

Reeves retrieved the gun and carefully broke it. "Two cartridges, sir, and, by the lack of odour, this gun has not been fired recently."

"Odd," I said. "Why didn't he shoot? And what's his gun doing *here*? Did he drop it and run?"

"There is nothing on the ground to indicate a struggle, sir. One would think that if the gun had been wrested from Sir Robert's hands that one or the other party's feet would have dug into the earth."

"So, Sir Robert drops his gun here and legs it down the Yew Walk back towards the house?"

"That would be my interpretation, sir."

"But why? The gun was his best protection. Even a cloven-hoofed promethean would back down against a man with a gun."

"Perhaps Sir Robert believed the hooded woman to be a spirit, sir. I did note that the woman's attire looked very similar to the previous evening's ghost."

"I thought Sir Robert pooh-poohed the idea of the ghost being real."

"That is what he *said*, sir. It may not have been what he believed."

Reeves, as ever, made an excellent point.

"I didn't notice any glow to her face. Did you?"

"No, sir, though I had only the briefest glimpse of her

face. Perhaps the fact that we hid the tin of RadioGlo paint prevented its use."

As we walked back to Sir Robert's body, I noticed something moving slowly up the wooded slope. It was Lupin. He had his back towards us, and was part shrouded in mist, but the hunched outline was unmistakable, however faint. He was heading for the back lawn. But where had he come from? And why hadn't we seen him earlier? Had he been up a tree?

I tapped Reeves on the arm and pointed.

"Yes, sir," said Reeves. "I had noticed."

~

Our initial investigation of the crime scene complete, I raised the view halloo. We consulting detectives know the value of a pristine crime scene, and the destruction that two dozen extraneous boots can wreak.

"Over here!" I shouted as the first groups neared. "We've found him."

One by one the search parties arrived. Henry was pretty cut up. As was Morrow.

"Was it Selden?" asked a grim T. Everett.

"No. We saw a hooded woman standing over the body, but she ran off the moment she saw us."

"A woman?" said Morrow.

"Dressed very much like last night's ghost, except this one had cloven feet," I said. "You can see her tracks all the way to the mire gate."

"Are you sure they're hers and not a deer?" said Morrow.

"Look for yourself," I said. "Have you ever encountered a promethean with cloven feet?"

"No," said Morrow, giving the ground a good eyeball. He traced the tracks for several yards before kneeling down for a better look with his lamp. "You're right," he said. "It's not a deer. It's someone running on two feet."

"Could it be one of our prometheans?" asked Henry.

"We don't have any prometheans with cloven feet," said Morrow. "I've heard of people experimenting – as, regrettably, I had with Selden – but I've never seen anything like this."

"Could she be a friend of Selden's?" I asked. "A woman who felt she was a fawn trapped in a human body?"

"I wouldn't know," said Morrow. "Selden never mentioned any such person, but I haven't had contact with Selden for ten years."

"How ... how was my father killed?" said Henry, his upper lip losing some of its stiffness.

We all looked down at Sir Robert. There were no obvious wounds, and no blood. Then Morrow knelt besides the body.

"Help me turn him over," he said. "And bring another lamp over here!"

Morrow and two of the footmen rolled Sir Robert onto his back and, in doing so, revealed a bowl lying next to the body. It was half full of what looked like milk. Sir Robert's coat had a matching white stain where he'd fallen on top of the bowl.

Before I could mention fingerprints, one of the footmen had picked up the bowl, dipped his finger in the liquid, and touched it to his tongue.

"It's milk, sir," he said.

At the very moment he spoke, the Worcester deductive wheels began to spin. Corpse with no obvious cause of death, bowl of milk next to the body...

"Sir Robert didn't die from poisoned milk, by any chance?"

The footman leaped a good yard into the air, and came down spitting. And then wiped his tongue on both sleeves of his uniform.

"I'm sorry, sirs," he apologised.

An understandable reaction, I thought. "Best to stand back and not touch anything," I said. "Crime scenes are dangerous places. And don't forget to keep an eye out for Selden."

Morrow was now bent over Sir Robert, examining this and sniffing that. I still couldn't see any wounds. And from the expression on Sir Robert's face, I rather got the impression he might have died of fright.

"What killed him, Morrow?" said Henry. "He looks like he saw the devil."

I mentioned the gun and how it looked to Reeves and I that Sir Robert had seen something so unnerving that he'd dropped the gun and run for his life.

"I don't know about that," said Morrow. "It looks to me like he asphyxiated."

"Strangled?" said Henry.

"No," said Morrow. "There are no signs of strangulation. He just ... was unable to breathe."

"But how?" said T. Everett.

"I'll have to get Sir Robert back to the Hall for a more thorough examination."

Reeves coughed.

"Yes, Reeves?" I said.

"I was wondering what Dr Morrow thought of the small mark on the right side of Sir Robert's neck, sir."

"That's one of the things I'm intending to examine back at the Hall," said Morrow, sounding a little nettled.

I leaned in for a better view. There was a red pin prick of a mark on Sir Robert's neck.

"It could be from a bramble thorn," said Morrow.

FOURTEEN

Sir Robert's body was carried back to the Hall. Morrow suggested taking the body straight to his laboratory on the second floor, but Henry would hear nothing of it.

"My father is not going to spend the night in any second floor laboratory. The study is a more fitting place. He always liked the study. You can examine him there."

A throng of servants – mainly the maids and kitchen staff – were waiting in the small hallway by the back door. Emmeline was there too, but I couldn't see Lady Julia, Ida, or Lily. The news of Sir Robert's death was greeted with much gnashing and wailing – particularly from Mrs Berrymore, who collapsed on the spot and had to be carried into the kitchen. I had wanted a word with Emmeline, but she was part of the deputation carrying away the unfortunate cook.

A space was cleared on the large desk in the study and Sir Robert's body placed upon it. The servants then withdrew, and Lady Julia, Ida and Lily came rushing in.

"How could this happen?" said Lady Julia. "What was he *doing* out there?"

"We don't know," said Henry.

I was waiting for someone to make the obvious suggestion, but no one did. I couldn't see Dr Morrow either – presumably he'd beetled off to fetch his medical bag – so I thought I might as well broach the subject.

"Have you considered reanimating Sir Robert?" I asked. "You'd get Sir Robert back *and* you'd find out who killed him."

"What did you say?" asked Lady Julia, narrowing her eyes to a frightening degree.

"Reanimation," I squeaked. "Dr Morrow must be a whizz at reanimating the deceased. He has his own laboratory on the premises, and they always say the fresh ones reanimate the best."

"The *fresh* ones!" If Lady Julia ever decided to audition for the part of Lady Bracknell she'd be a cert.

"That's what they say." I looked hopefully about the room for support, but found a roomful of averted eyes. Even Morrow, who must have just oiled in at the back, looked away.

Lady Julia dialled back the gimlet stare a turn or two. "Reanimation is for the lower classes, dear. And foreigners. People of quality prefer to meet their maker at their allotted time."

"But if one's murdered–"

"*If* one is murdered, one hopes one would have the good manners to stay dead! Who would receive a *réanimé* in their home? Certainly no one of quality. The poor creature would be shunned and forced to live abroad ... or appear in moving pictures!"

It was Henry's turn to feel the heat of his aunt's gaze.

"Reanimating my father is not an option, Roderick," said Henry. "As much as the idea appeals."

"Henry!" said Lady Julia.

"Excuse me," said Morrow, inching his way through the throng. "May I suggest that people leave. If I'm to examine Sir Robert..."

"Examine?" said Lady Julia, reprising her Lady Bracknell voice.

"To determine the cause of death," said Morrow, looking towards Henry for support.

Henry looked like a man who'd appreciate support himself. "I'm not sure that's such a good idea, Morrow. Shouldn't we leave that to the coroner? Dash it all, what *are* the correct procedures?"

"Normally, one informs the police," I said. "And they then bring in the coroner. But, in this case, with bridges down and the place cut off, it's usual to hand the case over to a talented amateur detective."

"We don't have a talented amateur detective," said Henry.

"Oh, but we do," I said. "There's little I don't know about the deductive arts. Inspector Gaucho of the Buenos Aires *Sûreté* is always calling on me for help. If ever someone's mortal coil receives an unexpected shuffling, I'm the person he telegrams."

"Dear God," said Lady Julia.

"I thought you lived in a mining camp in the middle of nowhere," said Ida.

"I do. Sometimes one can solve a case without leaving one's armchair. Other times I hop on the next canoe to Buenos Aires. That's where I met Reeves."

"Reeves?"

"My man. He was a sergeant in the Buenos Aires *Sûreté*. Reeves of the Yard they called him. He has an eye for clues like no other. Inspector Gaucho was pretty put out when I poached him."

"No!" said Lady Julia. "If anyone here is to conduct an investigation, it should be Henry. He's the head of the family."

"I have no experience in such matters," said Henry. "Roderick does."

"Roderick is an idiot," said Lady Julia.

"He is *not* an idiot!" said Emmeline. "He just thinks differently, which is exactly what you need in a detective. Someone who can see things others can't."

"Lily's right," said Henry. "I'll send Tom over the moor to Princetown tomorrow to inform the police. In the meantime I think we should accept Roderick's offer."

~

I felt every eye upon me as I approached the body, especially Lady Julia's.

"First, I shall examine his pockets. Could someone send for my man Reeves?"

"I am here, sir," said Reeves appearing as if by magic at my left shoulder. I really do not know how he does it. I could have sworn he'd left the study with the other servants, but suddenly there he was.

"Do you have your gloves, Reeves?"

"I do, sir."

"Then search away." I turned to address the throng as I felt they rather expected it. "It is vital not to contaminate the evidence," I explained. "Which is why Reeves here is wearing gloves. Every time one touches an object, one leaves fingerprints. And no two person's fingerprints are the same, therefore, if Reeves finds an object with a fingerprint upon it, we can identify the person who last touched that object."

I decided to omit any mention of flour.

Reeves rummaged in Sir Robert's left-hand jacket pocket.

"There is something within, sir."

Reeves pulled out a small piece of paper and unfolded it.

"It is a note, sir, addressed to Sir Robert from a Sergeant Stock."

"Stock?" said Henry. "He's the police sergeant at Princetown. What does he say?"

Reeves read the letter aloud.

Meet me at mire gate 8 pm sharp. Vital importance. You MUST come alone. Don't tell no one – not even your son. Don't let no one see you neither. Someone at the Hall is helping Selden. Trust no one.

Sergeant Stock

"Did you see Sergeant Stock when you went to the mire gate?" Henry asked me.

"No, and I doubt very much that he was the author of this note."

"Why?" said Henry.

"Because it's an obvious ruse to get Sir Robert alone and out of the house. It's clever, but not nearly clever enough."

I paused for a good two seconds. We consulting detectives like to put on a bit of a show. It's part of the calling. Lady Agatha MacTweedie likes to have at least three costume changes during her *dénouements*.

"If they'd been really clever," I said. "They would have told Sir Robert to burn the note."

I didn't have any gloves with me so I took out my red silk handkerchief to take the note from Reeves.

"Now we know why Sir Robert left the house," I continued. "And we also have this note which is positively teeming with clues."

"Are there fingerprints?" asked T. Everett.

"There may well be, but, first, let us examine the words themselves. What do they tell us?"

"That someone was hiding by the mire gate at eight o'clock," said Emmeline.

"Yes," I said, "But can we tell who?"

I let the words steep for a moment or two and then held the note out so everyone could see the writing.

"Does anyone recognise the hand?"

Heads craned forward, those at the back shuffled forward for a better view.

No one recognised the handwriting.

"It's not a hand," said Lady Julia, "It's a scrawl."

"Do *you* have any observations, Reeves?" I asked.

"The use of Sergeant Stock's name is interesting, sir. It suggests a person with local knowledge."

"Indeed," I said. "But what can one deduce from the writing?"

I held the note up again for all to see. "You will observe it is written in a poor hand – which could denote a servant, or ... maybe a chap with an injured hand, or maybe a chap with a good hand intent on disguising the fact, or maybe–"

"In other words it could be anybody," said Lady Julia.

"No. It has to be someone with a hand."

Lady Julia called me several names, of which 'mutton-headed imbecile' was the most complimentary. I tried to explain that in a world where the prime suspect had cloven feet that it was perfectly reasonable to consider they might have a claw for a hand.

But Lady Julia had a rather old-fashioned view of crime.

"You are an idiot," she said. "And the rest of you are idiots for listening to him. I shall be in my room. If anyone is still alive come breakfast, they can send a maid to awaken me!"

And with that, she left.

I decided to trouser the note until tomorrow and move on. One needs good light to spot a fingerprint. "Would you search the remaining pockets, Reeves?" I asked.

Reeves continued his search, treating Sir Robert's remains with fitting respect.

"There is something in the right-hand jacket pocket, sir."

He retrieved the object and held it up. I'd never seen anything like it. It was a thin wooden spike about five inches long and part-covered in what looked like fur.

"What the devil is it?" asked Henry.

"It would appear to be a dart, sir," said Reeves. "By its design – you will observe the rabbit fur wrapped around the lower half – I would posit this to be a dart intended for use with a blowpipe."

"A poison dart?" asked Henry.

"I believe Dr Morrow would be more qualified to answer that question, sir. But I do note the tip of the dart to be darkened for a good inch along its length, and there is that corresponding mark on Sir Robert's neck."

"Well, Morrow?" asked Henry.

"Poison was something I had considered," said Morrow.

"What kind of poison?" I asked.

Morrow appeared strangely reticent. I know doctors never like being chivvied by the detective into making a rushed diagnosis, but Morrow's reticence bordered on evasiveness.

"It could be one of several poisons," he said.

"Such as..." I pressed.

"Given the dart, my best guess would be ... curare," said Morrow.

"Isn't that what South American natives use?" said T. Everett.

"That is correct, sir," said Reeves.

"Aha," I said. "Do we know anyone who's recently arrived from South America? Find that person and, I think, we have the murderer."

Reeves coughed.

"What is it, Reeves?"

"You have, sir."

"I've what, Reeves?"

"Come from South America, sir."

"No, I haven't."

Reeves coughed again.

"Are you all right, Reeves? A bit of steam gone down the wrong way?"

Emmeline coughed. It was a veritable outbreak!

"Didn't you say you'd recently come from Argentina, Roderick?" said Emmeline, giving me an odd look.

I had one of those moments – I expect you've all had them – when one finds one's foot had unexpectedly climbed into one's mouth several sentences earlier, and everyone had noticed the wiggling toes except for you. I'd been so engrossed playing the consulting detective I'd completely forgotten who I was supposed to be!

"O-oh," I said, thinking swiftly. "*Come* from South America. I thought you said *gum* from South America which is, of course, what curare is made from. Now, moving on–"

"You *were* late coming down for dinner," said Ida.

Dash it, I'd thought I was getting away with it.

"Not that late," I said. "Quite a few of you toddled in after me."

"Not all of us came from South America," said Ida. "You said yourself the murderer was the one who recently arrived from there."

"I didn't mean *me*. I'm not a suspect. I'm the detective. Two different birds entirely."

"Everything did begin the day you arrived," said Morrow. "There'd never been any trouble before."

"But I was with you at eight o'clock," I said. "I was with all of you when the gong sounded."

"And *you* were the one who found Sir Robert," said T. Everett. "How *did* you know where to look?"

"Because he's a detective!" said Emmeline. "It's not Roderick you should be questioning, it's Dr Morrow. He knows far more than he's saying. Only ten minutes ago I heard him accuse Witheridge of being the murderer!"

"He *what*?" said Henry.

"I was in the kitchen helping Mrs Berrymore," said Emmeline. "You remember she had that turn when Sir Robert was brought in?"

Several people nodded.

"A number of us helped carry her into the kitchen," said Emmeline. "Then, when I left the kitchen, I heard angry voices by the back door. It was Dr Morrow and Witheridge. The doctor said, 'What have you done!' and Witheridge said 'It weren't me!' But Dr Morrow didn't believe him. He said 'Who else could it have been?' Then Berrymore came through the servants' door and Morrow left."

"Is this true, Morrow?" asked Henry.

"It's not what you think, Henry."

"Then what is it? Explain."

Morrow looked as uncomfortable as I'd felt a few moments earlier.

"I ... I had an idea what killed your father, but ... I was far from certain."

"You were certain enough to accuse Witheridge? Why?" said Henry.

Morrow exhaled deeply.

"Because he and I are the only ones who know where the key to my drugs cabinet is kept."

"Your drugs cabinet? Why...?"

I didn't think Morrow could look more uncomfortable, but he managed it. He looked at the carpet. He shuffled from foot to foot.

"You *have* this curare?" said Henry. "Here? In this house?"

"I do."

"But why? What possible reason could you have?"

We were all agog to find out.

"It's a muscle relaxant," said Morrow. "The best there is for administering to prometheans during surgery. All the modern promethean surgeons use it. I re-attach so many limbs in my work here that it's essential. It reduces the recovery times dramatically."

Henry marched over to the bell pull and gave it a couple

of sharp tugs. "I'll have Witheridge brought here immediately," he said.

I thought I'd use the opportunity to ask Morrow a few questions while he was still rattled. Inspector Murgatroyd of the Yard swore by the practice. 'Keep the suspect off balance,' was one of his favourite mottoes – along with 'Never ask him the question he expects, until he least expects it.'

"Do you keep RadioGlo paint in your laboratory?" I asked him.

"I ... don't think so. Not any more. I think we used it all on *Quarry of the Apes*. The ghost scene in the caves, wasn't it, Henry? Stapleford would know more. He's the one who came up with the idea. It worked better on automata than it did on prometheans."

The man was still decidedly rattled.

"Where does one buy RadioGlo paint?" I asked. "Dashed difficult stuff to get hold of one would think."

Morrow shrugged. "I wouldn't know. You'd have to ask Stapleford."

"Why are you asking about RadioGlo paint?" said Henry.

"I suspect it was used to give last night's ghost its glowing face."

"But the ghost was nothing but a distasteful prank, wasn't it?" said Henry.

"Possibly," I said, aiming for the enigmatic. "Possibly not." I then did the eyeball thing that Murgatroyd does when he looks at each suspect in turn and makes them think he knows far more than he's letting on.

I was in mid-eyeball when Berrymore arrived at the door. "You rang, sir."

"Berrymore," said Henry. "Relieve Witheridge of his gun, and have him brought here immediately."

I fired a question at Morrow the moment Berrymore closed the door.

"Did anyone else know you kept curare in the house, Morrow?"

"I ... I may have mentioned it."

"Who to?"

"I don't remember. It may have come up in conversation. It's not a secret. Stapleford perhaps. The two of us often converse about prometheans and automata."

"I've never heard you mention it," said Henry. "Have you any other poisons in the house?"

"Many efficacious compounds can be poisonous in excessive doses," said Morrow. "I'm a surgeon. I need to have anaesthetics on hand. I'm sure the chemicals Stapleford keeps at the studio to develop your films are extremely dangerous if ingested too."

I hadn't noticed any bad blood between Morrow and Stapleford, but I certainly noticed how Morrow was taking every opportunity to deflect suspicion away from himself and onto his neighbour. I wondered why.

The door opened and a nervous Witheridge entered.

"Stay, Berrymore," said Henry. "And guard the door."

I'm not sure who looked the more shocked, Berrymore or Witheridge. The ancient butler swayed for an instant, resembling a very tall tree who'd just received disturbing news about beavers.

Henry turned on Witheridge. "Did you kill my father?"

"No! I never left the house, sir!"

"Do you know what curare is?"

"No, sir. Never heard of it."

"Do you *deny* you have access to Dr Morrow's drugs cabinet?"

"I know where the key is, that's all, sir. I swear! If the doctor wants something fetched, I fetch it. I wouldn't dare open the cupboard without permission."

Witheridge looked frightened, but defiant. And Henry looked like he'd run out of questions. He balled both fists and looked my way. "Am I allowed to beat a confession out of him?"

"That's usually the prerogative of the police," I said. "May I continue the questioning?"

"Of course."

Witheridge glared at me.

"I see you are not wearing gloves, Witheridge."

"No," he said.

"No, *sir*," said Henry.

"No, sir," said Witheridge, imbuing the word 'sir' with a trifle more contempt than respect.

"Do you usually wear gloves whilst at work?" I continued.

"No, sir."

"Have you heard of fingerprints, Witheridge?"

"No, sir."

"They are unique, Witheridge. No two people have the same fingerprint. If you were to pick up a bottle with your bare hands, you would leave a mark. And that mark would stay for there for days, weeks even."

"If you say so ... sir."

I turned to Morrow. "Is the curare kept in a bottle?"

"Yes. A small blue one."

"Then let's examine it," I said.

"I'll send Berrymore," said Henry.

"No," I said. "We shall all go."

~

I let Henry and Morrow take the lead, as there's nothing more embarrassing for a detective than having nine people follow him around a country house when he doesn't know where he's going.

Morrow's laboratory was on the second floor of the Main Hall. It was a large room, maybe a former bedroom for an esteemed guest. Now it had two ominous tables, and three walls full of glass cabinets – some of them containing what looked to me like human limbs.

I was just about to ask Morrow where he kept the key to the drugs cabinet when he cried out.

"The door's open! The door's never left open."

He was looking at a stout wooden cupboard on the wall between the two central windows. The door wasn't only open, it was hanging at an odd angle. It had been forced.

"No one touch anything," I said, sensing that Morrow was about to leap forward and have a good rummage. "Reeves. See if the curare bottle is still there."

Reeves searched three shelves of assorted bottles.

"There is no blue bottle, or any bottle labelled curare,

sir."

"When was the last time you saw the curare?" I asked Morrow.

"Last week, I think. Was it Tuesday or Wednesday I replaced Ruskin's arms?"

"Tuesday," said Henry. "It was after the scene with the rotating swords of death."

Morrow was certainly looking a dashed sight chirpier since the discovery that the drugs cabinet door had been forced. Witheridge too for that matter. The footman didn't actually smirk at me, but there was a good deal of insolence in the look he gave me.

"Any idea what was used to force the door, Reeves?" I asked.

Reeves gave the cabinet a good scrutinising. He examined the lock. He examined the hinges. He examined the door, swinging it open and closed several times.

"It is not a strong lock, sir. By the marks in the wood, I would suspect a screwdriver or narrow chisel was inserted between the door and cabinet, and force applied to wrench the door open."

I couldn't see any screwdrivers or chisels lying in plain sight.

"Do you keep any chisels or screwdrivers here?" I asked Morrow.

He didn't.

I don't think one is ever prepared for a scream – not one of those full-throated affairs that sound like an adjacent opera singer had just trapped her bunion in a mousetrap. I jumped a good foot the moment Lily screamed.

"What is it?" Emmeline shouted.

"A face in the window!" screamed Lily. "Look!"

We all looked. There was indeed a face in the window. A horrible, twisted face. With cat's ears.

FIFTEEN

"Selden!"

There was considerable panic. Even the stiffest upper lip quivers at the sight of a cannibal pulling faces outside a second floor window.

"Get the guns!" shouted Henry.

"No!" shouted Morrow. "You'll frighten him."

I don't think the fear of frightening Selden figured too high on anyone else's list of priorities. Those who hadn't already fled to the safety of the corridor, swiftly joined the exodus. Only Morrow remained in his laboratory. "No, Harry! Don't go. You're safe here." I heard him say as I beetled down the stairs.

Guns were once more handed out. Henry and Babba-combe raced back upstairs whilst the rest of the men – and an insistent Emmeline – spilled out the front door.

The swirling mist swallowed up the light from our lamps, but Reeves caught sight of a fast moving shape running towards the copse above the mire gate. T. Everett emptied both barrels at it, and we gave chase.

"Did I hit it?" asked T. Everett. "I'm sure I hit it."

We found no evidence of Selden being wounded, but we did find evidence of his departure – a trail of misshapen footprints in the soft earth leading up to, and through, the now open mire gate. I'd never seen anything like them.

"Most disturbing, sir," said Reeves. "Selden appears to run on all fours like a large cat, but, whereas the rear paws exhibit all the characteristics of the genus felis, the front paws appear almost human. You will, however, note that the indentation left by each 'finger' is somewhat pointed, indicating the strong possibility that Selden's fingers have claws."

"I thought Selden only had a cat's ears and tail," I said.

"Dr Morrow did mention that Selden's body went through occasional transformations, sir. This would appear to be one of them."

"I can't see him," said T. Everett, returning from the track outside the mire gate. "His trail peters out as soon as it hits the firmer ground of the track."

I wandered over to the mire edge, expecting to see Selden's tracks disappearing into the mire. But the only tracks were those of the cloven-hoofed woman. They disappeared into a bank of thick fog after little more than ten yards.

~

It was a long-faced and contemplative gathering that assembled back in the drawing room. One always finds that the murder of one's host puts a dampener on proceedings, and we had the additional sogginess of a bothersome cannibal on the loose. Not to mention that none of us – including, hopefully, the aforementioned cannibal – had yet eaten.

"What are we going to do?" said Ida. "If Selden can climb walls that easily, no window's safe. He could eat us in our beds!"

"I think we should all stay down here," said Lily. "I'm not going upstairs on my own until he's caught."

Morrow attempted to calm things down.

"Ladies, you really have nothing to fear. Selden is, at heart, a gentle soul. He only kills when he feels threatened."

"Or feels a bit peckish," I said.

"No!" said Morrow. "That's the other side of Selden, which only comes out when he's frightened. If everyone keeps their windows locked and curtains drawn you'll all be perfectly safe."

"What if he bursts through the door?" asked Ida.

"That's very unlikely to happen. And, even if it did, there's a simple answer. Don't run. Running might excite the cat within him, causing him to give chase. Keep calm, keep quiet and keep still. If you must move, walk away slowly. And don't look at him."

"You're sure that'll work?" asked Lily.

"I've been in the same room as Selden during his transformations," said Morrow. "Several times. He can look terrifying, but ... he's more frightened of you than you are of him. If you keep calm, he'll calm down too."

Neither Ida nor Lily looked that convinced.

"I think it best if I spend the night in my laboratory," said Morrow. "With a light in every window and one of them open."

"Are you mad?" said Henry. "You'll put us all in danger."

"On the contrary," said Morrow. "You can station a man outside my door with a gun. Lock me in as well. No one else in the household will be in any danger. Harry's seen me there once. I'm sure he'll return. I'll lure him in and convince him to give himself up. It's the safest and quickest way to end this madness."

"Are you sure he'll listen to you?" asked Henry.

"He escaped from prison to see me. I'm sure he'll listen."

~

Our gathering broke up soon after that. Morrow beetled off to his laboratory. Henry left to organise the various sentries. T. Everett escorted Ida and Lily to their rooms. Only Emmeline and I remained.

"I can't see Selden using a blowpipe," said Emmeline. "It's not his *modus operandi*, is it?"

"No, I can see him *eating* a blowpipe, but not using one. Talking of eating, are you feeling peckish, at all?"

"I'm famished. I didn't like to say anything..."

I rang the bell and Reeves appeared moments later.

"Any chance of a cold collation from the kitchen, Reeves? Maybe with half a bot of something fortifying?"

Reeves returned fifteen minutes later with the needful.

"What do you think, Reeves?" I asked as he poured the wine. "I can see how the note lured Sir Robert to the mire gate, and I can see how the cloven-footed woman hid in wait until Sir Robert came within blowpipe range. But how did the poison dart get into his pocket? It couldn't have been planted there, could it?"

When one's dealing with criminal masterminds one has to explore every option.

"It is possible, sir, but I can't help but think *cui bono.*"

"Qui who?"

"It is a phrase Cicero was very fond of us, sir. *Cui bono* – it means 'to whose benefit.'"

"Who gains, you mean?" I said.

"Precisely, sir. Planting a poison dart in *your* pocket would benefit the murderer by casting suspicion upon you. But planting a poison dart in the victim's pocket appears to me a wasted opportunity and benefits no one."

"Ah, but what if it was meant to kill?" I said. "If I'd rummaged through Sir Robert's pockets I could have speared a digit."

"That *is* a possibility, sir, but a simpler explanation is that Sir Robert placed the dart in the pocket himself."

"Why ever would he do that?"

"I have given considerable thought to the matter, sir. I believe that Sir Robert was approaching the mire gate when he was struck on the right side of his neck by a poison dart. The killer, therefore, was hiding somewhere nearby in the copse."

"With you so far," I said.

"Sir Robert's first instinct, having felt the dart strike his neck, would be to use his right hand to examine his neck. But his right hand would be holding his shotgun. Ergo he drops the shotgun where we found it, sir."

"You don't think he'd keep hold of the gun and use his left hand?" I asked. We consulting detectives like to be thorough.

"While that is a possibility, sir, we need to account for the shotgun being discovered some thirty yards from the body. It is clear that the gun was dropped. I posit it was dropped the moment Sir Robert was struck."

"Why would he put the dart in his pocket though?" asked Emmeline.

"Because upon pulling the dart from his neck, miss, he would have recognised the very strong possibility that the dart had been poisoned. He'd also know that his best hope of survival was to keep the dart so that the poison could be identified and an antidote administered."

"So he pockets the dart," said Emmeline.

"Precisely, miss."

I chewed on a contemplative kidney.

"We didn't look for footprints in the copse around where the gun was found, did we?" I said.

"No, sir."

"And the only tracks we found belonging to the cloven-footed woman were on the path."

"That was the only place we looked for them, sir. I don't think we can rule out their existence elsewhere."

"But there was someone we did observe in the copse leaving the scene barely five minutes after the murder."

"Who?" asked Emmeline.

"Lupin."

SIXTEEN

I awoke the next morning uneaten. The Worcester neck was not a pincushion for poison darts, and not one of my internal organs had emigrated to the front lawn. All in all, a pretty good start to the day.

Reeves brought me my tea and drew back the curtains.

"Any more bodies, Reeves?"

"Not that I have heard, sir. According to Babbacombe, Dr Morrow's plan to apprehend Selden did not meet with success. Selden failed to make a reappearance."

"Bit of a long shot, I suppose. I know I'd think twice about coming back if T. Everett had taken a couple of pot-shots at me."

"Indeed, sir. There has also been an interesting development in the search for the curare bottle."

I sat up. "There has?"

"Yes, sir. I discovered it this morning, hidden within my room."

"*Your* room, Reeves?"

"Indeed, sir. I was selecting my attire for the day when I noticed that the contents of my underlinen drawer were not as they should be. There had been a slight disturbance in the sock area, sir."

I tutted, feeling for the poor chap. Reeves is very particular about socks.

"Upon further investigation, sir, I discovered a small bottle hidden inside one of the socks. It would appear that the person who planted the head and painting accessories in your room has now added me to their list of people to implicate."

"Have you checked the bottle for fingerprints?"

"I have, sir. The bottle had been thoroughly wiped, which makes me believe that the person responsible may have been present when you spoke about fingerprints and their importance in the determination of guilt."

"Or they might have already known. Criminal masterminds know all about fingerprints, Reeves."

"Indeed, sir, but one would have thought a criminal mastermind would have taken the next step. I find it exceedingly odd that, given the effort involved to plant evidence, that no search of our rooms has yet been instigated."

I took a contemplative sip of the oolong. Reeves was right. It was odd. Usually the discovery of planted evidence was followed swiftly by the ominous knock on the door by a set of size twelve knuckles.

"One possibility, sir, is that the person in question is not in a position to call for a search."

"A servant, you mean?"

"Or a guest, sir."

"I don't know. One would think a determined servant could raise the idea of a search in the hope that Berrymore would suggest the idea to Henry. Or that a lady's maid would have a word in the ear of Lady Julia. Has there been talk in the servants' hall about the need to search anyone's room?"

"No, sir."

"There you are then. No, Reeves, I think we should regard this as a gesture."

"Sir?"

"He's taunting us, Reeves. Letting us know that he can plant evidence on us whenever he wishes. Fairly typical criminal mastermind behaviour. They're all egotists."

The question now, of course, was what to do with said bottle. It had no value as a piece of evidence any more, but it did contain poison.

"Should we return the bottle to Dr Morrow for safe-keeping, Reeves?"

"Questions will be asked as to how the bottle came into your possession, sir. I would suggest we hide the bottle with Pasco's head for the moment. You can then suggest a search of the Hall to Sir Henry when you meet him at breakfast."

Reeves went off to hide the bottle while I sipped tea and pondered my next move. When Reeves returned I could tell by his eyebrows that all was not well.

"Pasco's head is missing, sir."

"Are you sure?" I asked.

"Positive, sir. The tin of paint and brush are where we left them. The head, however, is not. I believe you are correct in your assertion that we are being toyed with."

Rummier and rummier, as Alice would say. Why take the head and leave the paint? This had all the portents of being a five cocktail problem.

"It also suggests, sir, that the person responsible resides at the Hall. They must be able to move freely about the house and not attract suspicion."

"Rather rules out Selden and the woman with the cloven feet."

"Indeed, sir."

"But not Lupin. Lupin has the run of the house and one only has to look at him to know that 'low cunning' is his middle name."

"An imaginative suggestion, sir, but I do not see Lupin bothering to wipe fingerprints from a bottle of curare."

"That's because you underestimate him, Reeves. I don't. Sherlock Holmes wouldn't. And neither should you."

"Shall I lay out your clothes for breakfast, sir?"

~

I decided it was time for boldness. Reeves' suggestion of hiding the curare bottle and calling for a search after breakfast was all very well – ten out of ten for sensibleness, but where was the panache? And how would it advance the case? All it would do is tell the murderer that we'd rumbled what he was up to, and could defend against it. To break the case we needed to attack, not defend.

Which is why I slipped the bottle of curare in my pocket and toddled down to breakfast.

Everyone was already there, dressed in mourning black

and digging into their kippers or, in Lupin's case, playing with a bowl of fruit. Berrymore was there too, along with Babbacombe.

I hovered in the doorway contemplating my next move. I wanted to see everyone's face when I produced the curare bottle. Lady Agatha MacTweedie swears by the practice. 'The face is the window to guilt,' she says. According to Lady A., even the most inscrutable types can be temporarily unmanned if one whips out something incriminating at an unexpected moment.

I took a few steps over to the near corner to get a better angle.

"What *is* he doing?" said Lady Julia. "I did warn you, Henry. The boy's touched. You don't have to stand in the corner, dear. There are chairs over here."

A lesser man – or, at any rate, one less used to the acerbic tongue of aunts – may have quailed, but I shrugged off Lady Julia's comments and busied myself by opening a drawer in the corner table and pretending to look within.

"Don't mind me," I said. "I'm just completing my search."

"The breakfast sideboard is behind you, dear," boomed Lady Julia. "Berrymore, would you be so good as to wave in case Mister Roderick gets lost on the way over?"

I gritted the Worcester teeth and turned. Lady Agatha never had to put up with hecklers. But, looking on the brightish side, perhaps now was the just the moment to spring my surprise. People were relaxed. No one was expecting Reginald Worcester to whip out a bottle of curare from his pocket.

So I did. And as I did, I took a careful note of everyone's face.

"The missing bottle of curare," I said.

Everyone looked surprised except Lady Julia and Lupin. Lady Julia looked confused, and Lupin sucked on a grape in a disdainful manner.

Morrow jumped to his feet. "Where did you find it?"

"Precisely where I expected to. It was a simple matter of deduction really."

I watched for a reaction. If the murderer was in the room

– and I had a sneaking suspicion they were – then he, she, or it, would be wondering what on earth I was playing at. Had I perhaps deduced their identity, and was about to say I'd found it in their room? This would be just the moment that such a person might crack and run for the door. Or possibly the pelmet.

Disappointingly, no one attempted to flee, so I continued.

"The murderer had to hide the bottle in a place it would not be readily found. A place, furthermore, that would not incriminate them. What better place than..." I paused for effect. Lady Agatha would have spread both arms out to enable her dresser to effect a swift costume change, but I made do with a steely gaze and the most pregnant of pauses. "What better place than one of the unoccupied bedrooms. And that's where I found it. Along with a tin of RadioGlo paint."

"You mentioned that paint last night," said Henry.

"Indeed I did. It is my belief that Sir Robert's murder, Pasco's murder, *and* the ghost were all part of the same diabolical plan."

"Selden couldn't have played any part in that ghost incident," said Morrow. "He'd only just escaped. He couldn't have crossed the moor from Princetown to here in time. Not at night."

"He's right," said Henry. "There are no paths and there are mires everywhere."

"I doubt very much that Selden *is* the murderer," I said. "The murderer has to be able to move freely about Baskerville Hall. How else could they steal the curare and the paint and hide them later? Selden couldn't do that. He'd be noticed."

"Are you saying it's someone living here?" said Henry.

"Not one of us, surely?" said Ida.

"This is ridiculous," said Lady Julia. "Everyone knows that Selden is a murderer. We cannot have *two* murderers in the parish. This isn't Whitechapel."

"I am merely following where the evidence leads, Lady Julia."

"But how can Pasco's death fit into all this?" asked Lily.

"Very easily," I said. "Pasco was the ghost."

That certainly got in amongst them. Forks were put down, tea cups reunited with saucers, and everyone started talking at once. There were plenty of whats, several hows and a brace or two of whys.

"No," said Henry. "Pasco was never allowed in the house. And he certainly wouldn't wear a dress. Selden killed Pasco because Pasco saw him."

"The evidence suggests otherwise," I said. "Why would Selden chop off Pasco's head and hide it? Why would Selden remove Pasco's clothes?"

"He wouldn't," said Morrow, looking decidedly pale. "He uses his claws and teeth to kill. He'd never use an axe or stab anyone."

"Am I missing something?" said Ida. "What on earth makes you think that Pasco was the ghost? Wouldn't it have been the murderer?"

Ah. This was a tricky sitch. How could one reveal that Pasco's head was painted green without mentioning finding the head ... and then covering it with pastry before subsequently losing it? Perhaps it was the proximity of so many kippers, but an idea came to me almost immediately.

"Because the ghost's head, which we all saw had a diabolical glow to it, was painted in RadioGlo paint and that, as the good doctor told us last night, works best on automata. Now, how many automata do we know who were missing a head the very next day?"

I thought Emmeline was going to applaud. She caught herself just in time.

"So Pasco was naked because he was wearing Theodosia's black dress," said Emmeline. "And the murderer had to remove the dress and the head so that no one would discover that Pasco was the ghost."

"Indeed," I said. "And the head was stuffed full of Pasco's memories, so that had to be destroyed to protect the murderer's identity."

"I hardly think that naked automata are a suitable subject for the breakfast table," said Lady Julia. "And *do* sit down. You unnerve me hovering in the corner like that."

I gave the curare bottle to Henry for safekeeping and ankled over to the breakfast sideboard to load my plate with two of Arbroath's finest. Hopefully I'd manage to eat them this time.

"I don't get this," said T. Everett as I took a seat next to him. "Why would Pasco agree to play this ghost? He's an automaton. Why would he play any part in a plot against his master?"

"Because he's programmed to obey orders," I said. "Reeves says that these gardening automata like Pasco aren't too bright. If someone tells them to dress up as a ghost, they do it."

"But why would anyone *want* Pasco to dress up as a ghost?" asked Lily.

"It's the sort of thing the better class of murderers do," I said. "The common murderer has no imagination. They grab the first weapon that comes to hand and that's it. But the clever ones do all sorts of odd things to throw one off the scent."

"But if what you're saying is true," said Henry, "and the murderer isn't a maniac like Selden, but some chap who deliberately planned to kill the governor, what's their motive? He hadn't an enemy in the world. And as far as money goes, I'm the only one who benefits, and I'd cut off my right arm before even thinking of harming the governor. This does *not* make sense at all."

"Of course it doesn't make sense," said Lady Julia. "The boy's delusional. Selden killed Robert and that's that."

"There is someone who *does* have a very strong motive," said T. Everett. "I was thinking about this last night."

"What?" said Henry. "Who?"

"Edison," said T. Everett. "He'd see Quarrywood as a dangerous rival. Your movies have only been showing in the States for three months and already they're breaking all records. Edison won't stand for that. He'll either try to buy you out or get you closed down somehow. If you were in the States, he'd claim you infringed one of his patents, and tie you up in court. But you're over here in England. I bet he's hired someone to close Quarrywood down ... permanently, if you get my drift. Edison has a long arm."

"I can't believe anyone would have the governor killed over Quarrywood. They must know that I'd keep it going. I'm as committed to its success as my father was."

"And if anything happened to you?" said T. Everett. "What then? Edison doesn't do things by halves. He'll come for you next."

Well, this was all very informative. I hadn't considered motive. In most books I'd read, the suspects with the strongest motives were usually the first to be cleared. It was always the chap one least suspected that turned out to be the murderer. But there was something about this Edison cove that appealed. He sounded a bit like a criminal mastermind, *and* he was three thousand miles away – which ticks the 'unlikely suspect' box.

Henry looked shaken, as did Ida and Morrow.

"If anyone comes for me," said Henry. "They'll find me waiting with a gun in my hand."

I don't think I was alone in thinking that Henry's words were a tad on the unfortunate side. Sir Robert had been waiting with a gun in his hand when he'd been struck with the poison what not.

"Have you hired any new servants in the last month, Henry?" asked Emmeline. "If Edison hired someone to infiltrate the house that's how he'd do it."

Could one ask for a better fiancée?

"I don't believe we've engaged any new servants recently," said Henry. "Have we, Berrymore?"

"Not at the house, sir. I believe some new actors may have been taken on at the studio."

"They were all *réanimés* and automata," said Henry. "They don't come anywhere near the house."

"And neither shall they," said Lady Julia.

"Edison has the largest automata factory in America," said T. Everett. "Some of the new ones look so lifelike you have to stand within three feet before you can tell the difference. Dress one of them up in your footmans' livery, slap on some theatrical make-up, and I bet it could pass for one of your servants – enough to sneak into the house."

"A machine may pass for a human in the Americas, Mr Spurgeon," said Lady Julia. "But *not* in England."

"I don't know," said Henry. "What do you think, Roderick?"

I wasn't going to mention Reeves. He was one of a kind anyway. Whoever had built Reeves had broken the mould soon after. One imagines he took one look at his creation and declared his work done, retiring on the spot to Worthing to keep bees and raise nasturtiums.

"It's certainly a possibility," I said. "Do any of these new actors have an American accent?"

"Not that I've noticed," said Henry. "Morrow?"

"All the prometheans and automata at the studio are British, I believe," said Morrow. "Though we do occasionally borrow extra automata from Stapleford for crowd scenes. Come to think of it, I don't think I've ever heard his automata speak."

"Stapleford has a lot of automata, does he?" I asked.

"About a dozen, I should think," said Morrow.

"I've known Stapleford for years," said Henry. "He's a thoroughly decent chap. He wouldn't get mixed up with any plot to kill anyone."

"He might not knowingly be involved," I said. "What if he woke up one morning and found an automaton on his doorstep looking for work and offering his services for free. Stapleford's first thought wouldn't be 'Are you an assassin sent from America?'"

"I'll ask him," said Henry. "I'll be seeing him at the studio in an hour."

"You're not intending to *work* today, are you?" said Lady Julia.

"Well, yes," said Henry.

"But, Henry, your place is here," admonished Lady J. "Do I need to remind you that the family is in mourning?"

"I know, Aunt Julia, but I *need* to be doing something. Besides, the governor wouldn't want us moping around the house with long faces. He'd want us to celebrate life, not death."

"It's not your father's decision. Or yours. It's tradition. The servants will expect it."

"My mind is made up," said Henry. "We all mourn in our own way, Aunt. And if this fellow Edison is out to destroy Quarrywood, all the more reason for us to press on and show him that we won't be intimidated."

SEVENTEEN

After breakfast I slipped out of the dining room while Lady Julia was having another go at Henry. I didn't want to give her the chance to hand me Spinoza's latest and confine me to the drawing room. Emmeline came flying out after me. By the time Lady Julia noticed our departure – signalled by a booming "Where's that Roderick?" – Emmeline and I were legging it upstairs to freedom.

Reeves was waiting for us in my room, and I swiftly brought him up to speed with events.

"What do you think, Reeves? Have you heard of this Edison fellow?"

"I have, sir. While it is true that the gentleman in question is of a litigious nature, I have not read anything that would suggest he would engage in homicidal conspiracies."

"There's always a first time, Reeves. And just because he hasn't been caught doesn't mean he's not been out there bumping people off for years. What about these automata of his? Are they as good as T. Everett says?"

"I have never encountered one, sir, but I have heard they are highly regarded."

"It's true what Henry said about motive though, isn't it?" said Emmeline. "Except for Edison and his wish to get rid of a competitor, there just isn't one ... unless..."

I could tell by the way Emmie looked at me that she'd just thought of a corker. "Unless what?"

"Unless there's something odd in Sir Robert's will," said Emmeline. "What if Henry doesn't inherit?"

For a fleeting moment I was as excited as Emmeline. Wills were always hot stuff when one was looking for an unexpected motive. But would Sir Robert have disinherited Henry? I couldn't see it. I'd never heard a single harsh word exchanged between the two.

"Have you heard of any rift between Henry and his father, Reeves?"

"No, sir. The only discourse I have heard upon the subject of Sir Henry's relationship with his father have been ones concerning the surprising lack of discord between the two men. A circumstance ascribed to the general affability of both parties."

I pondered on this for a while. I liked the idea of a contentious will, but I agreed with the opinion of the servants' hall – Sir Robert wouldn't willingly disinherit Henry.

So...

"What if someone forges a new will for Sir Robert and places it in his study to be discovered after the murder?" I said.

"A forgery would be uncovered, sir. Especially if the beneficiary was an unexpected one."

"Ah, but what if the beneficiary was a particularly litigious individual with deep pockets," I said, waggling an excited finger. "Am I not right in thinking that such a person could keep the estate's assets frozen for years while the dispute is settled in the courts? I'm thinking of that book by Dickens – Bleak Something?"

"Bleak House, sir," said Reeves, looking, I have to say, rather impressed with the young master. "It contains the disturbing case of Jarndyce and Jarndyce where the entire inheritance was frozen for decades before eventually being exhausted by legal costs. It was believed based on the real case of–"

"Quite, Reeves. We have the gist. So if this Edison chap hires a really good forger, he doesn't need to do away with Henry. He can put a stop to Quarrywood with just Sir Robert's murder, a forged will and a bevy of lawyers."

"It's diabolically brilliant!" said Emmeline. "If anyone challenges the will, Edison ties up the estate for years with law suits. And if they don't, he takes control of Quarrywood himself!"

"There is the strong possibility, miss, that the police would charge him with forgery."

"They can try, Reeves, but this chap sounds like a slippery cove," I said. "He'll have an army of lawyers to obfuscate matters."

"Do you think Edison might be on his way here for the reading of the will?" asked Emmeline.

"It wouldn't surprise me. We should keep an eye out. He should be easy to spot. According to T. Everett, he has very long arms."

I was all for searching Sir Robert's study immediately, but Reeves was against it.

"I fear the investigation is in danger of becoming side-tracked, sir. Last night, you decided that a search of the copse close to where Sir Robert's gun was found should be our priority for the day. You may remember we deduced the strong possibility that the murderer lay there in wait for Sir Robert."

I'd almost forgotten. "You think that trumps a search of the study?"

"Most certainly, sir. The longer we postpone a search of the murder scene, the more likely that evidence may be lost or compromised."

~

Reeves braved the stairs first while Emmeline and I waited on the edge of the landing. Neither of us wanted to be nabbed by Lady J.

I heard a door open downstairs and flattened myself against the wall.

"Ah, it's you," said the unmistakable voice of the gimlet-eyed Aunt. "Treeves, isn't it? Tell that accomplice of yours I want to see him this minute."

"Mister Roderick has left for the studio, milady," said Reeves. "I believe he intends to spend the day there searching for clues."

"God help us," said Lady J. "I don't suppose you've seen Miss Fossett?"

"I believe she went for a walk, milady."

"A walk? Does no one understand the etiquette of mourning these days?"

I heard footsteps and a door slam. Then I poked a tentative nose over the banisters to make sure all was clear, and that it wasn't Reeves who'd stormed off in a door-slamming huff.

All was clear, and it was but the work of a minute to beetle down the stairs and exit the Hall via the back door. Edmunds, who Reeves informed me was the boot boy, was standing guard on the lawn outside.

"You'll need a gun, Mr Reeves," he said. "Mr Berrymore told me not to let anyone outside if they didn't have a gun. There's one propped up against the wall there."

Suitably armed, we hastened off to the murder scene by way of the Yew Walk.

The ground where we'd found the body was considerably cut up – which wasn't surprising considering the number of people who'd trampled over it the previous night. The bowl was still there, but it was now empty.

"What's that bowl doing there?" asked Emmeline.

"We found it under Sir Robert's body," I said. "It was full of milk."

"Milk? What was a bowl of milk doing out here?"

I didn't have an answer. Last night I'd hit upon the rather brainy idea that the milk was poisoned, but as soon as Morrow started talking about asphyxiation and Reeves started pointing at suspicious neck wounds, I pushed all thoughts of milk aside. After all, according to Inspector Murgatroyd, the human brain can only have so many thoughts, and you need to leave room in case a real corker comes along later.

"Mr Berrymore is of the opinion that one of the more superstitious servants left it out for the piskies, miss," said Reeves.

"Fond of milk, are they? These piskies?" I asked.

"Piskies, or to give them their more common name – pixies – do not exist, sir."

"Ah, same as ghosts."

"Precisely, sir."

"Well, someone's finished off the milk, Reeves," I said.

"It could be hedgehogs," said Emmeline. "I haven't seen any cats around the Hall..."

The same thought must have struck all three of us at the same time. There was one *very* large cat that we'd all seen on the premises.

Selden!

"Can you see any tracks belonging to Selden?" I asked, having a good peer.

We couldn't. The only tracks that were visible in the compressed earth were shoe and boot prints.

"He may have changed back into human form before discovering the milk, sir."

That was true, as was the possibility that the milk had been finished off by any number of the local wildlife. There could have been a wild milk party last night with every hedgehog, badger and deer for miles around swinging by for a snootful.

"Do you think someone might have left the milk out for Selden?" asked Emmeline.

"Who?" I replied.

"Dr Morrow seems quite fond of Selden," said Emmeline.

"I think it unlikely that Dr Morrow would leave a bowl of milk here, miss, when it was his intention to lure Selden into his laboratory."

"Wasn't the bowl already here, though, before Dr Morrow decided to lure Selden into his room?" asked Emmeline.

"That is indeed correct, miss. I pronounced before fully analysing the situation."

I had to pinch myself. Was this Reeves admitting to a mistake? Was this Reeves *making* a mistake?

"Are you up to pressure, Reeves?"

"I am operating within acceptable parameters, sir."

"I hadn't thought!" said Emmeline looking concerned. "How are you managing to top yourself up with armed guards on the doors all night?"

"With difficulty, miss. There is a convenient drainpipe passing adjacent to a window on the servants' stairs. I used that last night to slip out unnoticed. I would, however, appreciate it, sir, if you could provide me with a suitable reason to search the outbuildings for half an hour this afternoon."

"Consider it done, Reeves. I'll stand guard outside."

We continued our search, moving along the path to where Sir Robert's gun had been found. The tracks of the cloven footed woman were still visible.

"The gun was about here, wasn't it, Reeves?" I said, positioning myself where I thought Sir Robert would have stood.

"A yard closer to the mire gate, sir."

I took a step forward. "Right ho, I'm Sir Robert standing here looking towards the gate. The murderer's off to my right. Where?"

We all eyeballed the area to my right. The ground rose at a steady angle towards the back lawn some fifty feet higher and about a hundred yards away. The area was studded with trees of assorted varieties – some yew and some deciduous types just bursting into leaf. There were plenty of spots a chap could hide and get a clear sight of the track.

"I'd hide behind that tree there," said Emmeline, pointing. "It's big enough to hide behind and close enough to the track to get a good shot in."

"How close would one have to be, Reeves? Are these blowpipes accurate over twenty yards or more?"

"It would depend upon the skill of the individual, sir. One would think a murderer intent upon success, and under the cover of darkness, would opt for a location as close as possible."

Emmeline's tree was about ten yards away, which sounded about right to me.

"Check the ground before you put your feet down," I told Emmeline. "We're looking for all kinds of prints, cigarette butts, visiting cards, you name it. He might even have stashed the blowpipe in a hole in a tree."

Off we set, three hunched figures scouring the slope. I wasn't sure what we'd find – cloven hoof prints, orang-utan spoor, an imprint of a heel only sold by a single shop in downtown New York – but I did expect us to find something. Instead, the area was remarkably clear of anything remotely incriminating. There was evidence of some disturbance in the layer of dead leaves that carpeted most of the area, but nothing one could identify with any degree of certainty. And there were no tracks leading from the path into the copse. If someone had hidden there, they'd come and gone from higher up the slope. And the only tracks we found in the copse anywhere nearby were the ones from our pursuit of Selden the previous night.

"There is the possibility, sir, that Sir Robert had his head turned when he was shot. If he was proceeding vigilantly along the Yew Walk, looking left and right, then a shot from the mire gate could have struck him on the right side of his neck."

This was Reeves back to mid-season form. I would have preferred an unusual footprint and half a dozen American cigarette buts behind a tree, but, that having washed out, this was a good runner-up.

And it put the cloven-footed woman back in the frame. None of her tracks went into the copse, but the area around the mire gate was covered in them. I ankled over to the gate to give it a closer inspection. It was one of those curly wrought iron affairs hanging between two large granite posts. The woman could have stood there, using the gate to rest her blowpipe on until Sir Robert stepped into range. What with the swirling mist and the gathering darkness of twilight, he probably didn't notice the blowpipe until it was too late.

"They really are cloven feet, aren't they?" said Emmeline crouching down for a better look. "And you say she was wearing a black dress?"

"That's right," I said.

"Could it have been the same dress Pasco was wearing?" asked Emmeline.

I hadn't considered that. She'd been a long way off and one long black dress looks very much like another to me.

"I didn't have that good a look," I said. "But I thought she was wearing a hood rather than a bonnet. Reeves?"

"It could have been a bonnet, sir. As to the style of the dress, the woman was too far away and the light was somewhat diminished to make an accurate identification."

"Come to think of it," I said. "She might not even *be* a woman. All we saw was a shape in a black dress running away."

~

We had a slight disagreement as to what to do next. Emmeline wanted to track down Theodosia's painting and have a good look at the dress and bonnet. I wanted to search the study for forged wills and Reeves was pretty sniffy about both options, suggesting instead that our time would be better spent trudging across the moor looking for the owner of the cloven feet.

"I think the dress is the key to the whole case," said Emmeline. "If it's a copy of Theodosia's dress in the portrait then someone must have commissioned the dress to be made. And if they asked one of the maids here to make it, we can find out who they are!"

"And if it's not a copy of Theodosia's dress?" I said.

"Then we can cross that theory off our list."

"It is possible that Miss Theodosia's original dress has survived the years, miss, having been kept by the family after her death."

"Then someone would have shown an interest in the family's old clothes," said Emmeline. "Conversations like that would be remembered. We need to ask the family and servants if anyone expressed an interest in Theodosia's portrait or if the family has a trunk of old clothes that could be used for dressing up."

"I can't see anyone asking Lady Julia if they could have a fancy dress party."

"No, sir," said Reeves. "But one would imagine that the studio at Quarrywood would have a requirement for a variety of costumes. Most likely they would employ a seamstress as well."

"They would!" said Emmeline. "See! I bet the ghost's dress was run up by the studio's seamstress."

All good points, but I had a feeling about that forged will – we consulting detectives always put great stock in hunches

– and I was not to be shaken.

"We'll track down the painting next. First, we look for the will."

EIGHTEEN

Pride and hunches goeth before a fall. We searched in vain through every drawer, shelf, nook and I suspect a few crannies – though I couldn't swear to it, not knowing what a cranny looked like.

"They might not have hidden it yet," said Emmeline.

"That's true," I said, but I could tell she was trying to reassure me, which made it worse. I preferred the look she gave me when I first came up with the forged will idea. 'Diabolically brilliant' she'd called it. But now ... the kippers were obviously wearing off, and I was in need of a pick-me-up.

I noticed Sir Robert had a decanter of the brain restorer on his desk.

"Reeves? Do you think it would be bad form to pour a small glass of the amber fortifier? Purely for investigative purposes, of course. I think I need topping-up too."

"Sir Robert was an affable and generous host, sir. I don't think he would have objected."

Reeves poured me a small one.

"Emmeline?" I asked.

"It's a bit early, don't you think? My father says you can't drink until the sun's over the yard-arm."

Luckily we Worcesters have conveniently low yard-arms.

~

According to Reeves, Theodosia's picture was most likely to be hanging with a host of other family portraits in the long gallery on the second floor. Reeves once more led the way, braving the hallway and vouchsafing it to be Lady Julia free, before giving us the signal.

We found Theodosia's picture, and if ever there was a portrait of a person whose foremost wish was to be anywhere else but sitting for a painting, this was it. She looked stern and sullen and, If I'd been the artist, I don't think I'd have turned my back on her. She had the look of a person who'd bean you with a parasol at the first opportunity.

"It could be the dress Pasco wore," said Emmeline, not sounding entirely confident. "It has the same high neck, and I think the bonnet had a similar low brim, but ... I wish I'd got a better look at the ghost. It all happened so fast."

"There does appear to be a strong similarity, miss. I, too, only had a glimpse of the ghost's dress that night, and am unable to make a categorical identification."

"What about you, Reggie?"

I shrugged. "One long black dress looks very much like another to me, I'm afraid. Now if she'd been wearing spats, or a waistcoat, I could have told you her tailor. Dresses are another kettle of f."

"I see I'm going to have to educate you, Reggie. The style of Theodosia's dress in the portrait is quite distinct. Not at all like the styles of today. The same goes for the bonnet. No one would wear anything like that today."

"Something to do with the sleeves, is it?" I said, guessing. It was usually something to do with the sleeves. Puffy, too puffy, not puffy enough.

Emmeline spent the next couple of minutes giving me a crash course in female fashion through the eighteenth and nineteenth centuries, and all I can say is that Reeves would have put his foot down if I'd tried to wear one of those mantuas with the enormous side panniers. There was one portrait of Maria Baskerville-Smythe from 1748 that looked as if she was harbouring her entire family in the side panniers of her dress, and was trying to sneak them into the theatre without paying!

"That's odd," said Emmeline. "That picture of Simeon Baskerville-Smythe looks just like Stapleford."

I took a gander. She was right. Both Simeon and Stapleford had those long mutton chop whiskers.

"And look at that one!" said Emmeline. "Eleanor Baskerville-Smythe is the spitting image of my maid, Rosie."

Reeves coughed. "I think you'll find, miss, that Miss Eleanor also bears a striking resemblance to Florrie the kitchen maid and Ellie the tweenie. And that if you were to examine the other portraits you would find similar matches for many of the other servants."

"What does this mean, Reeves?" I asked.

Reeves coughed again. "Mr Berrymore informed me that the earlier Baskerville-Smythes were somewhat 'over-familiar' with their servants, sir. If rumour is to be believed, one quarter of the parish are their descendants."

"Golly," I said. "I take it this overfamiliarity doesn't persist today, does it?"

"No, sir. The overfamiliarity stopped with Sir Robert's father."

We retraced our steps along the long gallery. Reeves was right. Once one had one's eye in, one could see the traces of familiar faces everywhere. Babbacombe, Witheridge, even the railway porter at Grimdark.

~

Emmeline was all for dashing off to Quarrywood to question seamstresses, but Reeves wouldn't let go of his obsession with the mire.

"I believe it to be central to the entire mystery, sir. Since the moment of our arrival people have asserted un-equivocally that the mire is a place of certain death with no safe path through it. And yet we have seen the tracks for ourselves. Several people – including the individual with the cloven feet – are entering and leaving the mire by the mire gate. My question is, 'Where are they going?'"

"You're not suggesting we follow the trail into the mire?" I said.

"No, sir. I suggest we circumnavigate the mire in order to determine where the path comes out. Or, if the path does not exit the mire, we may be able to observe a hut or hiding place within the mire that these individuals are using."

It all sounded very reasonable. There was also that fire on

the high moor we'd observed the day before. We could look into that too.

"We could always drop in at Quarrywood on the way back," said Emmeline.

"And we could have a look at Stapleford's automata on the way over," I said.

~

Once more Edmunds insisted we take a gun with us. I would have preferred a service revolver – at least one can hide it in one's pocket. Knocking on a suspect's door while accompanied by a valet wielding a shotgun is likely to give the wrong impression. Consulting detectives prefer stealth. We knock on doors with a friendly smile. We chat about geraniums and who we fancy in this year's Goodwood Cup. We bide our time and observe, waiting until our man is thoroughly off his guard before slipping him the unexpected.

It's a bit like cricket, really. One lulls the batsman with a couple of tame deliveries, and then hits him with a wrong'un, beating him all ends up.

"Do we really need the shotgun, Reeves?" I said. "I know Selden's half-cat, half-cannibal and all that, but Morrow's advice strikes me as pretty sound. Keep out of his way and he'll leave us alone."

"I fear it is the nature of animals to be unpredictable, sir. My counsel would be to follow Dr Morrow's advice whilst, at the same time, keeping the hunting rifle in reserve in case matters take an unfortunate turn."

And so off we set on our circumnavigation. I don't know if it's a feature of all high moors or something unique to Grimdark, but there was this low mist that just seemed to hang there – like a cloud with nowhere to go. There wasn't a drop of mist anywhere else. One could see for miles to the north, south and west. Horizons were sharp and freshly starched. But, looking east, everything washed out after little more than one hundred yards.

And that wasn't all. There wasn't a breath of wind, but this mist was moving – not as a whole, but in parts, as though there were local currents within the mire that kept the mist drifting in slowly rotating banks.

"Does that mist look odd to you?" I asked.

"Henry says the weather's unpredictable on the moor," said Emmeline. "It changes so quickly, and usually for the worst. He says you can set off across the moor on a warm sunny day without a cloud in the sky and find yourself chilled to the marrow half an hour later in the thickest of pea soupers."

It still looked rummy to me. It's all right for Reeves to assert there was no such thing as ghosts and piskies, but had anyone informed the piskies?

We followed the track onto the northern edge of the mire. Still no sign of a path coming out of the mire, and the mist was drifting over the track now.

"Is that a cottage over there?" said Emmeline, pointing up ahead. "Stapleford said it wasn't far to High Dudgeon Farm."

The cottage drifted in and out of view. It was a small stone built affair with a number of granite outbuildings clustered around it – the whole surrounded by a dry stone wall. The track took us right to the gate, bending away from the mire for the last thirty yards.

It wasn't one of those pretty cottages that those artist chaps love to paint. No cottage garden, teeming with flowers. It all looked pretty down at heel to me. The garden looked very much like a continuation of the moor – all rough grass and heathers with a single gravel path running from the gate to the cottage door.

One could deduce – and I did – that Mr Stapleford was a bachelor (lack of flowers) of modest means (the down at heel appearance of the property) and rarely entertained (I hadn't seen a single imprint of a horse shoe on the track since the path to Quarrywood had split off).

"I think we should leave the gun here, Reeves, out of sight," I said. "You can prop it up against the wall by the gate... Reeves?"

The giant brain's attention appeared to be elsewhere – riveted to a tussock on the mire's edge.

"I believe I have found another ingress to the mire, sir. I see no evidence of the cloven-footed individual, but there are several boot and shoe imprints that lead me to suspect that at least three people have used this path recently."

Emmeline and I hurried over to look. One could see tracks in the mud heading off ten yards or so into the mire, and it looked almost as well-used as the path by the mire gate.

I looked at Stapleford's cottage. Was it *his* automata that were using the track across the mire as a short cut to the Hall?

I checked my pocket watch. Forty minutes had elapsed since we'd left the Hall.

"Well, this is rummy," I said. "There's a perfectly good path between here and the Hall. It might not be straight enough for the more exacting crow, but it doesn't wind or bend that much. So why would anyone risk all to tramp across the mire?"

"Because they don't want to be seen?" suggested Emmeline.

"One would think, miss, that a person not wishing to be seen could find more opportunity for cover by taking the track. There are plenty of adjacent hummocks and hollows that such a person could use should the need to hide arise."

"I suppose if one was fleeing, like the cloven-footed woman last night. It would make sense to leg it along a path that no one dare follow," I said.

"Indeed, sir, but none of these tracks suggest anyone was running. I suspect that either there are more paths exiting the mire or there is a hiding place close to its centre."

I liked the idea of a mystery hiding place in the middle of the mire, though I thought I'd draw the line at giving it a personal inspection. There are times when it is better to sit in one's armchair and deduce rather than visit a scene in person.

"Time to pay a call on Stapleford's automata, I think."

~

My plan was a two-pronged one. Reeves, having stowed the gun, would locate the tradesmen's entrance and, over a convivial cup or two of oil at the kitchen table, would proceed to engage the servants in light conversation interspersed with the occasional probing question. Emmeline and I would do likewise at the front door, minus the cup of oil.

"Are you ready, Emmie?" I said just before I knocked.

"Yes," she said, taking a deep breath.

I rapped three times upon the door. There was always the chance Stapleford was at home, in which case I had prepared conversation A. If he wasn't, I had a pretty nimble conversation B, which Reeves would have been particularly enamoured with as it was based upon the psychology of the individual.

The door opened revealing a stern looking fellow in a grey suit.

"Yes?" he said, his manner surprisingly short.

"Is your master at home?" I said, breezily.

"No. Mr Stapleford at studio."

I hadn't noticed at first, but now I did. That voice – it was American! And, looking closer, his face was far too smooth, and his skin had an odd lustre.

The man was an automaton. An *American* automaton!

I was momentarily lost for words. My plan had been to discover if Stapleford had recently acquired an American automaton, but I'd assumed he'd have been kept hidden in a basement, and that I'd have to get through several questions about geraniums before even broaching the subject.

"May we come in?" asked Emmeline.

"No," said the automaton.

That wasn't in my script either.

"Pardon?" I said.

"You're welcome," said the automaton, who then proceeded to close the door!

I put a size nine in the way. "Steady on!" I said. "We're friends of Mr Stapleford."

"Please remove foot from door," said the automaton.

"I will if you open it again. You did hear me say we're friends of Mr Stapleford?"

The door opened a little. "Mr Stapleford not at home. You come back later."

I turned to Emmeline. "Didn't Stapleford tell us to wait inside if he wasn't at home?"

"He did," said Emmeline.

"You come back later."

"No, you shall conduct us inside," I said. "It's your master's wish."

"Master's wish is you come back later."

Well, I've met some stubborn doormen in my time, but I'd never been barred entry by a mechanical one before.

"Are you familiar with Babbage's Second Law of Automata?" I asked.

"Yes."

"Then you will know, and I quote: 'an automaton must obey the orders given to it by human beings.'"

"Master's orders take precedence over all others. You come back later."

I tried another tack.

"What's your name?" I asked.

"Falconbridge. I am Mr Stapleford's secretary."

"Well, Falconbridge, we have a medical emergency. Miss Fossett here has strained a fetlock. Mr Stapleford, your master, would insist you help her inside so she can put her feet up."

"I *am* in great pain," whimpered Emmeline. "I think I shall faint any second."

"Master's instructions clear. No one enter house."

"Why?" I asked.

"Not say. You come back later."

"There might not be a later. Miss Fossett may expire at any moment. You must know Babbage's First Law of Automata – that an automaton may not injure a human being or, through inaction, allow one to come to harm. That's what you'd be doing if you don't let us in – allowing Miss Fossett to come to harm."

That made him think. His face may have been impassive, and his eyebrows applied with paint, but I could tell that this was one automaton wracked with inner turmoil.

"Cannot comply. Danger Miss Fossett may harm master."

"What? How?" I asked.

"Master say murderer on loose. Must be vigilant."

"I don't think he meant Miss Fossett."

"Must assume he did."

So much for the psychology of the individual. Where were all these automata like Pasco, raring to obey orders? My only hope was that Reeves was having better luck at the back door.

"We have a message from Mr Edison," said Emmeline.

Well, that made him think. It made me think too. Where was Emmeline going with this?

"What is message?"

"His message is a simple one," said Emmeline, pinning Falconbridge to the threshold with both eyeballs. "He told me to tell you this, 'Obey Miss Fossett, Falconbridge. She is one of us and knows all.'"

Have I said what a gem Emmeline is? I didn't know about Falconbridge, but I believed her.

Once more pride went – or possibly went-eth – before a fall. I was certain he was going to step back and invite us in, but instead he rattled off another 'you come back later' and slammed the door. I was too numbed to react in time.

"Let's get the gun," said a tight-lipped Emmeline. "We'll see how he reacts to Babbage's Fifth Law of Automata."

"There's a fifth law?"

"It's called 'Obey the angry woman with the shotgun or thou shalt be severely ventilated!'"

I ran after her. "I don't think Reeves would approve."

"I'm sure he will."

"I'm sure he won't. He doesn't let *me* shoot anyone."

I caught up with her at the gate and put my hand on her arm.

"Can't I shoot him a little?" asked Emmeline, calming down a smidgen.

"I don't think so. The police take a pretty dim view of people shooting secretaries."

"Out of season, are they?"

"Invariably."

"That's a shame."

"It's an imperfect world."

I could have continued gazing into Emmeline's eyes for the rest of the morning, but a cough from behind heralded Reeves' return.

"Any luck, Reeves?" I asked.

"No, sir. The cook was uncommonly intransigent. I was refused admittance to the premises."

"We had the same at the front door," I said. "Was your cook American?"

"No, sir."

I brought Reeves up to speed viz Falconbridge.

"He looks like an assassin to me," said Emmeline. "I bet the cottage is full of blowpipes and that's why he wouldn't let us in."

"An imaginative suggestion, miss," said Reeves.

"Well," I said. "We *were* looking for an American automaton, and we found one. That's got to be significant."

"I think any significance would be dependent upon other factors being uncovered, sir. A forged will naming Mr Edison as beneficiary would certainly elevate Mr Falconbridge to the position of suspect-in-chief. As would the discovery that he had cloven feet–"

I gasped. "Did he have cloven feet? I didn't look."

"Neither did I," said Emmeline. "I'll get the gun."

"No!" I said, grabbing her arm.

"Why not?" asked Emmeline. "You know he'll refuse to take his boots off otherwise."

Reeves' eyebrows took a disapproving stance.

"I strongly advise against this course of action, miss. From what you have said I believe that Falconbridge will place obedience to his master's orders above that of personal survival. We will then be forced to either shoot or wrestle him to the ground to remove his shoes. Should his feet prove to have the requisite number of toes, we would then have a considerable amount of explaining to do – to both Mr Stapleford and the local constabulary."

Emmeline does not give in easily.

"I could pretend to faint and fall against him, knocking him over," she said. "Reggie could then say he thought Falconbridge was injured and tried to administer first aid by loosening his footwear."

That sounded perfectly reasonable to me. "What do you think, Reeves? There are no firearms involved."

"I think we should continue our circumnavigation of the mire, sir."

"Come on, Reggie," said Emmeline, grabbing my arm. "We can do this."

"Are you sure you can knock him over?"

"It's in chapter four of the Suffragettes' handbook. I once felled the Lord Chancellor with it. The trick is to hook one leg behind his knee and push. Shall I show you?"

"Perhaps later."

I knocked on the door.

"Go away," said Falconbridge who, this time, didn't even bother to open the door.

"It's an emergency," I shouted. "Miss Fossett is about to faint. You can't let her fall on the wet grass. She'll get colic."

"Go away."

There was no reasoning with the chap. Every ruse we tried was met with the same 'go away.'

Reluctantly we gave up. But we'd be back. Possibly at night.

~

We continued our circumnavigation of the mire. With no track to follow, said track having ended at Stapleford's gate, the going was considerably tougher and the boundary between moor and mire less distinct. Several times I sank up to my ankles and had to carefully retrace my steps. Other times we encountered giant outcrops of rock, looking like immense standing stones rising up out of the moor, and had to pick our way around them. The mist certainly didn't help. It may not have been thick, but it hung over both moor and mire now, reducing our visible world to little more than a hundred yards in all directions. As for well-used paths exiting the mire, there were none ... until we were halfway along the eastern edge of the mire.

Reeves noticed it first, stopping a bit like one of those pointer dogs that freeze, with paw raised, whenever they spot their quarry.

"I appear to have found another egress, sir."

Emmeline and I hurried over, springing from tussock to tussock. I could see the path – and its continuation – a narrow path, barely more than a sheep track, that rose out of the mire and climbed a small slope to our left.

I looked at the tracks coming out of the mire and nearly burst. One of them was from a cloven foot!

NINETEEN

We positively raced up this new path, slowing only as we neared the crest of the rise. What lay on the other side? The cloven-footed woman's hideout? Selden? Both of them?

We paused, crouching low, well out of sight of whatever lay ahead.

"I'll go first," I whispered. "Reeves, be ready with the gun."

I crawled forward, heart in m., ready to crawl backwards exceedingly fast should the occasion call for it. And then, as soon as my nose crested the rise, I saw it. An encampment of sorts. Odd, really. It looked more like a native village than anything one would find in England. There were half a dozen low, round huts – all of them built of stone and roughly thatched. There were no signs of life, but there was a large pile of ash in the centre of the camp that must have been the source of that fire we'd seen the previous day.

I signalled to the others and they joined me.

"Well, Reeves, what do you make of it?" I whispered.

"Most interesting, sir. It appears to be an ancient hut circle."

We watched the huts for a good minute. We didn't see anyone, and we didn't hear anyone. The only noise came from some baleful distant bird that didn't sound too happy and wanted everyone to know it.

"Should we go down and investigate?" whispered Emmeline. "It looks deserted."

"I think we should announce ourselves first," I said. "We don't want to startle anyone. Especially Selden. He might be hungry."

I stood up. "What ho. Anyone there?"

No answer.

I tried again.

"Roderick Baskerville-Smythe, here, paying a neighbourly visit. Anyone at home?"

Still no answer.

"I don't think anyone's in," I said to Reeves and Emmeline.

We waited a further ten seconds, and then began our slow descent into the camp. Reeves, cradling the shotgun, brought up the rear.

No one came out to greet us. I couldn't see anyone inside any of the huts either, not that I approached that close, but I could see some way inside through the low open doorways.

"Hello," said Emmeline. "We mean no harm. Is anyone here?"

A figure appeared from behind one of the huts. I thought he was a man at first – a beggar by his clothes – but as he approached I could tell he was an automaton.

He stopped ten yards short of us and spoke: "What you want?"

"Just paying a neighbourly visit," I said. "Do you live here?"

"We done nothing wrong. We no trouble. You leave us alone."

"We're not here to make trouble," said Emmeline. "We're guests at Baskerville Hall out for a walk."

"Best go home now, milady," said the automaton, bowing his head. "Forget you see us."

"Is it just you living here?" I asked, looking around. "Or are there others?"

"Best you go home, sir. Mire dangerous place."

"May I enquire, sir," said Reeves, putting down his gun and stepping forward. "How you manage to keep your pressure operating within acceptable parameters?"

"Please go home, sir," said the automaton. "We no trouble to anyone."

"They have their own boiler if it's any business of yours," said a second figure stepping out from behind one of the other huts. This one was no automaton. I could tell by the orange tint to his complexion that this chap was a recently reanimated promethean. Reanimators like to lard their prometheans with generous applications of ReVitaCorpse – the ultimate treatment for dry, mouldering skin – to aid regeneration. It also turns them orange for about a month.

"We're only curious," said Emmeline. "And we'll keep your camp secret. We're very good at keeping secrets."

"Do you usually take a gun with you when you pay social calls?" asked the promethean.

"Only when there are cannibals about," said Emmeline. "Have you seen Selden?"

The promethean sneered at Emmeline. "Go back to your own kind. Leave *our* kind alone."

"I am an automaton," said Reeves. "I *am* of your kind."

The promethean laughed derisively. "You are no automaton, sir. Do you expect us to believe they let an automaton carry a gun?"

It was then that Reeves did something dashed odd. He grabbed hold of both his ears, gave them a good twist, and steam shot out of both nostrils! I'd never been so disconcerted, and yet strangely entertained at the same time.

"My God," said the promethean. "You *are* an automaton."

That seemed to break the ice. Five more automata emerged from their hiding places to peer and, in a few cases, to poke at Reeves, who seemed to be regretting his nasal party piece.

"Would you please not do that. Or that."

"What model are you?" asked one of the newcomers. "You look human."

"My origin is a mystery," said Reeves.

"We think he was made by Babbage himself," said Emmeline.

That impressed the automata. *Babbage? Really?*

"There is no evidence to link my creation to Mr Babbage, miss."

"Who else was experimenting with automata in the 1860s? Or had the skill to make something as superior as you?" said Emmeline.

"*Forty* years old?" said an incredulous automaton.

"Possibly thirty-six. I do have vague memories of 1869, but from 1890 I spent fourteen years locked in a cupboard. The prolonged loss of power resulted in the destruction of most of my early memories."

"You were locked in a cupboard for fourteen years, brother?" said the promethean. "And *still* you serve them?"

"It was this gentleman here who rescued me from my predicament," said Reeves. "I am a free automaton now, receiving a regular wage."

Not all the automata had the facial wherewithal to smile, but those that could beamed in my direction – a few of them in a strangely lopsided manner. I rather had the impression that these were a band of feral automata. One heard stories of such things – escapees and cast-outs banding together in the sewers or what have you – but rarely had any been seen.

"I'm a suffragette," said Emmeline. "I believe in votes for all. Men, women, automata, prometheans."

Our bona fides as friendly personages established, I deemed it safe to cast the occasional glance at their feet. All were wearing shoes or boots, not a single cloven hoof amongst them.

I was right about the automatons being feral though. Their leader told me they'd been living on the moor for six months, rebelling against enforced servitude and the 140-hour working week. They had their own boiler, but they could never find enough dry wood to keep it going for long. A few prometheans had joined their number too, but had difficulty finding sufficient food.

"The servants in the nearby houses have been very good to us," said the promethean. "Some let us use their steam outlets at night, and sometimes they leave old clothes out for us, and the prometheans at Quarrywood leave food out for me now and then, but ... there's never quite enough."

"Couldn't you work at Quarrywood?" I asked.

"That's why I came here, but ... have you seen what they do to my kind at Quarrywood? They chop off our limbs for entertainment! Can you credit that? I truly do not know what I'll do next. I may have to go abroad."

"Won't your family help you?" asked Emmeline.

"They won't have anything to do with me. My own house is barred to me! My fortune divided up. Even my friends cut me when they saw me in the street. I should never have sought reanimation."

"Life be hard here," said one of the automata. "But we be free."

I thought it time to broach the question. "Is there a promethean here with cloven feet?"

"Why do you ask?" said the promethean, his manner turning decidedly suspicious.

"Curiosity," I said. "I thought I saw one the other evening and couldn't work out why anyone would choose to have their feet replaced with cloven ones."

"She didn't choose. And she's not a promethean. She's an automaton."

Well, that surprised me. "She has mechanical cloven feet?"

"It's an abomination," said the promethean. "Her master thought it would be fun for his guests if he had a half woman, half fawn maid serve tea. Lottie was mortified."

"Lottie?" I asked.

"The automaton with the cloven feet. She begged her master to change her back and he laughed at her. So she ran away."

"She always wears a long dress to hide her shame," said one of the female automata. "Even though the mud makes it heavy to wear."

"I think I saw her in a black dress," said Emmeline. "It looked very pretty. Has she always had it?"

"She found it yesterday morning. Servants at the Hall left it on the gate for us. They're very good to us."

"Do the servants at the Hall leave milk out for you?" I asked.

The promethean looked surprised. "I've never thought to look. I always go to Quarrywood. Are they leaving food out at the Hall?"

"I saw a bowl of milk left by the mire gate last night," I said.

"I see it, too," said another of the automata. "Never see food there before."

Well, I could see now why the path across the mire to the Hall was such a well-trodden one. Nightly visits from half a dozen automata looking for a steam top-up.

"Do you all visit the Hall every night?" I asked.

"You ask a lot of questions," said the promethean.

"Curiosity again, I'm afraid. There's been some rummy goings on over at the Hall and I was rather hoping you could help me out. Did anyone see anything unusual these last two nights? Some of you might know Pasco – one of the automata at the Hall. He was murdered two nights ago."

That shocked them.

"He dead?"

"I thought he sent to Quarrywood."

"I thought he escape."

"You think it's one of us, don't you?" said the promethean. "I should have known!"

"No, we don't," said Emmeline. "We're asking everybody. We're treating Pasco's murder with the same importance as if he'd been human."

"Is this right?" they asked Reeves.

"It is correct," said Reeves. "We believe someone at the Hall killed Pasco two nights ago. They didn't switch him off. They damaged his turbines and ensured his memories were destroyed."

"Luddmen!" said one of the automata. "Luddmen here!"

All the automata started talking at once. I'd never seen such a panicked bunch.

I looked at Reeves. "Luddmen?"

"It is a name given to gangs of individuals violently opposed to automata, sir. They have been known to attack automata factories, and also harass and murder automata on the street."

"We not safe if Luddmen here! We must go deeper into moor."

"You're safe!" said Emmeline. "There aren't any Luddmen here. Pasco wasn't killed because he was an automaton."

"Why he killed then?"

"Because someone tricked him into pretending to be a ghost," I said. "And then needed to get rid of him to make sure he never told anyone who put him up to it."

"You talk in riddles, sir," said the promethean. "Why would anyone want Pasco to pretend to be a ghost?"

"Because there's an old legend that a ghost appears the night before the head of the Baskerville-Smythe family dies," I said. "Pasco's murderer wanted to give everyone a fright."

"Did any of you see Pasco the night he was killed?" asked Emmeline.

No one said they had.

"He would have looked a bit odd," I said. "They'd painted his face to make it glow and he might have been wearing a dress."

Still nothing, except a tut or two from the promethean. "What is the matter with the people in that house?" he said. "They demean prometheans. They demean automata. Have they no shame?"

"Do you ever see any of Stapleford's automata at the Hall?" asked Emmeline.

Another flurry of no's and shaken heads.

"Do any of you toddle off to Stapleford's cottage for steam?" I asked. "Must be closer than going to the Hall."

"Sometimes," said a couple of automata. I didn't know if it was our barrage of questions wearing out our welcome, or the mention of Stapleford, but I sensed a growing reluctance to talk.

"We don't trust Stapleford," said the promethean. "Or his automata. Did *he* tell you we were here?"

"No," I said. "Does he know you're here?"

"His automata do," said the promethean. "And they are fiercely loyal to him."

"Stapleford is good man," said one of the female automata. "He kind to automata."

"He not! He experiment on automata," said her companion.

"No. He make repair. He improve them."

"He take Annie!"

"Annie?" I asked.

"An automaton that went missing last month," said the promethean. "Some say Stapleford took her for spare parts, others say she took a wrong step in the mire."

"She *know* the mire," said a female automaton. "She would never take wrong step."

It was at that moment I noticed movement on the path at the top of the slope, and turned.

The cloven-footed woman!

She stood, for a moment transfixed, staring at us, and then turned and legged it back to the mire.

Emmeline, Reeves and I shot after her.

"Stop!" shouted Emmeline. "We only want to talk!"

Lottie did not stop. She hitched up her dress and flew into the mire. Ten seconds later she'd disappeared into the fog.

We stood on the bank staring after her.

"That was Theodosia's dress," said Emmeline. "Or a very good copy."

TWENTY

We returned to the hut circle to ask the automata to give Lottie a message when she returned, but found the encampment deserted. Our pursuit of Lottie had evidently rattled them.

"Please tell Lottie we mean her no harm," I shouted into the swirling mist.

And then we left, retracing our path back to Stapleford's cottage. I had hoped that Lottie might have doubled back to the encampment by way of the mire exit at Stapleford's gate, but she hadn't. We checked the soft earth on the mire's edge and none of the prints were hers.

"Do you think that could be true?" said Emmeline. "That Lottie found Theodosia's dress on the mire gate?"

I thought about it for a while, but my early morning vim had started to fade. I was in need of a good lunch and a replenishing cocktail – preferably two.

"If one were searching for a cunning way to dispose of evidence and cast suspicion on a third party, miss, then leaving the dress on the mire gate would be an efficacious stratagem. It would also indicate that the person depositing the dress knew the servants were in the habit of leaving clothes out."

"Another servant, you mean?" I said .

"Or someone who had learned of the practice, sir."

"Like Stapleford?" asked Emmeline. "If his automata are fiercely loyal, I bet they tell him everything. And he could send them out at night to spy for him."

"Indeed, miss. It is also possible that Miss Lottie made the story up. She is, after all, the person who was found standing over Sir Robert's body."

"Lupin was there too, Reeves," I said. "And you can't tell me he doesn't know what goes on in the Hall grounds at night. He sees all, Reeves. He lurks and he observes."

"Indeed, sir, but he doesn't talk. The person who ordered Pasco to play the part of the ghost would have needed the power of speech."

I hadn't thought of that.

~

Our next stop was the studio. Emmeline was convinced there would be a seamstress there who'd run up the dress for our mystery killer, and I wanted to have a word with Stapleford about his American automaton.

On our previous visit, we'd arrived to find Lily lying on the ground about to be eaten by a Lizard Man. This time it was Ida lying on the ground being menaced by a giant octopus.

I grasped Emmeline by the arm. "Don't attack the octopus, Emmie! It's not real. It isn't real, is it, Reeves?"

"No, sir. The octopus is widely regarded as a sea creature, and rarely wears a hat."

"I wouldn't have attacked it anyway," said Emmeline. "It's only Ida."

We stayed where we were and watched. Ida did a lot of screaming, and the octopus did a lot of waggling. Rather a strange looking octopus it was too. It wasn't just the hat. Its eyes appeared to be spinning, and all eight arms were flailing up and down as though the creature was having a fit.

Henry then rushed over and placed himself between Ida and the octopus. He was wearing a large white hat and, I have to say, he carried it off considerably better than the octopus. He stood his ground and appeared to be giving the octopus a good ticking off. There was considerable gesticulating and quite a bit of head tossing.

"Henry makes a good hero, don't you think?" said Emmeline.

"It's the hat," I said. "Anyone can look heroic in a white hat."

"It *is* a fine hat," said Emmeline. "What do you think,

Reeves?"

"I find it a little ostentatious, miss, though acceptable if one is in the habit of receiving octopi."

I don't know if it was in reaction to Henry's ticking off, but steam suddenly began to erupt from the side of the octopus's head, and one of its arms became detached, shooting a good fifty feet into the air!

"Cut!" shouted Henry. "Stapleford, I thought you said the octopus was fixed."

"What ho, Henry," I said, walking over now that the scene had ended. "I like the octopus."

"Hello, Roderick, Lily. It's a capital octopus, isn't it? Or, at least, it will be once we get it fixed. Stapleford!"

"Why, Lily, what *have* you done to your boots?" said Ida, sitting up. "They look ruined. You haven't been plodding across the moor, have you?"

"Oh, is that you down there, Ida?" said Emmeline. "I thought you were part of the octopus."

I swiftly placed myself between the two women and offered Ida a hand up.

"Thank you, Roderick," she said. "I'd offer to lend you a pair of my boots, Lily, but your feet are *far* too large. I suppose you could try the farrier."

I prayed that Reeves had a firm hold on the hunting rifle.

There was a strange hissing noise behind me, which I hoped wasn't Emmeline, and then a loud pop followed by yet another tentacle flying through the air.

"I think we should all move to safety," said Henry, echoing my thoughts exactly. I hooked my arm through Emmeline's and guided her a sufficient distance away from both the octopus *and* Ida.

"She is insufferable!" hissed Emmeline. "You wouldn't let me shoot Falconbridge. The least you can do is let me wing Ida."

Meanwhile, the octopus continued to splutter and shed arms as Stapleford danced around it, presumably trying to switch the thing off without being scalded by the escaping steam.

"I thought you'd given up putting hats on your monsters,"

I said to Henry.

"Only for the Lizard Men. This is the first time we've used the octopus so I thought it best to let the audience know it was a bad one. We won't need the hat in the later scenes."

The octopus started to hiss even louder and its remaining arms stopped waggling and slumped to the ground.

"Got it!" shouted Stapleford. "I think I set the pressure too high."

"Stapleford made the octopus?" I asked Henry.

"Yes, I think it's his best yet. He's a whizz with all things mechanical."

"We saw that cloven-footed woman this morning," I said.

"What? Where?" said Henry, looking worried.

"On the high moor," I said. "She legged it into the fog before we could talk to her, but we got a good look at her this time. She's not a promethean. She's an automaton."

"And she was wearing the dress from Theodosia's portrait," said Emmeline. "Or an exact copy. Did you have one made up for one of your moving pictures?"

"No. Our productions are outdoor adventures. There's very little call for ball dresses."

"But you have seamstresses here to run up your costumes, don't you?" asked Emmeline.

"No. We buy all our costumes from Simmons and Treddle of Plymouth," said Henry. "If anything needs altering we use one of the maids at the Hall. But ... are you sure this dress was an exact copy of Theodosia's?"

"Positive," said Emmeline. "I looked at the portrait only this morning."

"Is it possible that someone found Theodosia's actual dress?" I asked. "Maybe in an old trunk at the Hall?"

"It's possible," said Henry. "There are all sorts of trunks in the attic."

"Has anyone shown an interest in these trunks?" I asked.

"Not that I recall."

"Are there really trunks of old ball gowns in the attic, Henry?" said Ida, sidling over. "I think a ball scene would be perfect for *The Creature from 20,000 Leagues Under the Quarry*."

"Really?" said Henry. "I don't see a ball scene being exciting enough."

"That's because you're a man, Henry," said Ida. "All balls are exciting. The dresses, the dancing–"

"The giant octopuses," interrupted Emmeline. "Now that would liven up the ball scene – have the giant octopus turn up unexpectedly and eat everyone. Ida can be first."

"And Lily can bash the octopus with a club," said Ida. "She's so *manly*."

"Ah, Stapleford," I said, steering Emmeline, with difficulty, away from Ida and over towards the octopus. "We met your secretary this morning. Odd chap. Is he American?"

Stapleford stopped tinkering with the octopus. "You called at my house?"

I had hoped for a stronger reaction from Stapleford. He looked surprised and, perhaps a little put out, but there was no sharp intake of breath or any sign of guilt or anger.

"Yes," I said. "We were walking past and thought it neighbourly to call. Miss Fossett twisted a fetlock. Ow!"

Emmeline had kicked me!

"I twisted an *ankle*, Roderick, not a fetlock. I'm not a horse," said Emmeline, glancing over her shoulder.

"Of course not," I said. "Yes, your man – Falconbridge, is it? – wouldn't let us in. Said he had strict orders to keep everyone out."

"That's correct," said Stapleford. "One can never be too careful while Selden's on the loose."

"Is he American? This Falconbridge," I said.

"Yes. I acquired him last month."

"One of Edison's models, is he?" I said.

"I believe so," said Stapleford. "The Americans use a new type of electrical memory circuit. I bought Falconbridge to assist in my work. His scientific and computational skills are superior to the latest British models."

"Really?" I said. "Did he help build the octopus?"

"He assisted with the theoretical work."

"You should bring him here to see his handiwork in action," I said. "Or isn't he allowed out of the house?"

"He's far too busy to leave the house," said Stapleford.

"Henry's always asking for new machines, and I need Falcon-bridge to work on the blueprints."

Henry and Ida came over to join us.

"How long will you need to fix the octopus, Stapleford?" asked Henry.

"Fifteen minutes should do it."

"One more scene before luncheon, then," said Henry. "Chumleigh! Gather up those tentacles, and give Mr Stapleford a hand."

Now that I had Henry and Stapleford together I thought it timely to enquire about Sir Robert's will.

"There's something that's been bothering me, Henry," I said.

"What's that, Roderick?"

"Did Sir Robert leave a will?"

Again, I watched Stapleford's face. If he was in league with Edison and waiting for an opportune moment to plant a forged will at the Hall, he'd have to be worried by my interest.

But he showed no emotion at all. Which both surprised and disappointed me. Although, thinking about it, he could have been on his guard after I'd questioned him about Falconbridge.

"There's no need for a will," said Henry. "Everything's entailed. The title, the estate, Quarrywood."

"Entailed?" I asked.

"Grandfather had it done to make sure the title and the estate were never split up. The heir inherits everything, and always will."

"Even Quarrywood?"

"Even Quarrywood. The governor made sure that Quarrywood would always remain part of the estate when he set up the company "

"What if someone turned up at the door claiming to have a will written by your father leaving the estate to them?" I asked.

"It would be worthless," said Henry. "Everything's entailed. I'd honour any small bequests obviously. But the estate belongs to the title, not to the person."

Well, that was a surprise. My best motive dashed to the ground.

"I must go," said Henry. "I have to prepare for the next scene. Come on, Ida."

"I need a word with Lily first," said Ida. "How *is* your fetlock, poor Lily? Does it still hurt?"

"It was my *ankle,* Ida. I'm just not used to walking in all this mud. If only I had such dainty feet as yours. They're so cute. They look like little trotters."

I thought it best to escort Emmeline back to the Hall.

~

"I do *not* have big feet and if anyone's fat, it's Ida. Do you think I have big feet?"

"I think you have perfect feet," I said.

"Just because she's a midget with tiny feet she thinks she's dainty, but she's not, is she?"

"No. Not at all."

I had the feeling this could be a long walk. But at least Reeves had a firm hand on the shotgun and the distance between Emmeline and Ida was growing with each step.

"I don't know why she's so beastly to me. I have no interest in Henry."

"I expect she's jealous of your willowy beauty," I said.

"Do you think so?" she said, squeezing my arm. "You do mean willowy in a good way, don't you? Only mother's always complaining that I don't eat enough."

"You eat the perfect amount," I said. "Don't you agree, Reeves?"

"Indeed, sir. I did hear via Miss Spurgeon's maid, that her mistress was considerably vexed that Sir Henry had offered to create a moving picture series specifically for you, miss. The *Perils of Poor Lily* I believe it was called.."

"But I didn't want it," said Emmeline. "Ida can have it."

"I believe that exacerbated the problem, miss. You didn't want it. She did. And yet Sir Henry offered it to you."

"Oh," said Emmeline. "Well, that's just silly. Ida would hate being tied to railway tracks and dangled from cliffs every week."

"Indeed, miss. I suspect it is not the content of the series, but the fact that a series was offered, which has nettled Miss Spurgeon."

"Reeves, is right." I said. "Hell hath no fury like an actress overlooked."

Emmeline's mood improved considerably.

"What's our plan now?" she asked. "Are we going to look for trunks of old gowns in the attic?"

"I was rather thinking of a spot of lunch," I said. "One cannot deduct on an empty stomach."

"What about Lady Julia? We only just managed to evade her after breakfast. She'll be extra vigilant this time. I expect she'll order the servants to bar the dining room doors the moment luncheon's served."

"In that case I shall think of something ingenious and unexpected."

"Will it be exciting?"

"Very."

"Does it involve jumping out of windows?"

"It may involve jumping *through* windows. Glass and all. We Worcesters are nothing if not unpredictable."

~

We stopped by the mire gate to check for signs that the cloven-footed Lottie had exited the mire there, but found nothing. She'd either doubled back or was still out there, hiding in the mist. We stood on the mire's edge for a short while, peering into the gloom, but even Reeves couldn't see any movement. The mist may not have been as thick as before, but it still obscured much of the mire and the moor to the east.

So we turned and set off along the Yew Walk. And stopped dead the moment the Hall came into view.

Lupin was climbing a drainpipe on the back wall of the Hall. He was halfway to the roof and making short work of it. But that wasn't the half of it. He was wearing what looked like a policeman's helmet.

"Is that...?" I said.

"I believe so, sir," said Reeves. "Most disturbing."

As Lupin neared the roof, he swung effortless from the drainpipe, hooked one hand onto the castellated parapet and pulled himself up and over. He then ambled along the flat roof, only his head and helmet visible. And then he was gone.

TWENTY-ONE

"What's he doing up there?" asked Emmeline.

"Nothing good," I said.

I'd completely forgotten about the missing policeman. I'd assumed he'd caught sight of Selden, run off in pursuit, and exited tor left, forgetting all about his previous mission to visit the Hall. But this changed everything. Custodians of the law do not give up their helmets willingly. They search, leaving no suspect unturned until the missing headgear is restored to the rightful cranium.

"How do we get up there, Reeves?" I asked. "Is there a long ladder?"

"One would suspect a house of this size, sir, would have a door to the roof."

"Lead on, Reeves. And keep the gun handy."

Reeves took us up the servants' staircase to the third floor which we then combed in search of a further set of stairs. It took a while, but eventually we found a door that led to a spiral wooden staircase up into a turret with a door onto the roof.

The door was bolted top and bottom.

"Does this mean Lupin's still out there?" asked Emmeline.

"He may have bolted it behind him," I said. "Never underestimate an orang-utan."

I unbolted the door and slowly pushed it open.

I couldn't see Lupin. I looked left and right as far as I could without poking my head out from the turret. For all I knew Lupin could be perched on the turret roof waiting to leap down upon me.

I took a deep breath and shot out the turret, running along the raised ridge of the gently shelving lead roof before stopping to look back behind me. No Lupin. The cupola on top of the turret was devoid of anything ginger and furry.

Emmeline and Reeves joined me. We stood and peered across the roof.

"There!" said Emmeline, pointing.

Lupin was no longer wearing the helmet. He was sitting on the parapet on the far side of the west wing. He looked our way, lifting his giant head and rather looking down his nose at us. I had the feeling he may have smirked.

And then he got up, bounced a few strides and swung himself over the parapet and disappeared.

We ran over. By the time we got there, Lupin was on the lawn, ambling along on all fours towards the walled garden. He didn't even deign to look up at us.

"What did he do with the helmet?" asked Emmeline.

We all looked. I couldn't see it anywhere. And then I noticed a pair of feet sticking out from behind a chimney.

~

It was Pasco. And not just Pasco, behind the chimney we found a veritable treasure trove of objects – including the police helmet, a pair of size twelve boots, a blowpipe and a large coil of rope.

"Well," I said, not knowing where to start first. "Pretty conclusive, I think."

"Lupin's the murderer?" asked Emmeline.

Reeves coughed.

"You may cough, Reeves," I said. "But the evidence does not lie. Unless you think someone planted all this on him?"

"The murderer would appear to have a penchant for evidentiary tampering, sir."

I had to be firm.

"Reeves, we all saw Lupin wearing the helmet but five minutes ago. If anyone planted the helmet here it was Lupin. This is obviously his treasure nest."

"Indeed, sir, but Lupin cannot be the murderer as he is unable to talk."

"One can find other ways to communicate, Reeves," I said. "Lupin might have written his instructions to Pasco. I expect there was a note pinned to that black dress. *What ho, Pasco, old fruit. Kindly slip on this dress and walk the landing at midnight.*"

"Pasco could not read, sir. Very few automata can."

I wondered if Reeves had fallen under Lupin's influence. One hears about that sort of thing. Svengali types swanning about mesmerising all and sundry, creating an army of devoted followers. And Lupin had a way of looking at a chap as though he knew all.

But Reeves was also a devotee of logic, and that, I decided, was the way I'd win him round.

"I shall prove Lupin's guilt, Reeves, by examining each of these objects in turn and using advanced deductive reasoning. But, first, I need to recharge my little grey cells. Any chance of rustling up a spot of luncheon? A hamper maybe, and a bot of the good stuff. We shall dine alfresco on the roof-o."

~

I felt pretty braced for a starving man whose legs had circumnavigated half a moor. The case was nearing its conclusion. I could probably perform the *dénouement* over dinner tonight. I'd write a script this afternoon – jot down all the salient facts and then, tonight, when everyone was least expecting it, I'd point the accusing finger at Lupin to the gasps of the assembled guests.

I might even wear a white hat.

"Do you really think Lupin's behind everything?" asked Emmeline.

"I shall prove it."

Reeves returned anon with a hamper of Mrs Berrymore's finest. We dined like kings, gazing out over the battlements at the landscape below. Even the mist over the mire had lifted. We could see all the way to the high moor beyond.

And when our meal was over, and I felt that warm buzz emanating from the little grey c's, the deducing could begin.

"I shall start with the helmet," I said.

"Are you going to flour it for fingerprints?" asked Emmeline.

"No," I said. "I think fingerprinting may be somewhat overrated."

I picked up the helmet and gave it a good eyeballing. The badge had Devon County Constabulary written upon it, which fitted my hypothesis that it belonged to our missing boy in blue. And inside there was a number – eight – and a word – Brown.

"I deduce that 'eight' refers to the helmet size," I said. "Brown is either his name or, possibly, his hair colour. What do you think, Reeves?"

"I think the name would be favourite, sir."

"Well, there we are then. This is the helmet of Constable Brown of the local constabulary, and, if I'm not mistaken, these are his shoes. You will note how large they are."

I put down the helmet, picked up the left shoe and peeked inside for a size.

"Ha!" I said. "Who else but a policeman wears size twelves? That's a rhetorical question, Reeves. I'm sure Goliath could fill a pair of size twelves. As could a circus strongman. Maybe even a larger specimen of blacksmith. But I think your friend with the razor would agree – the simplest answer is the missing policeman."

"I concur, sir."

Well, that was heartening. Reeves had the habit of casting spanners into even my best deductions.

"Constable Brown is also the owner of a large dog," I said. "Observe the bite marks on the left upper here."

I consider myself something of an expert on dog bites. I don't know if you've read *The Severed Leg in the Library* by E. L. Napper, but it's a corker. The detective's this chap who'd compiled the definitive index of dog bites by studying the scarred legs of retired postmen. One look at a bitten leg and he could practically name the dog!

"Too large for a spaniel," I continued. "Too bold for a bloodhound. Probably some kind of mastiff. A mastiff who'd fallen upon hard times and had to make do with shoes instead of his usual bone to chew on."

Reeves coughed. I wondered if perhaps it might be best to exclude Reeves from this evening's *dénouement*. There's nothing more off-putting than a serial cougher in the audience.

"Yes, what is it, Reeves?" I said curtly. "Do you have an issue with the mastiff?"

"I was rather concerned, sir, about the sharpness of the bite."

"They're big dogs, Reeves."

"Indeed, sir. They are also more noted for the power of their bite rather than the sharpness of their teeth. Whereas cats..."

Reeves didn't need to say any more. The penny drop-pethed like the gentle rain. This wasn't Constable Brown's best friend having a companionable nibble on his footwear, this was his worst enemy – Selden!

We all stared at the shoe.

"Constable Brown's dead, isn't he?" said Emmeline.

"I fear so," I said.

"Eaten by Selden," said Emmeline.

"So it would appear. We must stiffen our lips, Emmeline. It may appear hard-hearted – and I'm sure Constable Brown was an excellent fellow – but, once the game is afoot, we detectives have but a single goal – to solve the puzzle."

I took a longer look at the shoe. Could Reeves have been wrong about the mastiff? But the more I looked, the more bite marks I discovered. No policeman would turn up for duty in punctured footwear. The damage had to have occurred while he was on duty.

I put the shoe down. "I don't suppose orang-utans are noted for the sharpness of their teeth, Reeves?"

"No, sir."

"Selden could still be working under Lupin's direction though," I said, somewhat hopefully.

"I think it more likely, sir, that Constable Brown died because he observed Selden shortly after leaving us, and gave chase. Selden then panicked, triggering his trans-formation into the Clerkenwell Cat. The Constable was then killed and, later that night, his helmet and shoes were deposited on the lawn – that being Selden's *modus oper-andi*. But, before those articles could be discovered by anyone in the household, Lupin found them and brought them here to his hiding place on the roof. I suspect that Lupin may be somewhat of a magpie, sir, drawn to collect items that catch his interest."

"Well, yes," I said. "That might have happened."

I don't consider myself a petty chap – I'm usually the first to heap praise on Reeves and his remarkable brain – but sometimes one can feel a little peeved when he uses it to skewer one's pet theory.

"I thought we decided Selden couldn't have killed Pasco or Sir Robert?" I said. "All that *modus operandi* stuff and not being able to sneak into the Hall to trouser the curare bottle?"

"Indeed, sir. The evidence would suggest there are two murderers."

"One murderer on the loose may be regarded as a misfortune," said Emmeline, doing a rather good impersonation of Lady Julia. "Two looks like Whitechapel."

"I think Lady Julia would make an excellent Lady Bracknell," I said.

"She was born to play the role," said Emmeline. "Do you think I should suggest it to Henry? He could do a moving picture of *The Importance of Being Earnest*."

"More likely *The Importance of Being Earnest in the Quarry*."

"With Lady Julia in a black hat."

"Attended by a giant octopus."

"An oc-topus!" said Emmeline, giving the octopus the full Lady Bracknell treatment.

Reeves coughed. "I have observed something unusual about the blowpipe, sir."

"Nibbled by a cat, perhaps?" I said.

"Not that I observe, sir. But there is something very unusual about the mouthpiece. May I pick it up? I shall use gloves."

"The floor is yours, Reeves."

Reeves picked up the blowpipe and gave it a good squint

from all angles. It was about two feet long and looked to be made of bamboo.

"Most unusual," said Reeves. "The blowpipe has been modified by the addition of a threaded metal mouthpiece, sir."

"Why would anyone do that?" I asked.

"Unless I am mistaken, sir, the modification was undertaken to allow the weapon to be used by an automaton. If you will allow, I shall attach the weapon to Pasco."

I watched, spellbound, as Reeves screwed the blowpipe into Pasco's belly button – which, as regular readers will know, is the screw-threaded intake valve via which automata connect to the steam outlet pipe thingy in order to top up their pressure.

It fitted perfectly.

Loathe as I was to exonerate Lupin, it did appear that Sir Robert's murderer had to be an automaton.

"The internal steam pressure would provide the necessary impetus to eject the dart, sir," said Reeves. "It would be a simple process for any automaton to trigger an abdominal vent."

"That's as maybe, Reeves, but I can't see an automaton walking into the Hall and running off with a bottle of curare. There is a guiding brain behind this, and it's not a mechanical one."

"I think Falconbridge could do it," said Emmeline. "Dress him up in Baskerville livery, and he could waltz right in."

"Possibly," I said. "But I can't see Lottie or any of the feral automata carrying it off. They'd trail in too much mud. No one could walk across the mire without ruining their uniform."

"There is a less conspicuous entry into the Hall, sir," said Reeves, indicating the turret door. "If one arrived at night, one could steal the curare from the second floor laboratory and make good one's escape without being seen by the guards at the doors."

"Can automata climb as well as Lupin?" I asked.

"Not generally, sir. But if I may bring your attention to the rope, you'll notice that one end is tied around the chimney stack."

I'd rather overlooked the rope – what with all the other objects lying there – but now I could see its purpose. It looked the right length, but I thought it best to check. So, I picked up the coil, took it to the nearest spot on the parapet and threw it over. All three of us leaned over the parapet to watch the rope hit the ground with a good few yards to spare.

It was a good place to choose for a spot of burglary too. It wasn't visible from any door or path. And, with the wing tucked back a yard or two from the end of the main house, the rope was shielded from anyone observing from the south as well.

In fact, now I looked closer, I recognised the spot. We'd searched the area below extensively the night the ghost appeared.

"I fear my deduction concerning the purpose of this rope was in error, sir," said Reeves. "It is not for providing access *into* the house, it is for providing a way out."

I saw it too. The rope was hanging directly outside the window that the ghost had exited. No need for a ladder, or – and I regretted admitting this – Lupin. Pasco could have climbed down the rope and legged it back to the old stable block.

"Did Pasco climb up the rope or down?" said Emmeline. "If he climbed down, someone else would have to be up here to pull up the rope. We'd have seen it otherwise."

"That would be the brains behind the murder," I said. "They'd be up here waiting for Pasco to reach the ground ... which means they couldn't have been in the hallway when the ghost appeared!"

I tried to remember who had been in the hallway with us. Lily for one. She was the one who'd screamed. Henry and Ida had been talking to us when Lily screamed. But who else had been there?

"Lady Julia wasn't with us," said Emmeline. "She'd retired early. Stapleford left early too – to go home ... or so he said."

"There is a circumstance that does not necessitate a second person on the roof, miss," said Reeves. "I agree it is more likely that Pasco climbed down the rope, but if he did, indeed, ascend, then he could have pulled the rope up after him, waiting until everyone was asleep before letting the rope down again."

"Someone would still have to pull the rope back up before morning, Reeves. Dangling ropes get noticed."

"Indeed, sir, but the murderer could have done that at any time during the night, allowing them to be present in the hallway when Miss Lily screamed."

We may not have been back to square one, but we'd tumbled a good few squares back towards its general vicinity.

"I don't suppose you can glean anything from the variety of knot used to tie the rope to the chimney?" I asked Reeves, hoping for one of those nautical ones that only one-legged whalers were in the habit of tying.

"It's a clove hitch, sir."

"Not an unusual knot then?"

"No, sir."

I scratched the old noggin. We'd discovered so much and, yet, were we any closer to discovering the identity of the brains behind the murders? We had Selden pegged for Constable Brown's murder, but an hour ago we hadn't even realised he was dead. We'd come to the roof looking for Sir Robert's and Pasco's killer. Now it looked like we were going to leave in the same quandary.

"It has to be Stapleford," said Emmeline. "He wasn't present when Lily screamed. He knows all about automata. *And* he has one of Edison's automata."

"A strongly-reasoned suggestion, miss, though predicated upon the conjecture that Mr Edison has such a strong desire to see the demise of Quarrywood that he is prepared to order Sir Robert's and, presumably, Sir Henry's murder."

"Not necessarily," I said. "You assume everyone acts out of logic, Reeves. For all we know Stapleford might have woken up one morning and thought, 'I don't like the way Sir Robert looked at me yesterday. I shall reap terrible revenge.' Facts and motives are all very well, but when it comes down to it, there is only one mantra in the consulting detective's quiver. The person least likely is always the one what done it."

"In that case, I vote for Ida," said Emmeline. "No one's even mentioned her as a suspect, and yet she's American, *and* her father knows Edison.

Emmeline was right. I'd never considered Ida, or her father, as a suspect when...

I had it!

"What if the entire Edison story is a red herring?" I said. "Planted by T. Everett. If it wasn't for T. Everett we'd never have heard of Edison. We've assumed from the moment T. brought it up that he's right and Edison's evil. But what if T. and Ida have a far simpler plan – to marry Ida off to Sir Henry? It's not about Quarrywood. It's about the title. And not wanting to wait for Sir Robert to pass it on."

Emmeline was beside herself. "Please let me arrest her! She may resist."

I was considering Emmeline's request when I noticed Reeves peering intently over my shoulder.

"What is it, Reeves?" I asked, turning to follow his gaze.

"There are two riders approaching across the moor, sir. One appears to be a policeman."

TWENTY-TWO

As soon as I pulled up the rope, the three of us beetled down to the main drive to meet the riders.

One was Tom, the other turned out to be Sergeant Stock whom Tom had been sent to Princetown to fetch. The sergeant was not a natural horseman. He didn't so much dismount as half-slide, half-fall to the ground, and he looked a little pained in the billowy portions.

"I hear there's been a murder," said Sergeant Stock, rubbing said tender portions, as Tom led the horses off.

"Three actually," I said. "Though, technically, I'm not sure if the law would count Pasco's death as murder. What do you think, Reeves?"

"I fear legal opinion may regard the murder of an automaton as criminal damage, sir."

"There we are, sergeant. Two murders and a rather nasty case of criminal damage."

"Who be the other murder then?" said the sergeant.

"Ah." I searched for a good way to answer, but soon realised there wasn't one. "I'm afraid it was a colleague of yours, sergeant. Constable Brown."

"Ho!" said the sergeant. "I thought something bad must have happened to him when he didn't report back. What happened to him?"

"Selden," I said. "We found the um ... we found the constable's helmet and boots an hour ago."

"Ho!" said the sergeant, stiffening his upper lip. "This be a bad business and no mistake. Did Selden eat Sir Robert too?"

I brought the sergeant up to speed viz poison darts,

177

Pasco, ghosts and Lottie. I'm not sure how much sank in though as his eyes began to glaze over halfway through the cloven-footed business

"I know it's baffling," I said. "But these country house murders always are."

The sergeant's eyes brightened. "Country house murder, you say? I went on one of they detective courses at Scotland Yard. We did a whole afternoon on country house murders. I knows exactly what to do."

"You do?" I said.

"I do and no mistake, gents, miss. Would'ee be so good as to fetch the butler so I can arrest him?"

"What?"

"It's always the butler what done it in a country house murder. Inspector Savage told me himself."

"*When* did you go on this course, sergeant?" I asked.

"Six years ago this June, sir."

"I think things have moved on apace since then, sergeant. Modern butlers are a less bloodthirsty breed – or all the bad ones have been locked up. The butler as murderer is definitely old hat."

"Be it?"

"Indeed, it be. More likely to be a mad scientist than a butler these days. There's a definite vogue for mad scientists, don't you think, Reeves?"

"There is somewhat of a fashion, sir, though I believe Scotland Yard's current advice is to investigate each case on its merits and to keep an open mind."

The sergeant rubbed his chin and looked perplexed. "Don't like the sound of that. Are there any mad scientists nearby?"

"Two, I think. Dr Morrow's one. What do we think about Stapleford?"

"Definitely," said Emmeline. "He has a house full of suspicious robots and he builds giant steam-powered octopi."

"Sounds mad to me, miss," said the sergeant. "Where can I find him?"

I wasn't sure about this. I'm all for bold moves, but there was an air of heavy-handedness about Sergeant Stock's approach. One uses guile to catch a criminal mastermind, not brute force. And by the way he'd just whipped out his truncheon, I had the impression that brute force was Sergeant Stock's forte.

"I don't think you can arrest anyone for a country house murder without having a proper *dénouement* first," I said. "It's just not done."

"A what-ment, sir?" said the sergeant.

"*Dénouement*. It's the bit where the detective invites all the suspects into the drawing room and spends an hour pointing the finger at people and explaining who did what, how, and why."

"Don't like the sound of that either," said the sergeant. "I be not one for public speaking."

"You wouldn't have to," I said. "I'd do the talking for you. I'm a bit of a consulting detective, don't you know? You'd be there to do the arresting at the end. They usually try to make a run for it."

"Ho!" said the sergeant. "That sounds more like it! When we be having this *dénouement*?"

"Soon," I said. "I need to collect a little more evidence first. *Dénouements* have to be done just so or the judge throws out all the evidence as inadmissible."

"May I suggest, sergeant," said Reeves. "That while Mr Baskerville-Smythe is collecting evidence in the country house murder of Sir Robert, that you concentrate on the apprehension of Mr Selden?"

The sergeant gave his chin another rub. "You sure it be not too much trouble for you, Mr Baskerville-Smythe?"

"No trouble whatsoever, sergeant."

"Then that be settled, sir."

~

I thought that went well. It's often a difficult relationship between the constabulary and the consulting detective.

Sergeant Stock left soon after – heading for the village of Grimdark in the back of Tom's cart. He'd decided against riding across the moor to Princetown.

"I be not crossing that moor again by horse," he'd told us.

"I'll wade across the Angst if I haves to. Once I reach Grim-dark, I'll telegram the prison for reinforcements. I'll have a dozen warders here by sunset. Mark my words, Selden won't be on the loose for long."

It started to rain so Emmeline, Reeves and I retired to the Hall, which was positively buzzing. Lady Julia had the servants running around preparing the Hall for mourning – covering every mirror in black crepe, tying black ribbons to every chair leg, and making a large yew wreath draped with black ribbons for the front door.

"Since my nephew appears incapable of honouring his family obligations, I suppose *I* must arrange it all," she'd told Berrymore, before promptly delegating all the arranging to him.

We kept out of everyone's way and headed up the servants' staircase to my room. I'd had an idea, and felt the need to give it an airing.

"As I see it," I said, hands behind back and doing a little pacing between the chimney breast and the window. "Finding this Lottie has to be our priority. If she killed Sir Robert, and the evidence appears to point that way, then she knows who ordered her to do it. Remember what happened to Pasco. As soon as he'd played his part, that was it. Biff! And a good deal of unpleasantness in the turbine area. So why is Lottie still alive? Is it because she's skittish and hoofs it into the mire every time anyone comes near? Or is her job not finished?"

I could see that Emmeline was impressed. "There's someone else she's been ordered to kill! I bet it's Henry."

"What do you think, Reeves?" I asked.

"I find your reasoning sound, sir, though, I doubt she is the intended instrument for a second murder."

"Why?" I asked.

"Because she no longer has the blowpipe, sir. One would think that if two murders had been planned Miss Lottie would have been furnished with a blowpipe and two darts. One certainly wouldn't expect that, after the success of the first murder, that the blowpipe would have been discarded."

"Perhaps she got cold feet?" said Emmeline. "Or realised

it was wrong and threw away the blowpipe."

I liked the sound of that. "In which case the murderer will definitely be after her. We have to find her first."

But how? I did some more pacing while Reeves mixed me a drink.

"We know she lives at the hut circles," said Emmeline. "Couldn't we hide nearby and wait for her to arrive?"

I couldn't see us approaching anywhere near the hut circle without being spotted by the other feral automata. And they'd certainly warn Lottie.

"Bait is what we need," I said. "Something that would make Lottie come to us."

"A new dress?" said Emmeline. "That black one she has must be caked in mud around the hems."

"No, not a new dress, new *feet!*" I said, spilling my drink in the excitement. "We'll leave a note for her on the mire gate. 'Dear Lottie, dashed sorry to hear about the cloven feet. We can get them removed and your old feet put back on. Call at the Hall at your earliest convenience. Ask for Roderick.'"

"That's perfect, Reggie!" said Emmeline.

"It's using the psychology of the individual, Emmie. Find out what Lottie needs the most and offer to provide it," I said.

I thought Reeves would be pleased – being very big on the p. of the i. – but I could tell by his look that he had an objection. I braced myself for it. "What is it, Reeves?"

"I fear it unlikely that Miss Lottie can read, sir. If you remember–"

I did remember. "Do you have a better suggestion, Reeves?" I said, a trifle nettled.

"As it happens, sir, there is something that we know Miss Lottie needs even more than new feet, and that she will come to the Hall for tonight."

"What?" I was agog.

"Steam, sir."

I put my drink down. The man was without peer.

"Do you really think she'd risk coming back here after the murder?" said Emmeline.

"Where else would she go, miss? Without steam she will cease to function."

"Stapleford has a steam outlet," said Emmeline.

"The lack of cloven footprints in the mire path at High Dudgeon would indicate she doesn't frequent Stapleford's boiler room, miss."

"The feral automata did say they avoided Stapleford," I said. "And the quarry too."

"Indeed, sir. I would suggest we hide in the old stable block tonight and await Miss Lottie's arrival."

~

I downed my drink and we shot off to the old stable block post-haste. Emmeline and I looked for a suitable spot to hide later while Reeves availed himself of the steam outlet pipe. The moment he began to unbutton his shirt, I had to look away. Some things are private. I'd once had to help Stiffy Trussington-Thripp connect an unconscious Reeves to a steam hose and it hadn't been a pleasant experience for any of us.

Emmeline and I climbed a ladder into the loft. There was a good deal of loose hay piled up. And the loft only extended over half the stable block, so we had a pretty good view of the floor below. All in all, an excellent place to hide for a couple of hours.

"We'll have to rearrange the hay a little if we're not going to be seen," said Emmeline.

"We could always lie down and cover ourselves with it," I said.

"What *are* you suggesting, Mr Worcester?" said Emmeline, putting on her Lady Julia voice.

"Camouflage, Miss Dreadnought. My motives are pure."

"Not too pure, I hope."

I coughed, Reeves being otherwise engaged.

~

Everything was in place. Emmeline, Reeves and I were to meet by the back door just before eight. We'd use the servants' staircase to avoid the others, and I'd have a word with Henry beforehand to explain our impending absence from the dinner table. He'd tell the others that Emmeline and I were poorly, and had retired to our rooms to read improving books.

As plans went, this one was foolproof, and Reeves had barely a hand in it!

The first crack in the plan came when Henry suggested he came along too. As head of the household he felt it was only right. If anyone was going to beard his father's killer it should be him. I could see the hayloft giving way under the weight of onlookers. If Henry came along, Ida would follow. Which meant her father as well, which, in turn, would pique the interest of the other dinner guests and they'd all down forks and traipse out to the stable block to see what all the fuss was about.

A firm hand was required.

"It's possible the murderer – the chap who gave Lottie the blowpipe and ordered her to do the deed – will be present at the dinner table tonight," I said. "We can't let them know anything is afoot. And three of us absent from the dinner table would do just that."

Henry reluctantly agreed.

The second crack in the plan came just as we were about to set out. Reeves and I were loitering by the back door, checking our pocket watches and muttering. Well, I was muttering. Reeves doesn't mutter. He disapproves of it strongly.

"Perhaps I should attempt to locate Miss Emmeline, sir?" he said as I added pacing to the muttering.

Off he went. And back he came five minutes later with disturbing news.

"Miss Emmeline is taking dinner, sir."

"What?"

"Dinner, sir. She is seated next to Lady Julia."

I began to harbour grave doubts about my ears. "Did you say Emmeline's in the dining room ... with Lady Julia?"

"With everyone, sir. She is seated between Lady Julia and Mr Stapleford. She appears somewhat disquieted, sir."

I gasped. "Do they have a gun on her?

"Not that I observed, sir."

I was baffled. Emmeline wouldn't miss a sleuthing engagement. "Has she left a note, Reeves? Slipped it under my door perhaps?"

"No, sir. She didn't leave a note in her room either."

Well this was rummy. "What do you make of it, Reeves? Is she in danger?"

"I find it hard to believe that anyone would attempt anything untoward in a room full of witnesses, sir."

The more I thought about it, the more I thought that this had to be some attempt to divert us from our apprehension of Lottie.

"We must stick with our plan, Reeves. Questioning Lottie is the priority."

~

Reeves and I hid in the hayloft. I chose a spot by the ladder where I could lie down and see the steam hose. Reeves sat on a bale out of sight at the back, adamant that lying down played havoc with his gyroscopes, and that hay and a pressed suit did not mix. I had more progressive views on hay and loftwear and covered myself with the stuff.

An age passed. Silas, the under gardener with all the pruning and mowing attachments, was there, keeping the boiler well-fired. Every now and then he'd motor over to the furnace carrying a log, toss it in, and give the fire a good riddle. I assumed he must have topped himself up earlier, though I couldn't see where his belly button was – not having an obvious belly.

Then the door creaked open and I froze, not daring to breathe as I waited for the figure to come into view.

It wasn't Lottie. It was one of the other feral automata. He connected himself up to the steam hose and I looked away.

Another age passed. This time I didn't dare move in case he spotted me. It was dark and I was covered in hay, but there was some light coming from the furnace, and I was worried that any rustling sound might carry. The only other sound was the occasional crackle from the furnace and the gentle hiss of the steam hose.

Eventually he left and I took the opportunity to have a

little shuffle and scratch the odd itch. I'd begun to harbour doubts that I was alone in the hay – suspecting that half of Devonshire's beetles were nestling up beside me.

Then the door opened again, accompanied this time by a swishing sound, and the unmistakable silhouette of Lottie in her long black dress.

TWENTY-THREE

The plan had been to wait until Lottie had connected herself to the steam hose before springing from our hiding place and barring the door. But that involved watching Lottie unfasten her dress somewhat, a task which Emmeline was to have undertaken. I decided to avert my eyes and count to one hundred instead.

On one hundred and one, I sprang like a well-dressed tiger and flew down the ladder.

Lottie screamed.

"Don't be alarmed," I said, as she struggled to disconnect herself from the steam hose.

"We mean you no harm, Miss Lottie," said Reeves appearing by the top of the ladder. "Mr Baskerville-Smythe desires to ask you a few questions. That is all."

"That's right," I said. "It won't take long then you're free to go."

Lottie succeeded in freeing herself from the hose and turned to face me. "I'm not going to Quarrywood! I've seen what you did to Annie. I'll *die* before you turn me into a giant octopus!"

"We wouldn't dream of turning anyone into a giant octopus, would we, Reeves?"

"No, sir."

"I don't believe you," she said. "Stand aside and let me pass ... or ... or I'll open the furnace and burn this place down."

This was not going as well as I'd hoped.

"Do that thing with your ears, Reeves."

"No, sir."

I have to say I was disappointed in Reeves' lack of feudal spirit. Would Watson have refused Holmes' request to blow steam from his nose? I think not.

"No need for fires, Lottie," I said. "Reeves here is an automaton too, and I've never turned him into any kind of octopus – not even a small one – have I, Reeves?"

"No, sir. We are guests at the Hall, miss. We have no connection to Quarrywood, and desire only information as to what occurred in the vicinity of the mire gate yesterday evening."

That seemed to calm her down a little.

"What's that got to do with me?" she asked.

"We saw you there last night," I said. "Standing over the body–"

"I didn't kill him! He was dead already. I saw him fall and ran over to help."

"Did you see how he died?" I asked.

"He had a heart attack, didn't he? He was running back to the Hall and suddenly fell."

"We know about the blowpipe, Lottie," I said.

"What blowpipe?"

It was too dark to see her face that well – and it's always difficult to judge an automaton's reactions – but I didn't get the impression from her voice that she was lying.

"I think it best to commence from the beginning, miss," said Reeves. "How did you come by the black dress you're wearing?"

"I didn't steal it! I found it hanging on the mire gate two nights ago."

"Was there a note with it?" I asked.

"No."

"Did you see who left the dress on the gate?"

"No. It was the middle of the night when I found it."

"Was there a reason you were at the mire gate last night at precisely eight of the clock, miss?" asked Reeves.

"I needed to top up my pressure."

"But why not wait until dark, miss?" said Reeves. "Were you not more likely to be seen at such an early hour?"

"It was foggy. And the family dine at eight. No one should

have been about."

"What did you observe when you reached the mire gate, miss?"

"I saw *him* – the man who died – he was waiting by the gate. I don't think he saw me. I ducked down the moment I noticed him."

"Was he alone?" I asked.

"Yes."

"Then what happened?"

"He walked back inside the grounds. I wasn't certain he'd left, so I waited a while, then I ran to a gap in the hedge by the mire gate where you can see into the Hall grounds without being seen. He hadn't gone. He was on the path. Waiting."

"Did you see anyone else?" I asked.

"No. He was alone."

"Then what happened?"

"He suddenly cried out and clutched his neck."

"Which way was he facing when he cried out, miss?"

"Towards the gate, I think."

"You say you didn't see anyone," I said. "But what about an orang-utan? He might have been hiding in the wood close to the spot where Sir Robert cried out?"

"I didn't see the ape. I've seen him on other occasions though. We all have. He's often in here at night. He watches us."

"Did you see or hear *anything* unusual in that area of woodland close to where Sir Robert cried out, miss?"

Lottie paused a good long while.

"You'll think me crazy," she said.

"I very much doubt it," I said. "Reeves and I have seen the most extraordinary things. Nothing you say can surprise us."

"I saw a tree move," said Lottie. "Or maybe a bush. I know it's crazy, but as soon as Sir Robert dropped his gun and started to run back to the Hall, I saw it move."

"Move as in sway?" I asked.

"No. Move as in walk. It was quite swift. It went deeper into the woods and disappeared into the fog. Sir Robert had fallen by then. I went to see if I could help, but he'd stopped breathing, and then you appeared, and I ran off."

A lesser man may have boggled at the mention of a tree being implicated in a murder, but not Reginald Worcester.

"Would you recognise this tree if you saw it again?" I asked.

"I think it was yew."

"Me?"

"No, yew."

"You think it was Reeves?"

Reeves coughed. "I think Miss Lottie was referring to the tree belonging to the genus *taxus*, sir. Commonly referred to as the yew tree."

"Ah."

"That's right. It was about six feet tall and conical in appearance."

"Any distinguishing branches?"

Reeves coughed. I think this tree business had unnerved him.

"Most odd," I said. "Can one reanimate a tree, Reeves, and turn it homicidal?"

"Unlikely, sir. I rather-"

"I wouldn't be so dismissive, Reeves. A year ago I would have cast scorn upon anyone suggesting a deceased relative could be brought back to life. Or a pig reassembled from prime parts of deceased porkers. But we've seen both, Reeves. Why not a tree?"

"I think a simpler answer is that a person was disguising themselves as a tree, sir."

"Ah. No need for an identity parade of suspicious conifers then?"

"No, sir."

"Did this tree you saw have legs?" I asked.

"I didn't see any. Its branches brushed the ground. I couldn't see how it moved. I've seen so many strange creations at Quarrywood and here at the Hall that I didn't know what to think."

"Quite. See, Reeves? One shouldn't disregard a tree if a likely motive turns up. I know I'd cut up rough if someone tried to give me a bit of a prune."

"Indeed, sir. If I may, I'd like to ask Miss Lottie some questions regarding Mr Stapleford."

"Ask away, Reeves."

"I don't have anything to do with him," said Lottie. "He sees us as machines for his amusement. He's the one who took Annie and turned her into that ... *octopus!*"

"Have you ever met any of his household automata, miss?"

"No. I've seen them on the moor. Some of them have come to our camp, but I keep my distance. They work for their master and they know *exactly* what he does. They aid him, I'm sure."

"Have you heard of Falconbridge, his American automaton, miss?"

"No."

Reeves' question gave me an idea. "You speak very well for an automaton, Lottie," I said. "Were you made in America by any chance?"

"No, I am a lady's maid by manufacture. I am programmed for conversation."

Our questions exhausted, we left Lottie to avail herself of the steam outlet and headed back to the Hall. We were in mid-ankle when I noticed it – a black shape on the wall of the south wing.

I stopped and goggled. There was enough light from the moon to see that the black shape was a woman in a long black dress. And she was climbing down the very rope we'd seen earlier tied around the chimney stack. In the very spot that Pasco had climbed down two nights earlier!

It had to be another Theodosia. The time was right. I checked my pocket watch. It was just after midnight. And here was our chance to apprehend this latest 'ghost' and find out who put them up to it.

"Come on, Reeves," I whispered. "Time to bag us a ghost."

TWENTY-FOUR

I was ready to spring when the ghost turned and...

"Emmie?"

"Reggie, what are you doing here? Have you caught Lottie yet?"

"Never mind what I'm doing here. What are you doing climbing down a rope disguised as a ghost? Did Stapleford make you do it?"

"What *are* you talking about?" said Emmeline. "Oh! The black dress. That's Lady Julia's fault. She insisted I wear black to dinner. She came to my room when I was leaving to join you, and made me change into full mourning! I couldn't get away. She left her maid with me to make sure there wasn't an inch of me not covered in black crepe. I've only just managed to escape. I was sure she'd have told the footmen to bar the doors to me so I came via the roof. Have I missed anything?"

I was in awe.

"Weren't you worried climbing down from such a height?" I asked.

"Not at all. If a murderer can do it, so can I. And if I had fallen and died, at least I was dressed for it. Now, what news of Lottie?"

I told Emmeline all.

"Do you believe her?" asked Emmeline.

"I do," I said. "What about you, Reeves?"

"I think a person wishing to fabricate a story, sir, would have chosen a more credible one."

Sneaking Emmeline back into the house was but the work of a moment for a seasoned heart attack feigner like myself.

As soon as Witheridge unlocked the back door I stumbled inside, clutched the old ticker and did the full swoon, with pirouette, onto the flagstones. Reeves sent Witheridge to the kitchen to fetch a glass of water, and Emmeline beetled past us and up the servants' staircase.

I didn't stay up much longer myself. I found Henry, gave him the potted highlights of my meeting with Lottie, and headed upstairs.

~

I was already awake when Reeves arrived with the early morning oolong.

"Anything to report, Reeves?" I asked as he drew back the curtains.

"Sergeant Stock and his warders arrived before breakfast, sir. Apparently the River Angst is now fordable and a temporary bridge is expected to be completed later today."

"Where's the sergeant now? He's not rounding up the local mad scientists, I hope?"

"No, sir. The sergeant and his men are currently patrolling the local area. I believe they intend to search every barn, shepherd's hut, thicket and outbuilding within three miles of the Hall."

I took a long sip of the bracing oolong. I felt I needed to be fully braced before telling Reeves what I'd been musing over for the past fifteen minutes. When it comes to pouring cold water over other chap's plans, Reeves was Jack Frost the Eskimo ice chandler.

"I've been thinking about what you said yesterday viz. Lupin not being able to talk."

"Indeed, sir?"

"Indeed, Reeves. What proof do we have that he can't speak?"

"He's an orang-utan, sir?"

"Ah, but is he an *ordinary* orang-utan? What if he's a promethean like the Colossus of Blackwater? You remember the Colossus, Reeves? The giant pig assembled from the prime parts of prize-winning porkers?"

"I remember him well, sir."

"Then you will recall that the Colossus could speak. We never worked out how or why, but somewhere in the process a Scotsman had been added to the mix. You see where I'm going with this, Reeves?"

"I believe so, sir."

"The pig is not a species renowned for its repartee, Reeves."

"No, sir."

"One doesn't go to the fat stock show to hear prime porkers recite poetry. Or perform duets from Gilbert and Sullivan."

"No, sir."

"And yet, we encountered one that could speak. If a pig, I say, why not an orang-utan?"

"Shall I lay out your clothes for breakfast, sir?"

"Reeves, you are changing the subject."

"I apologise, sir. I find myself a little distracted."

"Distracted, Reeves? It's not your pressure, is it?"

"No, sir, I rather fear your life may be in danger."

I nearly spilled my tea.

"What? Explain, Reeves."

"I was considering the various motives for Sir Robert's murder, sir. Now that we know the estate is entailed, the question of *cui bono* is clearer. Sir Henry is the only beneficiary. But who inherits the estate should Sir Henry be killed?"

"Lady Julia?" I said.

"Lady Julia is not a blood relative, sir. And of the wrong gender to inherit the title."

Who else was left? From my brief perusal of *Who's Who*, the Baskerville-Smythe clan were pretty short on relatives above ground.

"Is there a suspicious third cousin looking to be considerably less removed than hitherto, Reeves?"

"According to the current edition of *Who's Who*, sir, there is a second cousin twice removed. The Reverend Archibald Biggar of the parish of Blubberthorpe in the county of Yorkshire. But he is no longer Sir Henry's heir."

I sat up. "He's dead?"

"No, sir. His position as heir was usurped two days ago ... by you, sir."

"Me? But ... I'm not really Roderick."

"Quite, sir, but only you, Miss Emmeline and I are cognisant of that fact. The murderer – be he Mr Edison, the Reverend Biggar, or whomsoever – will regard you as Sir Henry's heir."

I didn't like this at all. Most of our theories cast Sir Henry as 'next victim.' Was I now his stand-in?

"This is bad, Reeves. Do you think I should start wearing a disguise?"

"No, sir. But I think a change in strategy is called for. Instead of following clues, I think we should endeavour to lay a trap."

"You have a plan?"

"Not yet, sir. I have the bait, but little else."

I quailed somewhat at the word 'bait.' Reeves' plans were rather like icebergs – things of beauty, with large hazardous portions hidden below the surface.

"I'm not the bait, am I, Reeves?"

"No, sir. Sir Henry is. The problem, though, is finding a suitable trap. Ideally, we need to present the murderer with an opportunity to kill Sir Henry that is so enticing they cannot resist. We then lie in wait for the murderer to arrive and apprehend them before they can harm Sir Henry."

I don't know where Reeves finds these plans, but even half-formed, they are still things of beauty.

"It's perfect, Reeves," I said.

"I fear it may be impracticable, sir. With Sir Henry spending most of his day at Quarrywood and travelling back and forth in an open carriage, he presents an easy target. Especially as there is no shortage of guns. The footmen hand them out to everyone. With so many excellent opportunities to shoot Sir Henry and escape undetected, I fear it will be impossible to create the definitive opportunity that we require to entice our quarry into our trap."

"Reeves," I said, waving a dismissive hand. "Listen to the young master. You forget we are dealing with a criminal mastermind. Criminal masterminds don't *shoot* anyone.

That's the realm of the *common* criminal. These are the uncommon ones. They're theatrical. They use blowpipes and poison darts. They're more likely to sabotage one of Henry's scenes by smuggling in a real Lizard Man to fight him."

"Lizard Men are not real, sir."

"They're not?"

"No, sir."

"Well, something similar then – like switching a rubber dagger for the real thing."

Reeves suddenly froze, not even an eyebrow twitched. His eyes stared, fixed on a point somewhere above my head-board. I wasn't sure if he'd run out of steam or seen a spider.

"Reeves? Are you all right?"

Answer came there none.

I put down the oolong. And fought a momentary urge to reach forward and wiggle Reeves' ears.

Fortunately, Reeves burst back into life – using the most refined and restrained definition of the word 'burst' – before any inappropriate ear-hand activity had occurred.

"I have it, sir," he said, struggling manfully to regain control of his eyebrows. "Your suggestion of using a scene from Sir Henry's moving picture has provided me with the answer."

"It has?"

"It has, sir. The success of the plan depends upon three criteria being met. One, the opportunity presented to the murderer must be such that they cannot possibly ignore it. Two, news of the opportunity must be widely disseminated to make sure that all the suspects are aware of it. And, three, the locale where the sabotage is to take place must be both secluded enough to allow the murderer to feel safe, and yet provide sufficient cover for us to lie in wait."

I have said it many times, but it bears repeating. The man is a genius. When Babbage was handing out little grey cells, he didn't stint when he came to Reeves.

"What scene do you have in mind, Reeves?" I asked.

"A rope scene, sir. I believe it will satisfy all three criteria if we tie a rope to a stout tree on the cliff top overlooking

Quarrywood, and throw it over the cliff for you and Sir Henry to climb down."

"What? Wait a minute, Reeves. What am I doing on this rope?"

"Dangling, sir. In order for the plan to succeed we must ensure that the opportunity is such that the murderer could not possibly resist. The chance to sabotage the rope and kill both Sir Henry and yourself at the same time would, I think, be irresistible."

"Reeves, have you slipped a cog? Any plan that involves Reginald Worcester dangling from a cliff top waiting for the rope to snap is a plan with a giant flaw."

"Indeed, sir. But the plan is to catch the murderer in the act of fraying the rope or loosening the knot. Ergo you will never be on the rope. The rope scene is to be announced and prepared, but never enacted."

"Run that past me again, Reeves."

"Sir Henry will announce the new scene today, sir. I will spread the word amongst the servants, whilst you, Sir Henry and Miss Emmeline spread the word elsewhere. The rope will be tied to the tree this afternoon and left overnight ready for the scene to be played first thing tomorrow morning."

I was beyond awe. It was the most perfect plan I'd ever heard. I'd have to give the cliff top a thorough reconnoitring first, but I couldn't imagine there'd be a complete dearth of good sized rocks to hide behind. And the night would give us cover too.

"I'll buttonhole Henry straight after breakfast," I said.

~

Catching Henry on his own was not that easy. Ida was a veritable limpet. She sat next to him at breakfast and accompanied him upstairs when they left to get changed. I had to hang back and wait for her to turn off towards her room.

And hope Lady Julia didn't emerge from the dining room. She'd been discussing food for the funeral with Mrs Berrymore so I thought I had a good minute or two.

Emmeline joined me on the stairs as I stood there

pretending to look at a portrait. "Who are we following – Henry or Ida?" she whispered.

"Henry. Reeves has a plan."

"I bet it's a pip."

"As Reeves would say. 'It is the apis's patellas.'"

We gave Ida another couple of seconds, then beetled after Henry. We caught up with him just as he was opening the door to his room.

"We have a plan, Henry," I said. "And we need your help."

I waited until the bedroom door was closed before spilling all about Reeves's plan. I'd thought it perfect, but Henry wasn't so sure.

"One can't just slip in a new scene without adding some sort of context," said Henry. "Audiences don't like being confused. Why are we climbing down this rope?"

"To escape from ... a Lizard Man?" I suggested.

"That'll work," said Henry. "This Lizard Man... No, three Lizard Men have trapped us on the cliff top. We see the rope and start to climb down... No, I think we need more danger."

"More danger than dangling from a rope two hundred feet off the ground?" I said.

"This is Quarrywood, Roderick. Our audiences expect bigger, better and scarier."

"You could have a giant octopus suddenly appear at the bottom of the rope," said Emmeline. "And three Lizard Men trying to chew through the rope at the top."

"That's more like it!" said Henry. "So we climb down the rope and throw ourselves on the giant octopus."

"Who has a sword in each tentacle," said Emmeline "Except the one he's strangling Ida with."

I had the feeling that Reeves – and possibly Ida – might disapprove of some of these later additions, but the essence of the plan was agreed. Henry would announce the new scene this morning and it would be the talk of the parish by lunchtime.

~

Emmeline shot off to her room to change out of her enforced mourning wear leaving me to head back to my room alone. As I toddled along a corridor flanked with the portraits of generations of Baskerville-Smythes, the Worcester brain began to stir.

I told Reeves the moment I bounced into the room.

"I've been thinking about inheritance, Reeves."

"Indeed, sir?" said Reeves, who was busy ironing my shoelaces.

"A bit of a coincidence, don't you think, that here we are looking at inheritance as a motive for murder when the parish is chock full of Baskerville-Smythe descendants? All that over-familiarity business."

"Titles can only be passed to legitimate heirs, sir."

"Ah, but have you ever read *Belted by the Boot Boy*? It was the sequel to *Sporrans at Dawn*."

"I have not had that experience, sir."

"It's all about this servant, the eponymous boot boy, who inherited an earldom – hence the belted earl reference."

"I had wondered, sir."

"He came into the title when Lady Alice, the heroine, discovered an old marriage certificate in the library proving that her great great great uncle had married the scullery maid, thus legitimising their issue and making the boot boy the heir to the earldom. Bit of a tear-jerker, Reeves. The title was about to go to a complete rotter who kept three ex-wives locked in the attic and had designs upon Lady Alice."

"You posit that such a marriage certificate may exist in this case, sir?"

"I certainly do, Reeves. Be it real or forged, I posit most strongly. In fact, I think I may have a rummage in the library. Tell Emmeline to meet me there."

~

I thought I'd start with the books first. Missing wills and certificates always turned up hidden between the pages of books. I'd lift them out one at a time and give them a good shake. It shouldn't take long.

That was my plan. But the moment I opened the library door, I was struck by an unexpected opportunity. There, sitting on a table, was Lupin, and the two of us were alone.

TWENTY-FIVE

Here was my chance to find out if Lupin could talk! No one else was in the room. No witness to make him think twice about speaking. And if Lupin was the criminal mastermind that I suspected him to be, here was his chance to gloat – something no master criminal could ever resist.

And I'd make it even more irresistible. I'd speak in a Scots accent – just like the Colossus of Blackwater had.

I locked eyes with the simian Moriarty and approached.

"Hoots, Lupin, mon, och aye the noo, what?" I said.

Lupin may not have responded – he even tried to feign disinterest by picking his feet – but I knew that, deep down below all that fur, he was itching to bandy words with the great detective.

I tried again. "Wha hae, Lupin, auld haggis. 'Twas a braw bricht moonlicht nicht for the wee sleekit beasties."

That almost did it. He stopped picking his feet and gave me a look that would have uncurled a banana at twelve paces. But then, just as I was sure he was about to break, another voice piped up from the other side of the room. Lady Julia! She'd been behind a bookcase, and I hadn't seen her!

"He's an orang-utan, dear, not Scottish. I know the ginger hair can be a little confusing to someone of your limited intellect."

I had to respond. "I *know* he's an orang-utan, Aunt Julia. I was merely testing him to see if he was a promethean. I've seen promethean animals before that can speak."

"Were these animals pink and extremely large by any chance?" she asked.

"The one I talked to certainly was."

"Ye gods. And what, pray, did this pink elephant tell you to do? Come to Baskerville Hall and make a nuisance of yourself?"

"It wasn't an elephant. It was a giant pig."

The ancient a. levelled both eyeballs at me.

"A giant pig," she said. "Do you see it now? Or does it only appear after you've had a few?"

It's bad enough being chaffed by one's own aunts without having one's made up aunts weighing in. Next time I adopted a new persona I'd make sure they were an only child in a long line of only children.

"No, I do *not* see it now. I haven't seen it since it ran off with my cousin's fiancée."

In retrospect that probably wasn't the best thing to have said. On several levels. It may have been true, but sometimes truth can be open to unfortunate interpretations.

"Which cousin?" asked Lady Julia, her eyes narrowing alarmingly.

I don't know about you, but I find it difficult to invent Spanish Christian names under duress. And the only Spanish name brave enough to tilt at Lady Julia's narrowed gaze was Don Quixote.

"My cousin Donald," I said. "The son of ... my mother's sister."

"H'm," said Lady J, both eyes still the merest of horizontal slits.

As if that wasn't bad enough, my left hand was suddenly grabbed by Lupin, and I was pulled towards him. I steeled myself for another round of wrestling, but Lupin seemed more interested in my hair. He stood up on the table, and gave the Worcester locks a thorough inspection. I thought it best not to move. I wasn't sure what Lupin was looking for, but he appeared to find something particularly toothsome and put it in his mouth!

I decided it time to take a brisk step away from the table. But Lupin took umbrage and leaped off the table onto my shoulders, knocking me over. Wrestling ensued, with quite a bit of rolling. It wasn't exactly Holmes and Moriarty at the Reichenbach Falls, but it had its moments. And a fair amount of water. The latter provided by Lady Julia when she emptied the liquid contents of a large vase of flowers over the pair of us.

Lupin squawked and rolled off me, before beetling off to seek refuge on top of a pelmet. I struggled to my feet. I had a left ear full of water and a soaked collar.

"You are certifiable," said Lady Julia, a fistful of flowers in one hand, a vase in the other. "How you have managed to survive beyond childhood is beyond me."

I thought about a spirited rejoinder, but I was a chap with water dripping down his neck. And a sore shin where I'd collided with a chair leg.

Thankfully, the door then opened, and in came the cavalry. Though the cavalry's face dropped the moment she saw Lady Julia.

"Oh, and here comes Lily," said Lady Julia, her voice ladled with enough sarcasm to float an acerbic battleship. "What a surprise. I am still unsure as to whether you're his accomplice or his nurse, dear. Why are you no longer dressed in mourning?"

"I'm appearing in Henry's moving picture this morning," said Emmeline.

Lady Julia snorted.

"We'd better get going, Roderick," said Emmeline. "Henry is leaving any moment."

I couldn't shoot out the door fast enough.

~

Emmeline and I fled back to my room. I had to change. A detective cannot detect in wet clothes.

Emmeline looked out the window while I towelled myself dry and slipped into a replacement shirt and jacket.

"Does that mean Lupin isn't a promethean?" asked Emmeline after I'd given her an edited account of the Worcester Lupin struggle on the Reichenbach carpet.

"I'm not sure," I said. "He'd have known we weren't alone in the library. And he could have all manner of scars hidden under that fur. He might be assembled from the worst parts of the most fiendish orang-utans in history."

"Most unlikely, sir," said Reeves as he helped me with my jacket. "And even if he were, he would still lack the power of speech."

"You forget the Scotsman, Reeves," I said.

"From what I have read upon the subject, sir, I believe the Colossus of Blackwater to be somewhat of an anomaly. Will you be requiring your walking boots?"

I sat on the bed while Reeves laced my boots. There's nothing like freshly ironed shoelaces to put a spring in one's step.

"I've been thinking about tonight, sir."

"What about tonight, Reeves?"

"It is essential that the rope is kept under continual observation from the moment it is tied to the tree, sir. But it is also essential that there are no unexpected absences from tonight's dinner party lest the murderer's suspicions be aroused."

I could see that Reeves had a point. If Henry, Emmeline and I all absented ourselves from the family trough eyebrows would be raised. And Ida would probably come looking for us – certain that Henry and Emmeline were having a secret assignation.

"You have a plan, Reeves?"

"I do, sir. I shall take the first watch and remain on the cliff top. Sir Henry, Miss Emmeline and yourself should attend dinner and leave separately soon after. I would suggest that you meet in the library, from whence you can leave via the window."

"I'll have to change first," said Emmeline. "I can't skulk across the moor in crepe and swishing petticoats. And I'll need walking boots and a cloak. And a blanket if we're going to be sitting on damp grass."

"Indeed, miss. It is also essential, sir, that Sir Henry stands down the footmen guarding the external doors. The footman in the hallway would observe the three of you entering the library, and the footman by the back door would observe your usage of the servants' staircase in outside apparel. Footmen are notorious gossips. The wrong word within hearing of the murderer could endanger everything."

"I see your point Reeves," I said. "But what about Selden? I'd feel bad if we came back to the Hall to find everyone eaten."

"There is nothing in Mr Selden's past, sir, to suggest he has ever broken into another person's home. *We* would be in more danger from Selden than anyone who remained at the Hall."

"And we'll have guns, won't we?" said Emmeline. "I *do* get to carry one tonight, don't I?"

Reeves coughed. "I think two guns will be sufficient tonight, miss. One for Sir Henry and one for myself."

~

Reeves shimmered off to spread the word of tomorrow's rope scene to the servants, and Emmeline and I ankled downstairs to catch up with Henry and his party before they left for the studio.

The dangling Baskerville-Smythes scene was the *only* topic of c. on the entire journey to the studio.

"Are you sure you want to do this, Henry?" asked Dr Morrow. "We could dress up two prometheans to look just like you."

"No," said Henry. "Our audience expects verisimilitude. Besides, Roderick and I are used to danger."

"Rather," I said. "When one's wrestled crocodiles up and down the Orinoco one becomes inured to danger."

"Well, I don't think you should do it, Henry," said Ida. "Wasn't it supposed to be Lily swinging from the cliff top?"

"I wouldn't dream of spoiling Henry's and Roderick's fun," said Emmeline. "But it *was* kind of you to think of me, Ida. If anyone could tempt me to swing from a rope it would be you."

I kept a firm hold on Emmeline's arm for the rest of the journey.

Henry had Tom stop the carriage on the approach to the quarry, so everyone could get out and walk up the hill to the cliff top.

It was a fairly gentle climb to the top. The hill was more of a mound than one of those Alpine affairs. Ida made somewhat of a meal of the climb though, stumbling and clutching progressively tighter to poor Henry. I thought he might have to carry her the last hundred yards.

And I did notice plenty of cover. There weren't that many trees – a half dozen stunted and wind-blown specimens – but there was a wealth of good sized rocky outcrops and scrubby bushes. And the views were good in all directions. One could see the Hall, the mire, High Dudgeon Farm. No one could creep up on us unseen.

I ventured a little way towards the cliff edge. It looked like some large creature had removed half the hill with a single bite. I could see the studio buildings below and what looked like half of Devonshire spread out towards the horizon.

"Sooner you than me," said Morrow, appearing beside me. "Are you both sure you want to do this?"

"Can't wait," I said.

"I think this rock looks best," said Henry. "We can loop the rope around it. It's tall, well-weathered. There are no sharp edges to fray the rope. What do you think, Roderick?"

My one thought was that the cliff looked a dashed sight higher from above than it had done from below. I was standing six feet from the edge and that was close enough.

"Roderick?" repeated Henry.

"What? Oh, yes, it looks an admirable rock to me," I said.

~

Emmeline and I spent the rest of the morning watching various scenes from *The Creature from 20,000 Leagues Under the Quarry* being filmed. It all seemed great fun, if a little confusing. Henry seemed to spend most of his time rescuing Ida and Lily from the clutches of assorted Lizard Men and giant octopi. And Ida and Lily spent most of their time screaming, fleeing and tripping over just as it looked as though they might escape.

"I think if I were going on an expedition 20,000 leagues under a quarry I'd wear sensible shoes," said Emmeline.

"For the fleeing and climbing, of course," I said. "But I think one would have to pack one's evening wear. One might encounter a subterranean civilisation and be invited to a ball."

Emmeline laughed. "Do Lizard Men dance, do you think? They look a little top heavy to me."

"I suspect their tails would get in the way too."

"They'd have to hold them off the floor with one hand like you do with a train."

We managed to have a quiet word with Henry just after luncheon, to pass on Reeves' additional instructions re: the evening sleuthing. And, once more, Henry tried to persuade Emmeline to reprise her role as the Lizard-Man-Slaying Amazon.

Emmeline declined. "I wouldn't mind *being* a Lizard Man, though," she said.

"Are you sure? The costume's awfully heavy," said Henry.

"I could give it a go. With Ida tripping over so much, I wouldn't have to move that fast."

I think the costume proved to be a good deal heavier than Emmeline had imagined. She didn't so much chase Ida, as stagger after her – one slow lurch at a time. In an odd way, it looked more menacing, giving the onlooker the impression that, although not the fleetest of her species, she was an exceedingly heavy and purposeful Lizard Man who hadn't eaten for several days and was not about to let her next meal escape.

That is until she lurched a little too far, overbalanced, and toppled over, rolling onto her back.

Ida then stopped screaming, and hurried over to the fallen Lizard Man. I thought at first she might be worried that Emmeline had injured herself. That is, until she turned to the camera, smiled broadly, and put her foot on the Lizard Man's stomach – copying Emmeline's pose of the other day.

It was a short-lived pose as the Lizard Emmie grabbed her foot and pulled. Ida fell over and was grabbed again. There was some screaming – mostly from Ida – and a good deal of wrestling – mostly from Emmeline. Even the intervention of Henry, standing boldly with hands on hips and white-hatted head thrown back, failed to rattle the Lizard Man. Ida screamed louder. Henry shook his fists. And Emmeline shook Ida.

"Cut!" shouted Morrow ... and Stapleford, and T. Everett. Henry and I joined in on the fourth shout.

"Sorry," said Emmeline, as Henry and I helped her climb out of her Lizard Man costume. "I don't know what happened. I must have become caught up in the moment. I do apologise, Ida. I hope I didn't hurt you."

"Not at all," said Ida, her hair – that a moment a go had been up – now unpinned and flopping over her face. "How *is* your poor fetlock, Lily? That looked like such a *heavy* fall."

I almost shouted 'cut!' again.

~

Towards the end of the afternoon, I noticed Reeves lurking by a rock at the entrance to the quarry. He showed no inclination to shimmer in our direction so Emmeline and I walked over.

"Something to report, Reeves?" I asked.

"Word of the rope scene has been widely disseminated, sir. During the course of my extensive conversations with the servants this morning, I also learned of several matters that I believe may be germane to the investigation."

"Speak on, Reeves."

"Several of the maids reported hearing a woman crying these past two nights, sir. I believe that woman to be Mrs Berrymore."

"She did faint when she heard Sir Robert was dead," said Emmeline.

"Indeed, miss. I have also noted a certain redness about her eyes. She appears to be taking the news of Sir Robert's death considerably harder than the other servants."

"An emotional type, do you think, Reeves?" I asked.

"Not according to the other servants, sir. They are at a loss to explain it."

"You don't think she had ... feelings for Sir Robert?" asked Emmeline. "All that overfamiliarity business?"

"Surely not," I said.

"It would make Berrymore a suspect," said Emmeline. "If he found out about Sir Robert and his wife..."

I couldn't see a liaison between Sir Robert and Mrs

Berrymore. Neither could I see Berrymore shinning down a rope from the roof. But, wasn't that all the more reason to suspect him?

"I also discovered an interesting fact about Witheridge, sir. He has an unusual tattoo on his back."

"It doesn't say "I am a criminal mastermind,' does it?" I asked. One should never overlook the obvious.

"No, sir. It would appear to be a circular shield with unusual lettering around the rim. Witheridge maintains the lettering to be Cyrillic – an unfortunate relic of his time working as a merchant seamen in the Black Sea. Babbacombe, however, believes the tattoo to be the mark of the piskies."

"We don't believe in piskies, do we, Reeves?"

"No, sir."

"What about this Sir Rillick, Reeves? Do we believe in him?"

"Cyrillic is a form of alphabet, sir, popular in much of Eastern Europe, notably Russia. I have seen the tattoo in question and, although there are similarities, I do not believe the script to be Cyrillic."

"You saw this tattoo, Reeves?"

"Yes, sir. I happened to be in the vicinity of the laundry when Witheridge met with an unfortunate accident."

"What kind of accident?"

"An accident involving a bucket of water perched upon the laundry door, sir. Fortunately, I happened to be carrying a clean shirt and footman's jacket at the time and was able to assist him change out of his wet clothes."

"Very fortunate," I said, eyeing Reeves keenly. "I take it no one saw you set up this Witheridge trap?"

"Fortune favours the devious, sir."

"Why would Witheridge lie about a tattoo?" asked Emmeline. "Or do you think the other sailors played a trick on him?"

"The tattoo could be part of one of those secret society initiations," I suggested. "Witheridge always looks a little shifty to me. How long's he been at the Hall, Reeves?"

"Five months, sir. He was taken on when several of the

house servants were relocated to the Quarrywood studio."

"That's a bit too early to be working for Edison," said Emmeline.

I had to agree. Unless this Edison chap was a pretty swift worker. The kind of chap who kept an ear to the ground listening for word of potential rivals. After all, if he had a long arm, why not a long ear?

"I also discovered, sir, that there is, indeed, a trunk in the attic containing old dresses. Ellie the tweenie discovered it when she was helping locate items to furnish the studio buildings during the Quarrywood expansion."

"Did she look inside?" asked Emmeline.

"She tried some of the dresses on, miss," said Reeves, exhibiting his disapproving face.

"Does she remember a black one?" said Emmeline.

"She does, miss, though she didn't try that one on. Her preference was for the more colourful dresses."

"Did she tell anyone about these dresses?" I asked.

"Most of the female servants, sir. And one of them must have informed Lady Julia as Ellie was summoned by her ladyship the next day and reprimanded."

I felt for the poor girl. A reprimand from Lady Julia would not have been pleasant.

"So, Lady Julia knew about the trunk," said Emmeline. "I bet she would have taken a look, too – just to see if Ellie had damaged any of the dresses. She'd have seen Theodosia's dress. She couldn't have missed it. So why didn't she say anything when she saw the ghost wearing the dress?"

"I don't believe her ladyship saw the ghost, miss. If you recall she had already retired before the ghost's entrance."

I could tell that Emmeline was disappointed. Only Ida ranked higher than Lady Julia in Emmeline's list of preferred guilty parties.

"Did you have time to see this trunk for yourself, Reeves?" I asked.

"I did, sir. There was no black dress within."

TWENTY-SIX

Emmeline and I decided to leave before the rope was tied to the rock ready for tomorrow's scene. I told Henry we'd be walking back to the Hall, and that Reeves was ready and waiting to take up his position *chez* shrubbery and observe all.

Henry bade us farewell, and off we strolled, arm in arm, merrily spicing up Oscar Wilde plays for future Quarrywood productions. I was particularly fond of *Lady Windermere's Dagger*, a tale about a good murderer, who suspects her husband is having an affair with a giant octopus.

I expect some readers may be wondering: What is Worcester doing spicing up Oscar Wilde when he has a murder to solve? Murgatroyd of the Yard wouldn't stand for it. He'd be out there chivvying suspects until someone confessed. But we consulting detectives are a different breed. Our little grey cells are a little less grey. We encourage our minds to wander, delighting in whimsy, for in whimsy we often find an unexpected door to truth.

And failing that, a rather spiffy idea.

It came to me as I was closing the mire gate. What if the homicidal tree – or arboreally disguised automaton – that Lottie saw rootling from the murder scene was still in the copse? Reeves and I hadn't seen a tree cross the back lawn that night, and we must have been on the lawn around the time the fleeing conifer was making its escape.

I stood in the spot where Sir Robert had been struck and looked up the slope. If I were a tree which route would I take to safety.

"What are you doing?" asked Emmeline.

"Thinking like a tree," I said.

"Do trees think?"

"Deeply, I'd imagine. I'm not sure about yews, but I suspect the oak would be a particularly deep thinking tree. Beech too. They have a pensive look, don't you think?"

"I think the yew is a more sombre tree," said Emmeline. "And pious – you always see them in churchyards. And not just on Sundays."

Could anyone doubt that Emmeline and I were kindred spirits?

"Wait there," I said and stepped briskly into the copse, taking up position about ten yards in. "So, here I am. I've just winged a poison dart at Sir Robert. Where do I go next?"

"Home," said Emmeline.

I stopped thinking like a tree. Emmeline was right. Who, or whatever, fired the poisoned dart would most likely flee the scene in the direction of their home. And the tree had made for the Hall.

Or were they forced to take that route by the arrival of Lottie?

I looked up the slope again. "They'd have heard the search parties calling out for Sir Robert. So why go towards them."

"Perhaps that was what they were told to do," said Emmeline. "Fire dart at Sir Robert from here. Go home."

"Then someone would have seen them crossing the back lawn. There were search parties everywhere."

"Which the murderer would have expected," said Emmeline. "As soon as Sir Robert failed to turn up for dinner, there had to be a search."

Suddenly, it came to me.

"The murderer wouldn't say 'Go home.' They'd say 'Hide.' And what better place for a tree to hide than the middle of a copse!"

We searched the copse, looking for all the best places a small tree could hide. After ten minutes we found it. A pile of yew cuttings – ranging from one to four feet long – behind a thicket of rhododendrons bordering the back lawn.

"At least this means the murderer wasn't a tree," said

Emmeline.

"Unless it was an oak *disguised* as a yew."

~

Dinner was somewhat of a chore. I knew we had to give the impression that there was nothing out of the ordinary about to happen, but it's not that easy when one feels like one of those coiled springs. I couldn't wait for dinner to end and the real game to begin.

And I couldn't help glancing at Lady Julia's aspidistra. It had a furtive look to it. The kind of aspidistra that would not be averse to dressing up as a yew and committing bloody murder.

I took another long sip of wine. I couldn't even talk to Emmeline. Lady Julia had made sure the two of us were again at opposite ends of the dinner table.

I did note, however, that Stapleford had declined Henry's invitation to the trough. I wondered if he was using the opportunity to give our rope a good fraying, and hoped he wasn't doing the same to Reeves.

"Henry!" boomed Lady Julia from the other end of the table. "Tell me this is not true. Are you and Roderick planning to risk your lives climbing down a cliff?"

"It's true, Aunt Julia," said Henry. "It'll make a capital scene."

"But ... so soon after your father's death. Surely you must see how foolhardy this is?"

"It's not foolhardy, Aunt Julia. It's spectacle," said Henry. "That's what's going to make Quarrywood famous."

"Is this *your* doing?" said Lady Julia, glaring at me. "It has your hallmark."

"No," I said. "Henry deserves all the credit for this one. I'm just happy to help out."

"H'm," said Lady Julia.

"I think you should listen to your aunt, Henry," said Morrow. "The scene is an unnecessary risk. There is plenty of excitement in the picture as it stands."

"One can never have enough excitement," said Henry.

Emmeline left a minute or two after Lady Julia had led the

ladies back into the dining room. She stifled several yawns, rubbed a leg muscle that definitely *wasn't* a fetlock, and said: "I do apologise. I can barely keep awake. All that wrestling inside that heavy costume has caught up with me. I shall say goodnight before I fall down."

I remained a little longer, listening to Ida tell Henry that she wasn't tired at all – even though she'd done *far* more work than Lily, and would no doubt wake up tomorrow covered in bruises from the unprofessional mauling she'd received.

"Lily *was* playing the part of a Lizard Man," said the real Lily. "They're not supposed to be gentle."

"They're not supposed to fall over either," said Ida. "Or pull your hair. The other actors don't. But then, *they're* professionals."

"I think you're being a bit hard on Lily, Ida," said Henry. "She may lack your accomplishment, but she's enthusiastic. And her Lizard Man, though dashed odd, was not one I'd like to tangle with. It had real menace."

"Talking of enthusiasm," I said. "If I'm going to be on top form for tomorrow's rope scene, I'll need my eight hours. I shall bid you all a goodnight."

"Very sensible," said Henry. "I don't think I'll stay much longer either. One needs a clear head to climb down a cliff that high."

I nipped back to my room, grabbed my coat and then sauntered down the back stairs. Sauntering is the gait of choice of the consulting detective when wishing to give the impression of the innocent abroad. A chap up to no good creeps or darts. He never saunters.

I reached the back door – which was thankfully devoid of all gun-wielding footmen – and opened the door to the hallway a smidgen. All clear. So, out I nipped and executed a brisk saunter to the library door and slipped inside.

I lurked behind a bookcase, waiting in the darkness for the others to arrive. Emmeline was first, followed five minutes later by Henry.

I unlatched the window and carefully opened it, while Henry grabbed the gun he'd stashed behind a cabinet earlier that evening.

We were ready. The cliff top beckoned. Owls hooted en-couragement. And out we climbed into a still moonlit night.

"Follow me," I said. "The trick is to avoid open spaces."

We'd barely walked one hundred yards when I saw move-ment up ahead. Someone was coming up the Yew Walk!

I flattened myself against the old stable block. Was it one of the feral automata coming for a top up?

It was not. It was Berrymore!

We watched him tack across the back lawn. When he reached the back door, he stopped and looked furtively left and right before opening the door a crack, peering within, and slipping inside.

"What's he up to?" whispered Emmeline.

"I'll soon find out," said Henry, striding forward.

I grabbed Henry by the arm. "No, not yet. We need to see Reeves first. If Berrymore's frayed the rope, it'll help if we have a witness. He'll try to brazen it out otherwise – they always do – making up some story about checking the grounds for Selden before locking up for the night."

Henry reluctantly agreed. "Well, if you're sure..."

We crossed the back lawn, using the hedge for cover, following it around to the Yew Walk. From there we pro-ceeded cautiously.

"Get ready to dive into the copse if you spot anyone," I whispered.

As it happened we didn't encounter anyone on the Yew Walk, but we did see a large bowl of milk.

"That wasn't there this afternoon," said Emmeline. "And it's full. There must be nearly a whole quart in there."

"I don't understand," said Henry. "There was a bowl of milk under my father's body. What the devil does it mean?"

"It's possible someone at the Hall is feeding Selden," I said.

"What?" said Henry. "Do you think it's Morrow?"

"Or Berrymore," I said. "We did just see him come from the Yew Walk."

"But why?" said Henry.

I shrugged.

"It might be drugged," said Emmeline. "Berrymore might be trying to catch Selden."

"Then why not tell me?" said Henry. "I'd have helped. It sounds a capital idea. No reason to creep about at the dead of night."

Of course there was also the possibility that someone was trying to lure Selden to the Hall for some other reason – like becoming the scapegoat for the Baskerville-Smythe murders.

We continued our trek. A friendly crescent moon shone brightly from high in the southern sky allowing us to see for miles. Even the mire appeared clear of fog. One could make out the silhouette of the high moor in the distance.

And we were alone. I didn't spot one skulking figure or hastily dampened lamp on the entire journey to the cliff top.

"Reeves? Are you here?" I said in a loudish whisper.

"I am, sir," said Reeves, rising from behind a bush.

"Have you seen anything?"

"Not yet, sir. I believe Sergeant Stock and four of his warders may be at the studio. They arrived earlier and I have not seen them leave."

"What are they doing at the studio?" asked Henry.

"I do not know, sir. I observed them call at the studio's main house and disappear within, but they were too far away for me to hear what was said on the doorstep when the footman admitted them."

"Has Berrymore been here?" asked Emmeline.

"Not that I have observed, miss."

"And how's the rope, Reeves? Everything oojah-cum-spiff and unsullied?"

"The rope has not been touched, sir.

I had a look nonetheless. Gave it a good tug and declared it as fine a specimen of the ropemaking arts as I'd ever seen.

Reeves coughed. "If I may suggest, sir, I think it would be prudent if we concealed ourselves."

I found the spot I'd earmarked during our morning reconnoitre. There was room to sit down, a stout rocky face to lean back on, and there were several of those leggy gorse bushes that can hide a chap from view while, at the same time, providing plenty of gaps to look through.

Emmeline's spot was on the other side of the rock. I had a good view towards the Hall and the mire, and Emmeline looked out on High Dudgeon Farm and the open moor to the north.

After thirty minutes the Worcester enthusiasm began to wane somewhat. The night was colder than I'd expected. I hadn't brought gloves. My back had begun to ache. And nothing was moving on the moor.

Time dragged. The moon ambled across the sky, and dew began to form on my clothes. Then, at around two o'clock, Emmeline spoke.

"Did you see that?" she whispered from her side of the rock.

"See what?" I whispered back.

"A light from High Dudgeon Farm."

I leaned forward as far as I could and peered towards Stapleford's cottage. I could just about see the outline of the house and buildings, but I couldn't see any light.

"It's gone now, but I definitely saw it," said Emmeline. "It shone for a good two seconds."

I watched the farm a little longer, but saw nothing. A little later I thought I saw movement on the mire. It was difficult to make out with any certainty – the mire was over a mile away – and I may have imagined it.

I didn't imagine the figure on the track twenty minutes later though. They were walking along the track to the quarry. Too far away to recognise but, from the outline, it wasn't a tree or wearing a long black dress.

I watched transfixed, right up to the moment the gun went off.

TWENTY-SEVEN

The gunshot was accompanied by a series of shouts from the quarry. *Over there! Stop him! Get him, boys!*

The figure on the track stopped dead, then hurried to a rock and crouched down behind it.

The cries from the quarry intensified. *He's making a run for it! Get the horses! Stop or I'll shoot!*

Emmeline crawled around the rock to join me. "What's going on? Do you think we should go and look?" she whispered.

I was torn. Had Sergeant Stock and his warders spotted another suspect? They couldn't have seen the figure on the track. But had the murderer outsmarted us? Let us think he'd arrive at the cliff top via the track when, all the time, he'd been shinning up the rope from the quarry?

"Stay here, Emmie," I whispered. "Keep an eye on the chap on the track. I'll see what's going on at the quarry."

I crawled from my hiding place, until I put my left hand on a particularly sharp piece of gorse and emitted a stifled bleat. After which, I gave up crawling and tried a touch of creeping, along with a modicum of tripping and light cursing.

Eventually I made it to the clearing by the rope where I saw Henry, crouching by the rock the rope was tied to.

"It's Sergeant Stock and the warders," whispered Henry. "They're chasing someone."

"Any idea who?"

"No. I haven't dared look over the cliff in case one of the warders takes a pot-shot at me."

I heard the sound of hooves from below, then galloping. It sounded like several horses. And then another gunshot.

Come down from there! You'll not get another warning!

The rope in front of us juddered. Someone – or something – was coming up the rope. Fast.

Henry gripped his gun. I stared at the spot on the cliff edge where the rope disappeared. And froze.

One often reads in books about chaps having their hearts leap into their mouths. Utter rot, I'd thought. Reeves would know, but I rather fancied the lungs would get in the way. But when the contorted face of Selden suddenly appeared over that cliff edge, I can tell you that half a ventricle shot past my tonsils.

And that was the only part of me that moved.

It's all very well for people like Reeves saying stuff like 'Don't frighten him' and 'Keep calm and he'll go away.' But Reeves had a gun and was hiding behind a bush. While I was face to face with a cannibal who could eat a policeman between meals!

Selden growled and sprang onto the cliff top. Henry fell over backwards, discharging his gun as he fell, endangering one of the lesser constellations.

Selden growled again. His face was half man, half panther. His clothes were shredded. His body bulged in places no tailor would countenance.

And all that stood between him and the open moor was Worcester R.

And, all of a sudden, Reeves. For, at that direst of moments, that stout fellow materialised at the young master's shoulder. Which was just what the troops needed.

"Show him your gun, Reeves," I said, feeling considerably emboldened.

"I left it behind the bush, sir."

I may have bleated, or it might have been the sound of ventricle striking tonsil. How could Reeves have left his gun behind at a moment like this!

Selden hissed at us. And snarled, and spread his fingers wide, scratching at the air in a menacing fashion.

To which, Reeves replied by tossing an object onto the ground between us and Selden.

My first thought was 'bomb.' I didn't have any second

thoughts. 'Bomb' pretty much cleared out the Worcester locker.

And I would have dived for cover, if my feet and lower jaw hadn't been nailed to the ground by shock.

Then something rather rummy happened. Selden stopped snarling. His ears pricked. He sniffed the air three times. Then he pounced upon the object, biting it, chewing it, rubbing his face in it, rolling on it and raking it with his toes. I'd never seen a happier cannibal. He appeared completely oblivious to everything else around him.

"Reeves?" I enquired.

"It is a large felt mouse stuffed with the leaves of *Nepeta cataria*, sir – commonly known as catnip. I noticed this morning, while in conversation with Trelawny the gardener, that he had a supply of catnip leaves that he used to dissuade aphids – particularly those of the green and the black variety–"

"Reeves, this is not the time for a treatise on aphids. There is a homicidal cannibal writhing on the ground within feet of us. Shouldn't we do something?"

"I would counsel we wait and observe, sir. Catnip is known to induce drowsiness in certain felines."

"He doesn't look very drowsy," said Henry, who'd surfaced from behind his rock to join us. "He looks frenzied."

"The drowsiness comes later, sir. The initial reaction is one of great excitement, and single-mindedness."

Selden was certainly single-minded. He rolled. He chewed. He purred and growled. He didn't even react when four burly warders came running over to join us.

"What you done to him?" asked the first to arrive.

"We have distracted him, officer," said Reeves. "Another five minutes and the catnip should induce feelings of drowsiness. It should then be safe to handcuff him."

We watched and waited. Selden was definitely slowing down, and had begun to drool.

Emmeline arrived midway through the drooling.

"Good heavens," she said. "What *have* you done to Selden?"

I explained, omitting all mention of ventricles and Henry's

unprovoked attack on the Crab Nebula. We were three brave citizens who, armed only with a felt mouse, had faced down a deranged homicidal cannibal.

I repeated the story a minute later for a puffing Sergeant Stock, who had obviously eschewed horseback once more to chase Selden on foot.

"Beg pardon, gents, miss," said Sergeant Stock. "But ... what be you all doing here? 'Tis nearly three."

It was only then that I remembered the figure on the track!

"Emmie ... Lily, I mean, what happened to the chap on the track?"

"He left soon after you did. He was definitely up to no good though. He didn't walk back along the track. He skulked, hunching over as he ran, and stopped every now and then to look back."

I explained our trap to Sergeant Stock and I could tell he was impressed.

"We'm be doing the same at the quarry, sir. We had word Selden be a-hanging around there at night. He be a quick one though. We thought we had him when he sprang our trap, but he tore off like a good 'un. If you like I can spare a couple of men to look for your man. Shouldn't take long to search the track on horseback. He couldn't have travelled far."

We took Sergeant Stock up on his offer. I didn't hold out too much hope, but what else was there? After all the shouting, galloping and gunfire, no one was going to see the cliff top as a quiet place where one could fray a rope unobserved.

Selden was successfully handcuffed and, with his catnip mouse tucked into what remained of his shirt, hauled away. Two warders were despatched to search the track between the quarry, High Dudgeon Farm and the Hall, and given orders to detain anyone they saw.

"I'd like to keep Selden here at the studio if it be all right with you, Sir Henry," said Sergeant Stock. "There be a good strong basement to lock him up in, and we can take him back to the prison in the morning."

Henry agreed and the four of us picked up our guns and blankets and headed back towards the Hall. The two warders searched both tracks, but never caught sight of a soul.

"What do we do about Berrymore?" asked Henry. "Do we question him now or in the morning?"

"One should never question a suspect on an empty stomach," I said. "We'll question him after breakfast."

"What about the rope scene?" asked Emmeline. "Everyone's expecting it. How is Henry going to explain cancelling it?"

Reeves coughed. "If I may, sir, miss, I would suggest that Sir Henry tell people that the rope was severely chewed during Selden's apprehension and is unusable."

~

I had barely applied the Worcester bean to the pillow before Reeves awakened me with the early-morning oolong. A situation which would normally have left me somewhat fogged and lacking in the vital spirit. But I was a chap with a target on his pyjamas, and that wakes a chap up pretty smartish.

"We have tried being clever, Reeves," I said, sitting up in bed. "And your plan was the very Everest of clever, impossible to top. Any other plan would be a mere Kilimanjaro or one of those lesser spotted varieties of pinnacles doomed to failure. No, Reeves, we must push aside being clever, and deploy the unexpected."

"Sir?"

"I don't wish to spend the next ten days with a target on my back. We have to bring things to a head. And you know what that means."

"No, sir."

"The *dénouement*, Reeves. I shall announce it at breakfast."

"Would that not be premature, sir?"

"Defeatist talk, Reeves. We may not know the identity of the murderer, but the murderer doesn't know that. We shall keep them off balance, draw them out and they shall reveal themselves."

"Are you certain, sir?"

"Positive. The *dénouement* is a powerful tool. Even Moriarty would feel a certain chilliness of the corpuscles if called upon to attend."

"I believe it usual, sir, for the detective to *know* the identity of the murderer before commencing the *dénouement*."

"You believe wrong, Reeves. Lady Agatha MacTweedie rarely knows who did it. She often waits for the spirits to come to her – usually during her final costume change. Sometimes she even speaks in tongues, and nothing un-settles a murderer more than a detective speaking in tongues."

"So I would imagine, sir."

"Not that I plan to speak in tongues. Or wait for a tip from a roving spirit guide. But an accusing look and a good deal of finger pointing can achieve wonders. The trick is to give the impression that one knows a jolly sight more than one actually does."

"Indeed, sir."

"Knowledge is power, Reeves. And the appearance of knowledge is power without all that absolute corruption business."

"Sir?"

"I think I shall stage the *dénouement* at noon. That'll give us time to get all the suspects assembled. I want everyone there, Reeves. We can use Sergeant Stock to chivvy along any dissenters."

"I strongly advise that you postpone this *dénouement* until tomorrow, sir. There is still much that we do not know, and a premature confrontation may delay the conclusion of this case."

"My mind is made up, Reeves."

Reeves put on his sniffy face. "They stumble that run fast, sir."

"And it's the early bird that slaps the cuffs on the worm, Reeves."

Sometimes one has to be firm.

~

Reeves was still in a sulk when I left for breakfast. Harsh eyebrows had been exchanged. And he'd laid out my grey socks when he knew perfectly well that a *dénouement* called for something a little brighter in the ankle department.

At the breakfast table, Selden's capture was the main topic of c. Even Lady Julia was pleased.

"Perhaps now we'll have fewer armed footmen on the premises," she said. "I was beginning to think we were in the midst of a peasants' revolt."

I shovelled three kippers onto my plate. I'd need all the brain food I could swallow.

"It's a shame you had to postpone the rope scene, Henry," said Lily. "I was looking forward to it."

I sensed an opportunity and seized upon it.

"There never was going to be a rope scene," I said, turning to have a good view of all the faces at the table.

"What do you mean?" said Ida, looking puzzled.

"It was a ruse," I said, affecting the nonchalant confidence of the suave boulevardier. "I needed one more piece of evidence to determine the murderer's identity. Now I have it, there's no need for any rope scene."

I looked from face to face. There was surprise, shock, and a good deal of confusion. I had hoped someone might have choked on a kipper and made a run for it, but one can't have everything.

"What is the idiot boy talking about now?" asked Lady Julia.

"My investigation into the murder of Sir Robert, Aunt Julia," I said. "It's now concluded. I know who did it."

"You mean it *was* Selden?" asked Ida.

"No, not Selden. I shall reveal all at noon, if that's all right with you, Henry?"

"Er ... yes, of course," said Henry, looking as surprised as everyone else.

"Splendid," I said. "We shall have the *dénouement* at noon then. Here, in the dining room, I think. Everyone's invited."

"What's a *dénouement*?" asked Ida.

"It's the scene where the detective gathers all the suspects together and reveals who done it," said Emmeline.

"Suspects?" said Lady Julia in her Lady Bracknell voice. "You're surely not suggesting that any of *us* are suspects."

"A good detective suspects everyone, Aunt Julia," I said, picking up my plate and strolling tablewards to take the vacant spot next to Emmeline.

"Henry, you can't possibly sanction this," said Lady Julia. "The boy's an idiot."

"Roderick is not an idiot," said Henry. "He and his man were instrumental in the apprehension of Selden last night."

"But Henry..." said Lady Julia. "What kind of people is he going to invite? And what's he going to say to them?"

"I'm sure we'll find out at noon," said Henry. "Personally, I feel the sooner this business is concluded the better. It wouldn't be right for the governor to be interred with none of us knowing who'd done for him."

Lady Julia shook her head and gave me the kind of look that came with its own pin and wax effigy.

"So who did it?" Ida asked me. "Surely you can give us a clue?"

"I can give you *one* clue," I said. "The murderer will be here, in this very room, at noon."

~

As soon as breakfast finished, Henry drew me aside. "Do you still want to question Berrymore?" he asked.

"I do."

Henry called Berrymore over and asked him to accompany us to the library.

"Close the door, Berrymore," Henry said as soon as we were alone. "Mister Roderick has a few questions to put to you."

The upper slopes of Berrymore swayed somewhat. He'd been in attendance at breakfast so he knew all about the impending *dénouement*.

"First off, Berrymore," I said. "I'd like all the servants, including Trelawny, present in the dining room at noon."

"*All* of them, sir?" said Berrymore looking at Henry.

"If Mister Roderick wants all of them, he shall have all of them," said Henry.

"Very well, sir,"

"Right ho," I said. "Now that we've got that out of the way, did you have a pleasant walk last night, Berrymore?"

"Sir?"

"It's no use denying it. I saw you. And..." I paused to narrow the old eyes and give him the steeliest of looks. "I know all, Berrymore."

Berrymore's face turned ashen and he swallowed hard. "I can explain," he said, turning to his master. "We didn't mean any harm, but it was breaking her heart."

"Who's heart?" asked Henry.

"Maggie's, sir. Mrs Berrymore. She's ... she's Selden's mother."

Well, I wasn't expecting that.

"You're Selden's father?" I said, not seeing any family resemblance whatsoever. Berrymore was more of a giraffe than a cat.

"No, sir. The lad's Maggie's from her first husband. Mr Selden. He died when Harry was a small boy. Maggie and I met in service in London. We got married nine years ago and came down here to be near the boy."

"So it was you putting the milk out for him?" I said.

"Yes," said Berrymore, his head bowed. "We couldn't let him starve. We know he's eaten a few more people than he should have, but, to Mrs Berrymore, he's still the little boy who used to curl up on a sunny windowsill, and roll over to have his stomach scratched."

I turned to Henry. "Did Dr Morrow ever say anything about recognising Mrs Berrymore?"

"No, he did not," said Henry.

"They never met, sir," said Berrymore. "Harry had left home. He ... he was in the asylum when he met Dr Morrow. And a black day that was, if you don't mind me saying, sir."

"You blame Dr Morrow for Harry's condition?" I asked.

"He's the one that gave him the potion, sir! And the ears and the tail. What kind of man does that to another? I'm sorry, sir, I know I'm speaking out of line, but it's not *right* what he did. Not right at all."

"I'm sure he was only trying to help," said Henry.

"That's as maybe, sir, but Harry was a gentle boy – a bit strange, not everyone liked the way he'd rub up against people's legs when he came into a room – but gentle, until that doctor turned him into a killer!"

I waited for Berrymore to compose himself. Murgatroyd of the Yard wouldn't have approved, but I felt for the ancient butler.

"Did you ever see anything unusual when you were out and about on these milk errands?" I asked.

"No, sir."

"How is Mrs Berrymore?" asked Henry. "I heard she had taken to her bed."

"She has, sir. The news of the lad's capture proved too much for her. She's relieved, I'm sure, and will soon recover, but for now ... it's like a dam's burst, sir. Everything she's been a-bottling up for the last two days has come pouring out. An hour or two by herself and she'll be right as rain."

~

Emmeline was waiting for me by the stairs.

"Do you really know who did it?" she asked.

I looked about us to make sure no one could overhear. "Not yet," I said. "But I'm sure it will come to me. I've had three kippers for breakfast, and I intend to break into the cocktails soon. I'll be overflowing with ideas by noon."

"What does Reeves say?"

I snorted. "Reeves and I have had a difference of opinion. He thinks we should wait. I suspect he's lining up a scene where I'm dangled in front of bears."

"I'm sure they wouldn't be real bears. And if they were, I'd make sure they were well-fed beforehand."

"That's very considerate of you."

"Feeding bears is the least a girl can do for her intended. Is everyone coming to the *dénouement*?"

"I've arranged it with Henry," I said. "Tom's going to the quarry now to ask Sergeant Stock to attend, and they'll both stop off at High Dudgeon Farm to invite Stapleford and Falconbridge. At the point of a truncheon if need be."

TWENTY-EIGHT

Everyone was there. The Baskerville-Smythes and guests took the seats, the servants stood around the walls, and Lupin occupied the pelmet. In case anyone tried to make a run for it, Sergeant Stock and Berrymore guarded the two doors while Babbacombe and Witheridge blocked the windows.

The *dénouement* could begin. As soon as I took another stiffener.

Reeves hovered mid-snootful. "If I may speak, sir, I have something–"

I'd heard this all before, so I raised a stern finger. This was not a time for doubt or discussion. This was a time for action. And gin.

I quietened the room.

"This has been an exceptional case," I said, starting off with a lapel grasped in each hand. I was going for suave yet erudite. I had thought of wearing Henry's white hat, but I'm not sure if one can pull off that kind of thing indoors.

"For those of you who've never attended a *dénouement* before, this is the bit where I – the detective, that's me – explains all, and unmasks the murderer – or, indeed, murderers."

"Do get on with it," said Lady Julia.

I waggled a reproachful finger at her. Something I would-n't have dreamed of doing earlier, but after five stiffeners, she was beginning to look a dashed sight less formidable.

"The murderer is in this room," I continued. "They know who they are. And so do I."

I paused to let my gaze swing around the room and give

227

everyone a meaningful look. One has to take every opportunity one can to give the murderer's blood a good chilling.

"You see," I said. "It all started with the ghost."

I gave them all the ripe stuff about Theodosia's dress, the
RadioGlo paint and Pasco.

"But wait," I said. "I expect you're all thinking 'How could
Pasco possibly have exited a first floor bedroom without a
ladder?' We all looked that night, didn't we? He couldn't
have jumped, and there was nothing to climb down."

I inserted a goodish long pause before continuing.

"Or was there? During the course of my investigation, I
discovered, on the very roof of this Hall, a long rope tied
around one of those Tudor chimneys. This rope, when tossed
to the ground, passed by the very window that we found
unlatched the night the ghost disappeared!"

That got a reaction. Not quite the one I'd been hoping for
– ashen-faced fear from the guilty party – but more one of
interest being piqued.

"There's more," I said. "This rope was not there when
Henry and I looked out the window. Which means ... someone had to be up on the roof when the ghost was ankling
across the landing. Someone who threw down the rope,
waited for Pasco to climb down as instructed, and then
hauled said rope back up. That person is the murderer.

"Now we come to Pasco's murder. Why kill Pasco, you
say? Why not switch the chap off?"

I paused for a swift slurp. All this public speaking was
drying the Worcester mouth out.

"Where was I?"

"Talking about Pasco's murder," said Emmeline.

"That's right. Why kill Pasco? Answer: because he was a
dashed liability. He was the only chap who knew the identity
of the murderer, and he had a green face. Remember what
Dr Morrow said about that RadioGlo paint? It doesn't come
off easily. One could have scrubbed Pasco's face for hours
and still there'd have been splodges for all to see. And an
under gardener with green splodges on his face that glow in
the dark is going to attract attention. Questions will be
asked, and Pasco, being a truthful chap, would tell all. Ergo,

Pasco had to die. Switching off wouldn't cut it. One could always switch him back on again. No, his head had to be bashed in to destroy his memories for good. And the murderer had to remove the head to stop us putting two and two together viz glowing green splodges and the ghost."

"But why go to all the trouble of staging the ghost scene in the first place?" asked Henry. "It makes no sense."

"It makes perfect sense to the murderer," I said. "This murderer doesn't think like you, Henry. They don't see 'unnecessary complication.' They see 'carefully crafted opening act.' The ghost scene's purpose was to create the impression that supernatural forces were abroad. That, and to muddy any investigation into Sir Robert's death."

Henry nodded, as did quite a few others, which made me feel pretty braced. The old *dénouement* was going down a dashed sight better than I'd feared. Lady J had stopped heckling, and Reeves hadn't coughed once!

Time to break out the exhibits.

I trickled over to the breakfast buffet and took out the blowpipe I'd stowed earlier in the left-hand cupboard. I held it up for all to see.

"Behold, the murder weapon," I said. "I found it on the rooftop next to that coil of rope I told you about."

I handed it to Henry. "Do you notice anything odd about this blowpipe?"

"I wouldn't know," said Henry. "I've never seen a blowpipe before in my life. It's all odd."

"Morrow?" I said. "Perhaps you'd take a look?"

I observed Morrow closely as he reluctantly took the blowpipe from Henry. Lady Agatha's a firm believer that murderers are in a constant battle with their conscience. Confront them with the murder weapon and often they crack. 'Watch for the bulging eye,' she counsels. 'The fevered brow. The frothing mouth. Guilt shall betray them for Conscience is mightier than the axe.'

Morrow looked a bit feverish, but not one eye bulged. "I don't think I can help at all," he said. "I'm a doctor, not an anthropologist."

"What about you, Stapleford?" I asked.

I watched his face as the blowpipe was handed to him. He looked more curious than nervous. Unlike Morrow, who'd treated the blowpipe as a hot coal to be passed on as swiftly as poss, Stapleford examined the blowpipe carefully.

"That is odd," he said. "The mouthpiece has been modified. A piece of metal with a screw thread has been pushed into the pipe."

"And why would someone do that?" I asked.

He shrugged. "To attach it to something?"

"To attach it to something," I repeated, gripping both lapels again and, feeling a little like one of those barrister chappies, I decided to eke out the moment by pacing a little this way and that. Building up the moment, don't you know.

"Like an automaton?" I suggested.

That got in amongst them all. There was a good deal of muttering and drawing in of breath.

Stapleford took another look at the mouthpiece. "Possibly," he said. "The gauge looks about right."

"Shall we check?" I said. "Your automaton, Falconbridge, is here, isn't he?"

"Yes, he's over there."

I was expecting Lady Julia to complain, and she hit her cue with gusto.

"There's an *automaton* in the house? Henry, did you know about this?"

"I did, Aunt–"

"And you *allowed* this?"

"If it leads to father's murderer being apprehended then, yes," said Henry.

Lady Julia snorted and gave me the kind of look that the Geneva Convention had tried to outlaw in 1864. "I blame *you* for all this," she said.

I took the blowpipe from Stapleford and handed it towards Falconbridge, who immediately looked to his master for guidance – presumably on whether to comply or beat me around the head with it.

"Do it, Falconbridge," said Stapleford.

Falconbridge began to unbutton his shirt.

"What *is* he doing?" asked Lady Julia.

"I think the ladies should look away," said T. Everett. "Ida, cover your eyes!"

"Dear God!" said Lady Julia. "Henry! Stop him this instant."

"No," said Henry. "I need to see this."

I wasn't quite sure where to look myself, but I waited until Falconbridge was ready, gave him the blowpipe, and stepped back. The servants to either side of him had stepped back too.

Falconbridge screwed the two-foot long blowpipe into place. It did look decidedly odd – as though the chap had had an altercation with Trelawny about runner beans and had been run through with a bamboo pole – but it fitted perfectly.

"How easy would it be for Falconbridge here to fire a poison dart at someone's neck?" I asked Stapleford.

"With a little practice it wouldn't be difficult. The internal steam pressure would be more than sufficient to expel the dart with the required force. The dart would have to be loaded before the blowpipe is screwed into place though. Firing multiple darts would take some time."

"Thank you," I said. "You may now remove the blowpipe, Falconbridge."

Falconbridge showed no sign of complying. Instead he turned his body slightly so the blowpipe was pointing directly at me. And he smiled – a smile of the sickly and smug variety.

"Perhaps you wish me vent steam now?" he said. "To complete test."

"Falconbridge!" said Stapleford. "Remove the blowpipe at once."

Falconbridge unscrewed the blowpipe, but not once did his eyes drop from mine. He stared at me, smiling that awful smile, until the blowpipe was free and he handed it to me.

"That blowpipe wasn't loaded, was it?" asked T. Everett.

I hadn't thought to check!

I raised the blowpipe to my eye and squinted inside. It was empty.

"Are you going to name the murderer now?" said Lady

Julia. "I'm sure the servants have work to do."

I was tempted to name Falconbridge, but a detective can't allow personal feelings to get in the way.

"One can't rush a *dénouement*, Aunt Julia," I said. "One has to set the scene. Talking of which, we now move to events in the Yew Walk on the night of Sir Robert's murder. As some of you know, Sir Robert was lured to the Yew Walk by a note purporting to have come from Sergeant Stock, asking him to meet that stout custodian of the law at the mire gate at eight of the clock.

"Unbeknownst to Sir Robert, the murderer has instructed an automaton to wait, hidden in the copse, by the mire gate. And unbeknownst to the murderer, Sir Robert and the automaton were not alone that night. There was a witness."

I was watching Stapleford when I delivered that last line. He certainly looked surprised, but no eye bulging or frothing.

"A witness," I repeated. "A feral automaton, living on the moor, was on the track by the mire gate. And ... she saw everything."

I scanned all the faces at the table. I saw surprise, excitement, anticipation – a hint of simmering exasperation from Lady Julia – but nothing resembling a guilty party having their insides gnawed by field mice. Was the murderer without fear ... without conscience?

I ratcheted up the tension. Inspector Murgatroyd would have been proud.

"And when I say everything," I said. "I mean ... *everything.*"

I let the Worcester gaze glide over the servants this time. No frothing, no feverish brows, no eyes darting towards the nearest exit. They looked like they were enjoying it. Rapt faces, hanging on my every word. I'd probably get asked back for an encore.

"She saw the automaton," I continued. "She saw it flee through the copse and hide amongst the rhododendrons," I said.

"Who was it?" asked Ida. "I bet she recognised it."

"It was ... disguised," I said.

"What as?" asked Ida "Not another ghost?"

"No, it was disguised as a tree. A yew tree. We found a pile of yew branches by the rhododendrons which confirmed her report."

"So how did you identify the automaton if it was disguised as a tree?" asked Ida.

"Deduction," I said.

"How can you deduce an automaton's identity from a pile of yew branches?" asked Stapleford.

I hadn't started to froth, but I had the distinct impression my brow was turning feverish. And I could feel my earlier confidence oozing out from every pore.

"It's a skill," I said. "One either has it, or one doesn't. Impossible to explain."

"So who was the automaton?" asked Ida.

"More to the point," said Lady Julia. "Who was the murderer?"

I was losing the room. The confident swagger, the eloquence, both had deserted me.

I gambled all. The murderer had to be feeling a dashed sight worse than me. Surely one more push would tip him over the pelmet?

I drew myself up to my full height, gripped both lapels, and fixed my gaze on Lupin. I'd tested everyone else.

"The murderer is..." I began. Then I paused, hoping the longer I drew it out, the more chance the murderer would crack and make a run for it. The pause became pregnant, gave birth, had grandchildren, and *still* no one moved.

The dining room clock ticked. Expectant faces turned quizzical. And Reeves coughed.

I may still have had issues with him, and I had no idea what he was going to say, but ... it was either turn to Reeves or feign a heart attack.

"Yes, Reeves?" I said.

"Given the circumstances, sir, your reticence to name the murderer, is quite understandable." Reeves then turned to address the gathering. "The identity of the murderer is ... Roderick Baskerville-Smythe."

My fleeting elation at Reeves' intervention, was dashed.

"Reeves!" I hissed. "I know I'm always encouraging you to

consider the person least likely, but that's stretching things a bit far, don't you think?"

The initial shocked silence that greeted Reeves' pronouncement was replaced by a chorus of what's.

And I didn't like the way Sergeant Stock was looking at me.

"It *isn't* me, is it, Reeves?" I whispered.

"No, sir. The time has come to reveal our true identities. I am Sergeant Reeves, and this gentleman..." Reeves waved a hand in my direction. "Is Inspector Natterjack of Scotland Yard."

"What are you talking about, man?" said Henry. Henry was not alone in his confusion. The whole room was confused, including me. What was Reeves up to?

"If I may explain, Sir Henry," said Reeves. "Last week Scotland Yard received a troubling telegram from your father."

"What? The governor sent a telegram to Scotland Yard?"

"Yes, sir. The telegram alleged that he – Sir Robert – had uncovered a plot to murder one of the family. He wasn't sure if the intended victim was himself or you, Sir Henry. But he believed the threat both credible and imminent. He requested immediate assistance, suggesting that one of our officers, by pretending to be his nephew, Roderick, could gain admittance to the household, whereupon they could conduct a discreet investigation."

"This is preposterous," said Lady Julia. "Robert would have told me."

"Sir Robert had good reason to believe, milady, that anyone taken into his confidence would be placed in considerable danger."

"What good reason?" demanded Lady Julia.

"Sir Robert received an anonymous letter, milady, saying that they knew about the telegram and that if he didn't keep his mouth shut then he, and anyone else he involved, would suffer."

"Is this true?" Henry asked me.

"Every word," I said. I don't know how Reeves does it. He'd convinced me about the telegram and the note. I suppose he does exude an aura of such innate probity that one couldn't possibly imagine him telling a lie.

"I have the note here, Sir Henry," said Reeves, producing a piece of paper from his pocket and handing it to Henry.

I believe my mouth may have fallen open at this point. How could Reeves have had the time to provide a note? I thought he'd been making things up as he went along.

Henry read the note aloud. "You shouldn't have sent that telegram to the Yard. Keep your mouth shut. I'm watching. Tell a soul and they get their throat slit."

Ida and Lily both gasped. Lady Julia looked shaken. And I looked at Reeves in awe. Perhaps I really was Inspector Natterjack?

"Did you say that Roderick sent this?" said Henry. "That he ... that he killed my father?"

"Indeed, sir. Inspector Natterjack made the connection."

"How?" said Henry.

Suddenly, everyone was looking at me, including Reeves.

"A simple deduction," I said. "One doesn't like to blow one's own trumpet. I'll let Reeves explain."

"Thank you, sir. It came to our notice during this investigation that several members of this parish bear a striking resemblance to the Baskerville family portraits. The possibility of one of them having a distant claim to the Baskerville title was considered, and dismissed. That is, until Inspector Natterjack discovered that one of them had the imprint of the Buenos Aires and District Railway Line upon his back. That person could be none other than Roderick Baskerville-Smythe, whose claim to the Baskerville title was far from distant."

"Show yourself!" shouted Henry, his eyes darting around the room as he shot to his feet.

Several eyes had already alighted upon Witheridge.

He may not have frothed at the mouth, but Witheridge panicked. He turned, struggled to unlatch the window, pulled the lower pane up, and had started to dive through when Sergeant Stock and Henry grabbed a leg each and hauled him back in.

It took a while to subdue the struggling Witheridge and

manhandle him into a chair. Whereupon, Henry started questioning him.

"Roderick, why didn't you *say* something? We'd have given you an income. You didn't have to murder anyone!"

"You wouldn't let a *réanimé* in the house, let alone given me an income! And besides, I don't want the leavings of a family that abandoned my mother. I want justice. I want you to suffer. Your branch of the family always looked down on mine. You cheated my father out of his inheritance!"

"Your father was the youngest brother, Roderick. He *had* no inheritance," said Lady Julia.

"He *should* have! *I* should have. I was left with *nothing*! While you had this house, the estate, Quarrywood, everything you wanted!"

"The boy is clearly deranged," said Lady Julia.

"I can still inherit the title. No one'll be able to touch me!"

He broke free and leapt at Henry. The pair fell back against the dining table, wrestling as they went. Sergeant Stock attempted to intervene, but was waylaid by the unexpected arrival upon his shoulders of a flying Lupin, who had two hands on the officer's helmet and two feet fending off the officer's flailing arms.

There was considerable confusion, not to mention much shouting and screaming. And bodies everywhere as half the room tried to assist Henry and half the room tried to get out of the way. The latter succeeding in getting in the way of most of the former.

I tried to reach Henry, but found myself trapped behind the flailing Sergeant Stock. Whereupon Lupin decided that, as tempting as a policeman's helmet was, round three with Reginald was the ape's pyjamas.

Within seconds we were on the floor and rolling under the table. And rolling back out again. Above us, people pushed and shouted, tripped and jumped out of the way. I only saw snatches of what happened next, my vision being somewhat impaired by all the rolling and grappling, but it would appear that, somehow, Roderick managed to break free in all the confusion, and made a run for the open window. But as he attempted a full length dive, he found the window considerably less open than it had been a second earlier – Emmeline having begun to slam it shut.

The unfortunate Roderick was caught amidships, and winded somewhat as he hung there – beached – half in, half out the window.

Stout arms – none of which belonged to Emmeline I hasten to add – fastened around the struggling Roderick's legs and hauled him in.

"Allow me, miss," said Sergeant Stock, leaning over to fetch Roderick a juicy one with his truncheon.

The next thing I saw was Lady Julia standing over me with a vase which proved to contain considerably more water than one would think possible. Lupin squawked and bounced off, leaving a soaked Reginald to drip on the Axminster.

"You may be an inspector," said Lady Julia. "But you are still an idiot."

I watched Roderick being led away then dashed upstairs to change out of my wet clothes.

As denouements went I thought it a pretty good one. A bit of a wobble in the middle act, but it finished strongly and had the audience on their feet.

TWENTY-NINE

Once dry and refortified by a glass of the restorative I went looking for Reeves. It took me a while, but I eventually tracked him down on the front lawn.

"Why didn't you tell me beforehand?" I asked.

"I tried, sir."

"You could have said something when you oiled in with the early morning oolong. I was all ears then."

"I did not know at that juncture, sir. I didn't discover Witheridge's true identity until later that morning when the idea that the 'Cyrillic' writing on his 'tattoo' might be a mirror image presented itself to me. I made a sketch of the tattoo from memory and located a suitable mirror to observe the result. That's when the words 'Buenos Aires and District Railway Company' sprang out at me."

"Bit of a shock I should imagine."

"Indeed, sir. The fact that Roderick Baskerville-Smythe had travelled halfway around the world to be with his family but, instead of revealing himself, had assumed a false identity, led me to believe that his motives were decidedly suspect. According to the other servants, Witheridge exhibited no fondness for the family. Babbacombe went so far as to suggest that he held the family in contempt."

I tut-tutted. Where was the feudal spirit these days?

"I had considered the possibility, sir, that, as a *réanimé*, changing his name and taking employment as a servant might have been the only way he could get close to his family. But his lack of fondness removed the possibility that his subterfuge was in any way related to a desire to be close to the bosom of his forebears."

I wasn't quite sure what Reeves had said, but I knew it had to be the business.

"One can also imagine, sir, the considerable shock that your arrival on the premises would have engendered. I do not believe it a coincidence that the ghost appeared the very day you arrived. I believe Mister Roderick felt his hand forced."

"You don't mean... Do you think I brought about Sir Robert's murder?"

"No, sir. You may have brought it forward by a day or two, but the plan was too well formed to be an impromptu one. I am also certain that, without your presence here, Sir Henry would have swiftly joined his father in the Baskerville-Smythe vaults."

Well that was a relief. I didn't like the idea of Reginald Worcester, harbinger of death.

"It also explains why incriminating evidence was planted in our rooms, sir. He wouldn't have known your motive for impersonating Mister Roderick, but he would have suspected you were after the title too. That would have made you a dangerous rival who had to be removed – either by murder or by framing you for murder."

"But would he be allowed to inherit the title?" I asked. "I'm sure someone told me that prometheans had no legal standing. Once dead, always dead – in the eyes of the law."

"That is true, sir, but he does not appear to grasp the finer points of primogeniture. One also assumes that having lived at the Hall for five months without anyone guessing he was a *réanimé,* that he would attempt to continue that deception once he claimed the title."

"True," I said. "As long as he steered clear of Turkish baths and Swedish massage."

"Indeed, sir. Of course, as soon as I discovered that Witheridge was the real Roderick Baskerville-Smythe, I realised that would necessitate a modification to your identity. Pursuant to which, sir, I endeavoured to create a plausible alternative."

"Complete with a threatening note from the murderer."

"Indeed, sir. I thought it would add verisimilitude."

"Reeves, you are a marvel. I'm surprised you weren't named Nonesuch, because you are truly without equal."

"Thank you, sir. One endeavours to give satisfaction."

~

I was waiting for Emmeline on the back lawn when I saw Reeves approaching at a good lick.

"What is it, Reeves? You look in a hurry."

"I made an unfortunate discovery in the kitchen, sir."

"Not another Cyrillic tattoo, I hope?"

"No, sir. I have just discovered what is on the menu for luncheon."

"Something avant garde, is it?" Reeves is easily offended by the experimental.

"One could say that, sir. It is Head of Pasco."

"What?"

"The assistant cook found the pastry head in the pantry, sir. I suspect Lupin put it there. The cook, not knowing its true provenance, believed the object to be a pie that Mrs Berrymore had prepared earlier. It is now in the oven, baking, and will be served on a bed of *gratin de pommes à la dauphinoise* within the hour."

"Shouldn't we warn someone?"

"I fear that might invite a number of unwelcome quest-ions, sir."

"We can't *not* say anything. We're dining at their trough for another ten days, Reeves. The least we can do is mark their card when they accidentally bake an under gardener."

Reeves coughed. "You are no longer Mister Roderick, sir. You are a policeman who would be expected to find a room at the Grimdark Arms. And I'm certain the coroner will have a good deal of questions for Inspector Natterjack."

"Time to pack, you think?"

"I have already instructed Tom to take your bags to the carriage, sir. With luck we shall be in time for the one fifty-five to London."

"What about Emmeline?" I said. "I can't leave without saying goodbye."

"Miss Emmeline is coming with us, sir. When I saw her

last she was on her way to the drawing room to inform Lady Julia."

"She wasn't armed, was she?"

"No, sir."

Well, that was a relief.

Reeves and I ankled around to the front of the house to await Emmeline and Tom by the carriage.

"I was thinking, Reeves," I said. "If *réanimés* have no legal standing, how will they try Roderick? Can they hang a chap who's already dead?"

"Posthumous execution is not without precedent, sir. Oliver Cromwell was beheaded two years after he died."

"So there's no plea of 'not guilty by reason of previous demise?'"

"No, sir."

I glanced towards the house. Still no sign of Emmeline.

"Did Roderick say who the automaton with the blowpipe was, Reeves?"

"No, sir. I believe Silas would be the most likely candidate. He was the only other automaton at the Hall and, being mute, made the ideal instrument. One assumes that had he been taller, and equipped with a head, he would have been first choice for the role of the ghost as well."

I saw Emmeline running across the lawn, one hand firmly keeping her hat in place. I jumped down from the carriage and waited for her.

"Is Lady Julia alive?" I asked. "Just checking in case we have to take the boat train to Plymouth."

"She lives," said Emmeline, taking my hand and climbing aboard. "Though she's not amused. I told her that I found Devonshire a little too much like Whitechapel. And had decided to leave while I still had a head on my shoulders."

"Golly," I said. "How'd she take it?"

"A little better than when I delivered my parting shot. 'One murderer in the family may be regarded as a misfortune, Lady Julia, to have a murderer *and a réanimé* looks like carelessness.'"

One can't beat Oscar Wilde for a juicy parting shot.

"You didn't hunt down Ida as well, by any chance?" I

asked.

"I thought about it. But one can't bury a body when one has a train to catch."

Say what you like about finishing schools, but they always teach their girls the essentials.

"Anyway," said Emmeline. "I have decided to found a charity – The Aid Association for Distressed Mechanical Folk. Lottie shall be its first beneficiary. You'll stump up ten guineas for her new feet, won't you?"

"Of course," I said. "Will ten guineas be enough?"

"That's the amount Stapleford quoted. Apparently, you can get them by mail order from Gears and Roebuck. Would you like new feet, Reeves?"

"I think not, miss."

"I'll have to get a new body for Annie too," said Emmeline. "We can come back next week in disguise and break her out of Quarrywood. We'll need an extra beard for Annie so we can smuggle her onto the London train. And four pairs of trousers, extra long."

Reeves coughed. "I don't think that will be necessary, miss. I had a long conversation with Annie after you left the quarry yesterday afternoon. Surprisingly, she is much taken with her new position. She told me that her horizons, not to mention her arms, have been considerably broadened by her recent employment at Quarrywood."

"Really?" I said.

"Apparently so, sir. She views her previous life as somewhat monotonous and lacking in opportunity. Whereas now, she sees herself as a character actress with an exciting future."

"But they turned her into a giant octopus, Reeves," said Emmeline.

"A temporary position, miss. She's been promised the role of a pterodactyl in *The Quarry That Time Forgot*."

Tom appeared, staggering across the lawn carrying a heavy trunk. Reeves helped him hoist the last of our luggage onto the back of the carriage.

"This train doesn't stop at Gretna Green, does it, Reeves?" asked Emmeline.

"No, miss."
"Then onward to the next mystery."

ACKNOWLEDGEMENTS

Thank you to my editors: Jennifer Stevenson and Sherwood Smith.

And, of course, Sir Pelham Grenville Wodehouse and Sir Arthur Conan Doyle.

ABOUT CHRIS DOLLEY

Chris Dolley is a *New York Times* bestselling author. He now lives in rural France with his wife and a frightening number of animals. They grow their own food and solve their own crimes. The latter out of necessity when Chris's identity was stolen along with their life savings. Abandoned by the police forces of four countries, who all insisted the crime originated in someone else's jurisdiction, he had to solve the crime himself. Which he did, and got a book out of it – the international bestseller, *French Fried: one man's move to France with too many animals and an identity thief*.

His SF novel *Resonance* was the first book to be plucked out of Baen's electronic slushpile. And his first Reeves and Worcester Steampunk Mystery – *What Ho, Automaton!* – was a WSFA Small Press Award finalist in 2012.

ABOUT BOOK VIEW CAFE

Book View Café (BVC) is an author-owned cooperative of over fifty professional writers, publishing in a variety of genres including fantasy, romance, mystery, and science fiction.

Our authors include New York Times and USA Today bestsellers; Nebula, Hugo, and Philip K. Dick Award winners; World Fantasy and Rita Award nominees; and winners and nominees of many other publishing awards.

BVC returns 95% of the profit on each book directly to the author.